You Let Him In

You Let Him In

JA Andrews

hera

First published in the United Kingdom in 2020 by Hera Books

This edition published in the United Kingdom in 2021 by

Hera Books
Unit 9 (Canelo), 5th Floor
Cargo Works, 1-2 Hatfields
London, SE1 9PG
United Kingdom

Copyright © JA Andrews 2020

The moral right of JA Andrews to be identified as the creator of this work has been asserted in accordance with the Copyright, Designs and Patents Act, 1988.

All rights reserved. No part of this publication may be reproduced or transmitted in any form or by any means, electronic or mechanical, including photocopy, recording, or any information storage and retrieval system, without permission in writing from the publisher.

A CIP catalogue record for this book is available from the British Library.

Print ISBN 978 1 80032 983 6
Ebook ISBN 978 1 912973 50 7

This book is a work of fiction. Names, characters, businesses, organizations, places and events are either the product of the author's imagination or are used fictitiously. Any resemblance to actual persons, living or dead, events or locales is entirely coincidental.

Look for more great books at www.herabooks.com

Printed and bound in Great Britain by Clays Ltd, Elcograf S.p.A.

For Peter Kewley, a colleague and a friend who has kept me focussed:
#ThePlan

Prologue

Michael

It's a shame we couldn't afford a detached property with a huge garden, but this part of Westbridge was at least more respectable than others within our budget. I didn't like being sandwiched by neighbours and overlooked by strangers, but I had a dream for something bigger and better. All I had to do was stick to the plan. All Jenny had to do was believe in me.

We had visited the property twice before, deciding it was the perfect home for us. I took care of arranging the mortgage with the best rates because I'm better with the finances than Jenny. All she had to do was sign on the dotted lines. I liked to keep everything organised, the skills of being an accountant, while Jenny could concentrate on being a great mother and a loving wife. This was meant to be the start of our new life together. I was genuinely happy too, we both were. I thought our lives from that moment onwards would only get better.

Jenny fell in love with our new home the second she walked inside. I set up a surprise for her in the master bedroom after I collected the keys: a woollen blanket on the floor, a picnic basket filled with goodies from our favourite bakery and a spectacular bouquet of flowers. I used to buy Jenny flowers every payday to show her how much I cared, how much she meant to me. I was her loyal husband, a father that Daniel could look up to and the head of my own family. I had responsibilities that empowered me to become successful.

'It feels like home already,' she told me, as we sat upstairs in the master bedroom. I knew Jenny liked surprises. 'It's perfect for us, a whole new chapter in our lives. I love it.'

I remember smiling at Jenny and wrapping my arms around her. I was lucky to have her by my side, I was proud of her. The musty smell from the carpets hit me. This property needed some minor modernisation improvements and painting throughout. Already, as I looked around the rooms, I could easily picture us living here. The commute to work wasn't far, a school for Daniel was close by, it was convenient – yet little doubts kept me thinking. How long would we have to live here? How long before I could achieve my dreams? I wanted something better.

'A perfect home, for my perfect family,' I replied. 'It's a good starting home for us. I know that Mum and Dad will be pleased, too, that we're not that far away.'

This was an exciting time in both of our lives. I wanted our new beginnings to be a fresh start. When Jenny used to visit me in my flat before we lived together, I could keep some aspects of my life separate. I never really talked to her in great detail about my work. When we moved in together there were some things I didn't want her to see, but I thought I had it under my control.

On the day we moved in, I looked at Jenny's face which was full of excitement, love and hope. She was overjoyed, but there was one little detail that was eating away at the back of my mind. Something that I couldn't bring myself to tell her.

Keeping everything under control was stressful, and with the stress came moments when I would almost slip up. All I ever wanted was for us to have a great future together without having to worry anymore. In my mind I had everything organised. I needed time, money and everyone to play their part in this life I was constructing for myself.

Dying was never part of the plan.

One

Michael

Jenny has no idea what stress and pressure I am facing: secrets that weigh heavy on my mind – but I can't ask anyone for support. I got myself into this situation, and it's all on my shoulders to get myself out of it. I only need Jenny to play her part, stay at home, look after our son and stop asking me questions. If I don't talk about my issues, then I'm exposing no lies. All we have to do is keep up appearances. The last couple of months have been unsettling, but I don't want to worry my wife or burden her with my concerns. I'm convinced that a few more months is all I need to get back to some sort of normality and a few more weeks maybe at keeping up this lie. We're already at the beginning of autumn and it's only three months until Christmas. That's going to be another expense we could do without.

'Did you get a good night's sleep?' I ask my wife as I hear her footsteps coming down the stairs. 'I don't think Daniel woke up again in the night, did he?'

Jenny yawns without even responding or acknowledging my question. She is wrapping the dressing gown belt around her waist. I've made her breakfast to show how apologetic I am for how tense I have been with her lately. Work has been playing on my mind, and it's not like she will understand. She has enough on her plate with Daniel.

'I see you've cooked his breakfast and got him up and ready this morning,' Jenny replies, giving me that same soft smile that made me fall in love with her. 'That's a nice surprise in itself. He woke up about three-ish but managed to eventually drop back off.'

'I was going to surprise you with breakfast in bed this morning, but you've woken up too early,' I say, thinking of ways to encourage her to get back up those stairs. 'Why don't you go back to bed and

I'll follow you up with the tray? Do you want any coffee or orange juice to go with it?'

Jenny sighs, but I see another smile trying to work its way out in my direction. She can tell I'm trying to make amends for snapping at her yesterday. I don't want to explain my whereabouts when I walk through the door at the end of the day. If I'm late home, it's because I've been working late in the office. It doesn't need an explanation.

'I'm up out of bed now, so I might as well stay down here,' she replies. 'Thanks for breakfast, what a lovely treat, and I'll have an orange juice, thanks, if you don't mind.'

I present Jenny her breakfast at the table – scrambled eggs on toast, just how she likes them – and in that brief moment I hear the postman pushing the letters through the letterbox. I know exactly what documents I've been expecting, but I need to get the post before Jenny does. She was meant to have still been in bed, but at least she made her way through to the kitchen after the mail had hit the floor. She's never normally up this early and I don't want her to get to the post before me.

Daniel is sat on the chair playing with the plastic spoon he should be eating his soft-boiled egg with. The toast soldiers have been smudged around the plate a few times, but this is his usual routine before eventually eating them one by one. All I want to do is run towards the front door, collect the post and head out. I doubt it will be that straightforward now she's downstairs.

'I love you,' I say. 'I hope you enjoy your breakfast. Daniel seems to be enjoying his by the mess he's making.'

'I love you too,' Jenny replies. 'It looks great, I'm starving. I didn't manage to eat very much yesterday. I spent most of the evening on the phone to Lizzie, stressing about changes at work. Once she gets going you know how difficult it is to shut her up.'

Jenny doesn't suspect anything. I laugh at her quip about Lizzie. Thankfully, she seems to be in a better mood this morning.

'Sorry I was late home last night,' I reply. 'Needed to tie a few loose ends up in the office. Deadlines, you know how it is.'

I watch my wife and son eat their breakfasts, but I'm too on edge to eat anything myself. I'll grab some breakfast biscuits later in the morning. I've been stressed about the post arriving on time. I was not leaving the house without it. At least once a month I have to go through this tension in case Jenny sees the damage. I've got backup plans and excuses coming out of my ears. As of yet, I've not had to use any of them.

'Daniel, stop playing with your food and eat it please?' I hear Jenny say. 'Do you want to go to the park later with Nanny and Mummy?'

Nanny?

'You didn't tell me my mother was coming over,' I say, walking through the hallway to pick up the post. 'Reminds me I need to catch up with her – and Dad too. Tell her that I'll pop round in a few days, or maybe we can all go over together one evening?'

'She's only coming over to pay Daniel a visit. You know how much she spoils him,' Jenny replies. 'And how overbearing she can be, telling me what's best for Daniel. Why don't you go round, or give her a call without me, give me a break from her?'

The text alert on my mobile phone goes off, interrupting our discussion over my mother. I thought it was in my trouser pocket the whole time, but I glance behind me to notice it in full view on the kitchen window. It's not like Jenny has ever been interested in going through my phone, but I couldn't refuse her if she asked.

'Who's texting you this early?' Jenny asks. 'You're not due in until after nine today, are you?'

'Let me just check – probably a spam email alert or something,' I respond, with the phone in my hand. 'It's only Brad, reminding me not to forget the reports on the manufacturing accounts we're working on together. You know what a slave driver my manager is.'

Jenny nods. I know if I discuss my work, she won't ask any more questions.

'I'm going to spend the day trying to see if I can find any more clients. I've been thinking about some self-employed accounting work, but there's no point until the start of the new tax year. No business wants their tax returns completed in the autumn.'

'Any post for me?' Jenny asks. 'Not that I'm expecting anything, most of mine drops in by email, but I bought Daniel some new clothes from the catalogue, didn't know if the statement was in?'

Another question that makes me feel tense because she doesn't normally ask. I bite my tongue so I don't spoil her mood. Little does she know that I've managed to hide most of the letters. Envelopes tucked inside places that are out of her sight.

'No, just junk mail,' I reply, 'I've left it on the side by the microwave. I'll be heading off in a minute.'

'Michael?' Jenny asks, her tone of voice more serious. 'Can we please talk about having a break away this evening, or even think about saving for a family holiday? We deserve something to look forward to, don't we?'

I can't count how many times over the last couple of months I have already explained that we don't have the money for a holiday. It's unlikely to be this year, possibly not even next year. I'm already under enough pressure to pay for everything in this house. She just doesn't get it.

'We can't afford it,' I say diplomatically. 'Again, we've talked about all this stuff, Jen. Why are you bringing it up now? Once the mortgage comes out and the other household bills, we are barely left with anything for treats.'

My reply has disappointed her, I can tell. I have to focus on my work. It'll be great when Jenny returns full-time, so it's less of a burden.

'I have to head off to work, Jen.' I say, walking closer to the door. 'We'll talk about it tonight. I promise. I'll see if we can use my parents' lodge down in Cornwall for one weekend soon. You know that Dad will moan about the loss of rental income, but Mum shouldn't be that bothered, she'll talk him round.'

Jenny walks towards me with her open arms, and cuddles me while resting her head on my right shoulder. I give her a couple of tight squeezes to reaffirm that I do love her. Despite the tension between us from our petty arguments lately, my family are my everything. I know that with persistence, I can bring in more money. Work is my number one priority right now.

'Shit,' I blurt out. 'I'm bloody late enough already, Jen. I must go.'

'Michael!' Jenny says sternly. 'Cover your ears, Daniel. Daddy is so naughty.'

We both laugh as I make my way to the front door. I ruffle Daniel's hair as I walk past him. He does tend to pick up words quite easily now; I should watch my mouth around him.

'See you tonight, little man,' I say, giving him a smile. 'Make sure that you eat all of your breakfast for Mummy.'

I have almost escaped, with the front door handle now in touching distance, when I spot my car keys still hanging on the coat hook where I left them yesterday evening. I go to reach them, but they drop to the floor. I bend down to pick them up just as quickly as they fell.

'What's that sticking up out of your trousers from your backside?' Jenny asks. 'Are you hiding something from me?'

'No, why would I do that?' I reply, nervously thinking on my feet. 'It's nothing much, just work stuff, the usual, you know?'

'Then why are you hiding it?' Jenny replies, more inquisitively. 'It doesn't have to be stuffed down the back of your trousers?'

Jenny's holiday talk distracted me, but now it comes as an excuse.

'It's a surprise. I didn't want you to see the receipt, that's why I'm hiding it.'

I watch the smile on her face. She doesn't doubt me for a minute. Jenny squeals with excitement, but at least she hasn't come any closer. I pull out the letter from the back of my trousers and place it inside my inner jacket pocket. Something I'll have to deal with later.

'Oh, I can't wait. What is it?' she asks, eyes wide and her hand on her heart. 'It's a holiday, isn't it? You know how much I've gone on about it.'

Her and that bloody holiday. We can't afford it. I'm still late.

'I'm sorry to say, it's not a holiday.' I break it to her gently. 'It's something I've been planning for your birthday. I know that thirty-one isn't exactly a biggie, but I wanted to do something special. You deserve to be pampered, so you'll have to wait and see.'

I watch her. She is still smiling. There are days like today when I feel I don't deserve her. She stands by me through thick and thin, and I repay her with these lies. She doesn't suspect anything, but I know in a few months, when serious money starts rolling in, this will all have been worth it.

'I'll see you tonight after work. Have a lovely day with my mother,' I say, just before I head out the front door while waving at Daniel. 'You might want to ask my mother about the lodge when you see her today?'

'I'll leave that to you.' The last words I hear before closing the door behind me. 'Have a great day at work.'

Fuck, that was a close call. But now I've got to plan a surprise for her birthday. If she had only stayed in bed I wouldn't have gone and made things worse for myself.

Two

Jenny

I look out of the window to see the bad weather looming over the horizon. It might even rain. It's been that long since Michael and I spent some time away together, just the two of us, I have forgotten what a holiday feels like. I see the constant beach adverts on the television and fantasise about them. I'm sure we'll venture abroad when Daniel is a bit older or when I can afford to save some money of my own after I return to work full-time.

I work a couple of days a week at the electrical contractor's in town as a sales administrator, and it frustrates me when I know I am capable of achieving more. I have a business degree and high hopes of running my own company in the future instead of working for someone else. I've often thought about the idea of my own employment agency, but at the moment I'm mostly filing and sending invoices by emails, or chasing up payments and dealing with complaints. I'm sure I will have more opportunities when Daniel is older. I remind myself that I'm in a fortunate position what with owning a house and having a husband who takes care of us, but I miss my family too.

Leeds will always feel like home to me. My family are there, yet I am isolated from them. I only came to Westbridge to study my degree, then had multiple jobs from one company to another before meeting Michael on the dating app and the rest is history. I was unsure about him at first, but he was very flirtatious and demanding. It was hard not to notice him with all the constant messages about meeting up. Michael eventually won me over with his charm. The more I saw of him, even when it was just quiet walks in the evening or a meal out, the more sincere he seemed… He always directed the conversation, one way or another, to his family. He is very close to his mother, and I admired that. At the time, he had no kids, no ex-wife, a career. He was everything I was looking for in a man. Coupled with him being generous, kind and caring, I knew early on I was falling in love with him. I knew we had a future together because I couldn't stop thinking about him. Every time we met it was like I was on a high.

Also, I've made some really great friends here who I'd miss. Especially Samantha and Lizzie from the office. They keep inviting me out, but I don't like to tell them I can't afford it. It would be like wasting money better spent on our son. He's constantly growing out of all his clothes.

Despite her bad qualities, Donna is the closest person I could have to a real mother down this way. I call her Mum because it gives us a sense of closeness as a family. She adores Daniel and, as annoying as she is, I know she means well.

My life consists of the same routines and it has done for a couple of years now. The house is always clean, the meals are cooked but I barely get enough sleep, and I am sure this contributes towards my frustrations. Our arguments are starting to put a strain on our marriage. It can't stay this way for much longer.

I don't regret having Daniel because he's the most important person in my life, but having a child has shifted me and Michael in different directions. This isn't the life I expected as a mother and a wife. I don't have fairy tale expectations, but I'd like Michael to spend more time with us. We need to get our spark back.

In the early days of our relationship, when Michael and I first met, he couldn't get enough of me. He'd barely leave my side. My phone would be in overdrive with the constant messages. Little things, like, what am I having for dinner, how am I feeling, where should we head out next? He was a little bit jealous at times too. It never bothered me, but random guys would come over and chat me up at a bar on a night out, and Michael used to shove right in between us at the bar.

'She's taken, mate,' he'd say, looking at me like he's come to my rescue. 'We're a couple.'

I miss the attentiveness and all that quality time we used to have with each other. I love him, but one of us needs to make changes. Since he has gone to some effort to surprise me for my birthday, I should do something nice for him too.

I'll surprise Michael with a lovely dinner. I'll try to make it a last-minute date night that might stir up some memories of when we used to go out more. It should set the mood, and we can focus our attention on each other.

I promised Daniel that we would go to the park today. The swings still scare him, but I've told him a few times this morning that Nanny is coming around to see him. He is more excited than I am to see her, but she gives me a break.

My phone alerts me as I'm scrolling through the stream of Facebook posts I'd been concentrating on: Donna's sent a text to get the kettle on. I watch her from the window as she throws her mobile into her designer handbag and clicks the button on the key fob to alarm her car before walking up the driveway. I throw a smile on my face and wave at her from the window to acknowledge I'm about to open the door.

'Nanny's here, Daniel,' I announce, leaving him playing in the lounge. 'I told you she'll be here today to see you, didn't I?'

Daniel glares up at me, annoyed that I distracted him from the television. He is fixated on the kids' channels that churn out quick ten-minute cartoons, but he imitates some of the behaviours on them too. Quite normal for a three-year-old, or so I discovered having asked my friends on Facebook if my child is developing as well as he should. I keep comparing the photos of all the other mothers on social media to me: the holiday pictures, the new house extensions, the jewellery from their husbands. It can get quite addictive, but I'm trying to not be so comparative of my home life with theirs. Michael and I have each other, our home, and we get by. I remind myself that there are others less fortunate than us, who'd give their right arm to be in my position.

I open the door to be greeted with a hug. Donna is pristine in her designer wear. I don't know why she insists on wearing her best outfits when she visits. Daniel is only a child, and she knows he loves rubbing his hands all over his food.

'Nice to see you again, Mum,' I say, 'I hope the weather holds out for the park. Daniel needs to get out and it would be good to get some fresh air.'

'It's certainly fresh,' she interrupts me, walking in while I still stand there with the door open. 'Where's Nanny's favourite little boy?'

'Nanna, look!' Daniel replies, 'Nanna. It's the telly bears.'

I take another glance at the sky before closing the front door. *Please don't rain*, I beg because I am thinking that two hours trapped with Donna talking about nothing other than her successful business will drive me up the wall. At least she occupies Daniel, which should give me enough time to clean the kitchen and bathroom in peace.

'Can I get you anything to drink, Mum?' I ask, 'Tea, coffee, juice?'

'No, thank you,' Donna replies, 'I'm trying to cut down on the caffeine. I might have some water or juice though, later on.'

'I'll just grab myself a coffee, Mum, and I'll be right in,' I reply. 'Daniel loves that bear program if you can't tell already. It keeps him quiet.'

I already know what she is doing. She's changing over the television channel to suit what she would rather watch. I know exactly what will happen next, and yes, Daniel starts crying. She can never leave him alone for a minute.

'This fluffy stuff doesn't educate kids,' Donna shouts out from the lounge. 'It's no wonder some kids are destructive when they only have this to watch.'

'He's only three.' My reply is followed by a sigh. 'The history channels will bore him senseless. I'd rather he was kept engaged than bored and screaming his little head off.'

'But at least he's learning something,' she responds. 'I've put on that antiques program. The one where they find old treasures from car-boot sales.'

I walk into the lounge with my coffee. Daniel has stopped crying, but he seems to be at that age where he has learnt to turn the waterworks on and off to suit; I don't make much of a fuss of them now unless he's hurt himself.

'Why would you bother giving up caffeine?' I ask. 'It's not like you smoke, or do drugs, is it? It's quite harmless really – are you sure I can't get you one?'

'I'm trying to be healthier, I should resist,' Donna replies, 'I'm also trying to lose a bit of weight. I'm afraid of turning into a fat, frumpy sixty-year-old.'

'You're a few years off from that yet,' I laugh out loud. 'You look good for your age, you know you do. I thought about a diet, but with all the running around after Daniel, he keeps the weight off me.'

'I might take up some exercise classes to give Pete a break from my constant nagging about the shop,' Donna replies. 'We were rushed off our feet these last few weeks.'

I know this is my cue to ask, and I'm not about to disappoint her.

'How is the shop doing?' I ask. Her face immediately lights up. 'Michael mentioned to me that you were thinking of expanding. You've both done really well?'

Donna straightens her posture as she relaxes on the sofa. Daniel is sat watching the car-boot program on TV, but I take this opportunity to switch back to the kids' channel. Donna doesn't question my authority over the television. I've diverted her interest.

'It's going really well. We've done better this year than last, but that's thankfully due to the hotter weather this year. Since we had a great summer, one of the best in a while, we are now also thinking of expanding to Newquay,' Donna explains. 'Cornish beach locations have the most tourist visitors, and we can negotiate branded products with our suppliers. Basically, it's all of the same products with different wording – you know, beach towels, ashtrays, magnets, glassware. You get my drift.'

'What about extra staff?' I reply, 'I thought you were going to retire early?'

'We could pay for a shop manager or extend Lou's responsibilities. We're almost retired anyway. I don't ever want to stop working completely and I couldn't hand over all of the responsibilities to Lou, who manages when we're away, but it's just something for us to think about.'

I nod and sip my coffee while Donna continues to discuss how well the shop has been doing. For a few more minutes I hear about how great they are at running the business and how much she is looking forward to her next holiday. I'd give anything right now for a holiday. Spain, Greece or the Canary Islands springs to mind.

'Talking of holidays,' I ask, perfectly moving into her holiday home discussion, 'have you let the lodge out much over the summer period?'

'That's done really well this year,' Donna replies. 'We covered all of the holiday park's site fees quite quickly. It never feels like a holiday for us when we're in it. It's great that it's close to the shop, but Pete is obsessed with letting it out for the rental income.'

I smile with envy. I can't bring myself to ask Donna if we can stay in the lodge for a weekend. I've pre-empted her reply telling me they would, but Peter doesn't want to lose the rental income. Michael can deal with his father's disappointment and can talk his mother round better than I could. He's the precious son. I'd better start thinking about going out. Daniel will be getting bored.

'Shall we walk Daniel to the park in a few minutes? He hasn't been in a while. Only to the one a few streets over.'

'Sure,' Donna replies. 'Oh, I know what I was meant to say to you.'

I shrug, hoping it isn't something more about her shop. I need to get Daniel ready, which is a job in itself.

'Go on?'

'We drove past Michael the other day as he walked into the Westbridge Central Hotel. You know the one by the main train station?' Donna says. 'He was dressed up like he was going for a job interview. I said to Pete, "Look at Michael going in there all fancy." It's a few hundred pounds a night. Even we couldn't really afford it.'

I'm confused because Michael hasn't mentioned visiting any hotel as far as I can remember. His office is in town, but he hasn't said a word. She probably saw him in his work suit. Michael is so handsome in the immaculate navy-blue suit he keeps for meeting new clients. He likes to make a good first impression.

'I know the hotel, but he was probably there on business. He's been doing a lot of late evenings lately, and said something to me about project work. Are you sure it was him?'

'He looked ever so smart,' Donna replies. 'It was definitely Michael. I'd recognise my own son.' She starts laughing. I don't doubt her, but I'm wondering if this has something to do with my birthday surprise. I know that hotel has a lovely spa – I've seen the pictures on Facebook. I even mentioned it to him, I'm sure of it?

It's all starting to make sense now. He's booked a weekend treat for my birthday. He would have caught me looking at Samantha from work's Instagram pictures. She's always living in a spa every other month or so, and Michael did say I deserve to be pampered, so maybe that was a clue?

How exciting. I shouldn't be so harsh on him.

'I'm ready whenever you are,' Donna says, standing up from the sofa. 'Do you want me to help you get Daniel ready? Is he going in his buggy or walking?'

'Yeah, that would great. Thanks Mum,' I reply. 'If you can put his coat on him, I'll go hunt out his reins. I'm trying to get him walking more and less attached to his buggy. The only downside is he keeps wanting me to pick him up. It's not far anyway.'

Donna straightens her blouse and trousers. I'm surprised she hasn't commented on the clothes I've thrown on for quickness – yesterday's jeans are still clean enough and the top from the wardrobe doesn't look like it needs to be ironed.

'Do you like my outfit?' Donna asks. 'This blouse was from a boutique we found when we stopped off shopping on the way to Dartmouth last weekend. Have a guess how much?'

In my head I hear the words 'boutique' and 'how much', so I intentionally compliment her by going overpriced. I'll keep her sweet.

'I don't know, but with something designer, and similar stuff I saw on the shopping channels,' I reply, 'I'd say about one hundred, one-fifty?'

'Almost,' Donna says, grinning. 'Seventy! A bargain, isn't it – for the brand?'

'It looks lovely,' I reply. 'What with the state that Daniel gets me in, I couldn't wear anything that expensive. It'd be covered in food and mud in no time.'

We all leave the house – and then what I had been dreading happens. No sooner have we stepped outside, then the heavens open with a vengeance. The rain pours down in sharp, heavy bursts, taking us by surprise. Now I know that my afternoon can't get any worse. Daniel will be tired, tetchy and disappointed about the park while Donna will bore me about her successful business.

'Shall we just go back inside?' I ask. 'Have a nice cup of coffee?'

Donna doesn't say a word but nods her head in agreement to signal the end of her caffeine cutback. Daniel isn't fazed by the rain, yet looks surprised about turning around as we walk towards the front door again.

I'm going to question Donna some more about seeing Michael at the hotel.

Three

Michael

Jenny is standing in the kitchen with a glass of wine in her hands. I lock the front door behind me as I prepare myself for the discussion that she will have about me being late home. I hang up my coat on the hook in the hallway before walking into the kitchen. I try to think of a few excuses about not texting. I know she's going to go mad.

'Where's Daniel?' I ask, only because the house seems unusually silent. 'Is he asleep?'

Jenny doesn't say a word but glares at me while shaking head.

'I'm sorry I'm late home,' I say apologetically, 'I've had a lot to catch up on in the office. Those accounts I mentioned this morning were all a bit out of order. I had to work so—'

'I'm so fed up,' Jenny interrupts me. 'Your mother's been here all afternoon flaunting her designer clothing in my face, telling me what is best for Daniel and going on and on about her shop.'

'I said I was sorry,' I respond, trying to deflect the conversation. 'You're looking great by the way – what's the occasion?'

Jenny looks at me – severely pissed off. I can see the effort that she has gone to, but she should have said something earlier. It's definitely not our wedding anniversary. I've never forgotten the date.

'Your dinner is in there,' she says, pointing to the oven which has a tea-towel hanging off the door. 'I wanted to surprise you with a date night, but you're normally home by now. It's ruined.'

I'm not all that hungry, but – given the effort she has gone to – I'd better pull out the plate from the oven and start to enjoy it. A flash of steam wafts up into my face as I open the oven door to release the heat. The plate is hot, and I can feel the burn through the cloth as I carry it to the table. Jenny downs the rest of her glass of wine with a gulp and pours herself another glassful. The atmosphere is tense – but nothing unfamiliar to us both, lately.

'This looks good,' I compliment her. 'You look good too. Thank you, I'm sorry again.'

'Why didn't you tell me beforehand?' Jenny asks. 'Why didn't you reply to my text messages. I left you a voicemail?'

'I was just busy. I've been working all day and then I had to make a few calls about those extra jobs I've been trying to secure. The signal must have dropped. I didn't get them until I was almost home.'

'Everything is always about you, isn't it?' Jenny says. I think she's drunk. 'Do you even think about what I may need? I know you're trying so hard, but we need you at home too. I might not work as hard as you in the office, but in the home I am always on the go, Michael. I need your support.'

I throw her a sympathetic look, unsure of what to say, but she continues.

'You know my family live miles away. It's not like I can even ask them.'

I lower my head because I don't know what to say. I'm doing everything I can to spare her the disappointment of finding out the truth.

Jenny sits down at the table to face me. I had no idea that she was planning this surprise tonight. I've let her down.

'I did go to a lot of effort tonight,' Jenny says. 'I made you a nice meal, and I asked your mother earlier if she could have Daniel for tonight so that we can spend some time together, alone. I thought it would be nice for us.'

I drop my fork, and it hits the plate with a cracking sound. I am about to disappoint her further. It's best I just close my eyes and blurt the whole thing out rather than butter her up. My stomach churns with the anticipation of her response. Why did she have to do this tonight of all nights?

'I have to go back out soon, but please hear me out,' I tell her, knowing this is going to cause more issues between us. 'I have a last-minute business meeting that's very important. I can't get out of it or cancel. I literally have to eat, get changed and head out the door. Before you say anything, it's for a new contract. I need this.'

I can see the colour flush her cheeks as the disappointment sets in. She'll get over it by the morning, I know she will. The redness in her face is glowing, but I can't look her in the eyes.

'I'm really sorry,' I continue, 'I should have text you or called, but I had no idea what you had planned. Maybe we could do this again another night. I'll speak to my mother and see she if she can have Daniel next weekend. I know how much you need a break. I'll mention the lodge and see if we can borrow it.'

'It only takes a few seconds, if that, to contact me,' Jenny snaps. 'It's not good enough, Michael. I've had enough. You should have told me sooner.'

'All right, I promise that next time I'll message you sooner,' I respond with annoyance in my voice. I sense an argument is brewing. 'The meeting tonight is really important. I can't get out of it. I have to be there.'

'We both have to make changes. This constant strain is driving me mad, isn't it you? Don't you want to spend more time with your son?' she asks.

'That's not fair. I'm doing my best,' I reply, holding it together mentally while the emotion in my voice changes its tone. 'We're not in that bad a situation. I know that I have been out of the house a lot with work lately, but I am doing this for us. Everything I am doing is for the benefit of this family. I promise you. Trust me.'

I don't know how to redeem myself other than to explain that I haven't much of a choice. I'm edgy and aware of the time.

'Jenny, all I can say is that I'm sorry. Can we talk about this later?'

I've been thinking of nothing but this business meeting all day. I've rehearsed my pitch to perfection. I expected Jenny to have made her own meal and to have left me to throw something in the microwave later. I'm meant to be having a business dinner this evening. I don't want to be late.

'Things are going to get better, Jen,' I say as I watch her swig back the glass. 'I do want the best for us all, even if you can't see that. You and Daniel mean the world to me. I love you both.'

'Fuck you,' she mutters, sounding half tipsy, 'I don't want to stay trapped in this house like it's a prison. I should be supported by my husband. Daniel asks for you all the time. I keep telling him Daddy's at work.'

'There's no point in me talking to you if you're getting drunk, is there?' I snap because I have to vent my frustration too. 'Why don't you have an early night and stop comparing our life to all those mummy bloggers on the internet? Just saying.'

I look at my phone to check the time as I rush through the rest of my dinner. I should have been in the shower five minutes ago, yet this awkwardness between us continues. I can't stay here all night arguing.

'I do love you. You do know that, don't you?' I ask. 'I couldn't do this without your support. I want you to understand that I am trying, really trying, to improve our lives. Tell me that you understand.'

'I don't understand you at times like this,' Jenny slurs. 'We have a beautiful home, a beautiful son, but I miss you. I miss the way we used to be.'

'What are you saying?' I ask, concerned, biting my lip to hold back. 'Do you still want me?'

'Admit it,' she says, letting go of the empty glass, 'this is hardly a happy marriage, is it?'

I look down at my mobile phone, then look up again at Jenny. I have very little time left to keep explaining myself. She is right that we were never like this in the beginning. Jenny was more bubbly when I first met her. We used to go out clubbing; sometimes, at weekends, we would even go to the casino in the early hours and get wasted. Jenny never questioned anything I said. I never had to prove myself.

'I know that things between us have been a little tense, more so recently...'

Jenny shakes her head and walks away from me.

'You don't understand anything I've been saying, do you?' she asks, interrupting me as I try to explain. 'Everything I've said to you means nothing, doesn't it?'

I look at her, confused, thinking I had made myself clear enough.

'You're drunk,' I reply. 'Why don't we talk about this again in the morning?'

'I've given up talking to you,' Jenny replies, putting her hands on her hips in disgust. I know exactly what is coming next. 'I'm going to have an early night. You just do what you've got to do. We'll talk about it tomorrow.'

Jenny walks past me, and although she is in one hell of a bad mood, I can tell she's already calmer than earlier. She finds it better once she has got the worst of it off her chest. I listen, and appreciate everything she does for our son and me.

I have a good feeling about this new contract.

'I'll be back tonight,' I explain, while Jenny holds on tightly to the bannister as she makes her way up the stairs. 'Thank you for understanding. I will make it up to you, I promise. I will change. I'll make it up to you.'

Jenny stops about three-quarters of the way to the top of the stairs, removes her hand from the bannister and turns her head to face me. She looks emotional and I can see she is tearful. I'm nervous about what she is about to say next.

'I've decided to go and spend a few weeks with my mother in Leeds,' she announces. 'I'm going to ask work for the time off when I'm next in, and I'll take Daniel with me to Leeds. It's for the best. I need some time away. It will give Daniel a chance to see his other grandparents too.'

'No, you can't do this to me,' I respond. My raised voice startles her. 'Please, not now. At least wait until I secure this contract. I could come with you.'

'I need some time out,' Jenny replies, the tears now streaming down her cheeks. 'I need a break. Not just from you but from everything that's going on in my head.'

'Please, Jen, I'm begging you. Don't take our son to Leeds?'

Jenny wipes the tears from her eyes. I watch her take a breath and I am suddenly concerned about our marriage. I wasn't expecting this tonight. I have a million different thoughts and outcomes racing around my head. I'm desperate for this contract, but I'm staring at my wife who needs me by her side. I have to take a chance and make my way to the hotel.

'Have you been seeing other women behind my back?' Jenny blurts out. 'Are you heading out now to see some bitch I don't even know about?'

The disappointment is like a knife through my heart. I feel a lump in the back of my throat. This is the first moment since we've been together that I have considered she could possibly leave me.

Jenny has never been like this towards me before nor questioned my commitment to her.

'No,' I reply firmly, looking her directly in the eyes. 'I'm *not* seeing other women behind your back. I'd never do that to you. Why would you even ask me that?'

I'm shaking with fear. I remind myself that Jenny will forgive me when she's sobered up. I know she'll understand when I explain it in more detail. I don't have time for this now. I'm going to be late.

'Your mother saw you at a hotel,' Jenny replies, looking distressed and uneasy. 'You never mentioned anything. Don't forget that I know you – I remember what you used to tell me about the women you met before me.'

'Work,' I snap. 'It's for work. You know I have to meet clients out and about – it's what I do. It was probably some tax consultancy conference.'

If she takes Daniel to her mother's, will she ever come back?

I am torn between doing the right thing and taking a risk.

'Jenny,' I say softly while she looks at me from the top of the stairs, 'get some rest and we'll talk about it in the morning. I'll try to come home early or take tomorrow off. I'm already late, and I have to go. If I pull this off tonight we'll be celebrating.'

'Whatever,' she replies. 'Just go.'

I don't like upsetting my wife but she's oblivious to every struggle I face when I leave this house. If I don't do this, I risk everything.

I grab my jacket, car keys, and head out of the door in a hurry.

Four

Michael

The autumn sunset has darkened the skyline between the time of leaving the house and arriving at the Taverton Estate Hotel for my business meeting. I'm sat in my car while patiently waiting for the right time to make my way to the hotel. I'm nervous too, but that's to be expected since there's a lot riding on this meeting tonight. I've been given one more chance – one more opportunity to convince someone I am the right man for the job. Tonight's contract meeting could solve the biggest of all my problems right now. It will buy me some time.

In the twenty minutes that it has taken me to drive through central Westbridge to the outskirts of Taverton I couldn't stop thinking about Jenny. I am disappointed with myself for walking out on her but – like all our other little spats in the past – it'll blow over. I'm certain that she'll calm down in the morning and see sense. I'm not going to allow her to take a trip to Leeds. Instead, I have to show her how much she means to me. I'm going to have to surprise her with a holiday for her birthday, somehow.

This contract will end all of our problems. I need this.

I pull up into the car park, wind up the window because the breeze is too chilly, and look at my watch to check the time. I admire the classic Swiss design. The compliments I receive for such an expensive watch give me a feeling of success. This is a watch I am proud to own, and it's always a talking point if spotted by an eagle-eyed fellow watch lover – but the reality is I'm struggling to maintain this image I've created. I do not want to be seen as a failure, nor do I want my family to be destroyed by the downturn in my luck. I can't let Jenny know the truth. Not yet. Tonight's meeting could save me from embarrassment and shame so I have to focus and hope that Jenny can forgive me for walking out tonight.

Sometimes you have to keep secrets from your wife, don't you?

I also think that the psychology of appearances is powerful. The truth is that I'm still paying for my watch on finance because I couldn't afford anything as luxurious as this outright. Having a family and two-bedroom house to pay for means I need to work hard if I'm to keep the truth from Jenny. It's all about the plan in my head. I'm confident that I can make it happen. If I don't, the consequences don't bear thinking about.

I hope that this new client has good taste and notices my designer suit with my expensive watch during our meeting tonight. I will be subtle and try not to look a show-off – but it's all in the psychology. First impressions count for everything. It won Jenny over all those years ago. I'm wondering if I have met this client before. I don't recognise the name – but I thought that setting this meeting here, at this hotel, would be a sign. A lot of big business happens here because the hotel is rural, private and expensive and all the clientele are upmarket. I had to take this chance despite letting my wife down. I did try to explain.

I hate myself at times for what I have put my wife through. We don't argue all that often, but I know how much she is hurting. I have brief moments of resenting her because of her obsession with social media and living a lifestyle that seems out of reach. I understand that she is frustrated being at home with Daniel on her own all the time, but it's not for ever. She will have a better job and a better income when Daniel goes to school. I will try, in time, to save more money. It's not going to happen overnight.

I should do the right thing by texting Jenny to apologise. If I call her instead, we will only end up arguing again. I'll let Jenny simmer for a while tonight – I might even sleep on the sofa to give her some space. If this meeting is as successful as I hope, then our money struggles should drastically improve. For me, it's the deal of the year. I love her for standing by me, and at times I probably don't deserve her. If I can win this contract, secure the extra work, then I will make more time for my family. I have to save our marriage.

My phone buzzes in my pocket. I feel the shake of it gently vibrate on my thighs.

'Please, don't be Jenny,' I whisper to myself. 'I don't want the stress. It could jeopardise everything.'

I pull out the phone, touch the screen to unlock it and see the message. I'm thankful that it isn't her.

> Can we meet a little later than planned at 7.30p.m.?

I reply immediately because I have already arrived and am waiting in the car park of the hotel.

> Not a problem. Looking forward to it. I am already here but will meet you soon in reception at the new time of 7.30p.m.

I look back out of the car window to see the hotel. The lower car park is small and packed with cars already so I've had to stay further back. I admire the intricacies of the building architecture as the white lighting shines over the arched windows. I see a small group of people walk out of the hotel, and I watch their every move. It appears to be a wedding party who are starting to congregate by the hotel entrance. I try to spot the bride but she must still be inside. This must have cost a bomb at this hotel but then again it's a weekday wedding so they might have had a cheaper deal.

My wedding day with Jenny was bliss because everything we planned came together with ease – no family arguments and I even managed to get to the church on time having been out all night at the casino with my mates. I didn't get a wink of sleep but all my close friends were insistent upon one last drinking session. I've realised that I hardly ever see them anymore.

Life one year to the next seems to pass by so quickly yet having Daniel has changed our priorities. That little man is the boy that turned us into a family. The late nights out – the Saturdays I would spend in the bookmaker's watching the horse racing and the random pub crawls I used to have – have all now come to an end. I think that both of us took our freedom for granted in our mid-twenties. Being married has changed us both.

Where did it all go wrong?

Jenny, who was Miss Evans up until our wedding day, had spent the whole day before with her parents David and Julie at a rental property on the outskirts of Westbridge. Neither of us had been married before but a church wedding was a huge deal. It was all Jenny had ever dreamed of. I can hardly believe that was five years ago now but both of our families helped with the costs and Jenny had the wedding of her dreams. I didn't think we'd even be able to find the house deposit but we did thanks to my quick thinking. Risks I took to find more money. I know I can do it again.

Jenny and I met on a dating site six years ago but despite the exchange of a few shared messages we never got around to meeting each other until a chance outing with a mutual friend some months later. The surprise of the circumstances encouraged us to talk and give each other feeble excuses as to why we never pursued any dates. For her, it was the annoyance of being bombarded with constant messages from guys only after one-night stands that drove her to delete her account. However, I felt confident enough to chat to women online but talked myself out of dates because in reality I was looking for a one-night stand. I had good intentions but when it came to the day of the date I had other plans with someone else. I assured her it was nothing personal. It's not like I stood her up or anything. I just cancelled last minute.

I remember how nervous I was about giving Jenny my number when we met again. I thought she'd think I was that workaholic from the dating site that never bothered to turn up on a real date. She gave me assurances that she'd call me – and I didn't have to wait long. Jenny called the very next morning to arrange a date. We both met each other a few times – once a week initially until, in a coffee shop, I blurted out an admission that changed the direction of our relationship forever.

'I'm falling for you big time.'

I watched her face light up. She threw her arms around me and we hugged before kissing each other. With all the hints and signals from our previous meets, I knew she was starting to feel the same way about me as I was her. These new emotions made every day exciting for us both. I knew that she was the woman for me. Jenny was better than all the others. She had class. There was something about her that drew me in and I wanted to spend more and more time with her. I was falling in love.

'I feel the same way,' Jenny replied. 'We're officially a couple now, aren't we?'

A few more months of meeting each other followed with Jenny staying round at my flat more and more for longer and longer periods at a time. It was a surprise when Jenny became pregnant but we then got married and bought the house before Daniel's due date. The three of us wouldn't have had much room in that small one-bedroom flat of mine in central Westbridge and besides it wasn't the most desirable of areas for a new family. It wasn't far from the university so it was full of students and bedsits. It wasn't practical for us as a new family.

Every now and then I think that a mortgage is a bigger commitment than marriage. On days like today after we've argued I imagine all the what ifs.

What if we ever got divorced? What if the house had to be sold? What if I lost everything? What if nothing goes according to plan?

I take another glance at my watch. It's still too early to stroll on inside. By looking at the distance between the car park and the entrance I guess that it would take me a couple of minutes at most to walk down the winding road. There don't seem to be any pathways other than a gravelled lane with fields either side where the grass looks like marshland. The wind is starting to pick up but I am thankful it's not raining.

I can feel the nerves starting to get the better of me and my stomach is queasy with anxiety. I have come well prepared and I have memorised my speech twice over. I have practised my pitch all day. I know that this business could provide long-term financial gain. I am desperate to make this a mutually beneficial partnership that works for us all. I need them to trust me as the best accountant for the job – just as my wife trusts me. I need this deal more than anything.

The wedding party crowds have disintegrated and the silence has become more noticeable. Those whispering voices with the odd cackle of drunken laughter can no longer be heard in the distance.

I see the moon in the sky behind the hotel as the night has become much darker. I'm shivering a little now but that could be the nerves kicking in. I know my pitch. I've memorised every word. It's time. I can do this.

I get out of the car, shut the door and press the alarm on my fob. I straighten my jacket while taking in a deep breath of the cold country air. There is a dampness to it. I notice way out on the horizon a mist forming over the fields as the night air sweeps in. As I start to walk down the winding road I can hear a car in the background. It soon becomes the only noise in the distance apart from the sound of the birds as they flock to the trees. The closer I walk to the hotel, the louder the sound becomes. I turn around and hear the sound of my wallet dropping as it falls from my trouser pocket. As I bend down to pick it up I see the beaming lights of a car approaching me. I step off the road and onto the grassy verge as any moment the car will pass.

I open the wallet to see the picture of my son looking back at me. I give a smile, remembering how much joy he has brought to our lives. Despite not seeing him take his first steps or hearing his first words because I was always stuck at work, I still care that he knows how much I love him. After the argument with Jenny tonight I made a promise to be more supportive and to be a better father to Daniel. Everything I am doing now is to try to secure my family a better future. I have to keep trying – but I fear I might lose them both.

I've always been a risk-taker.

I love them both so much. In reality, I don't fear that Jenny will *really* walk out on me but I understand her concerns. I owe her and I go through times of guilt and regret. She's my wife and I should be there for her but I can't let go of this deal. It could improve our lives.

The lights are bright – full beams on – as the car races down the road. Panic overwhelms me as I see it heading in my direction. For a split-second this fear has me frozen on the spot with a heavy sickly feeling in my stomach causing my body to start trembling. I am shaking head to toe as I turn to start running towards the hotel. The loud noise of the engine screeches and the pulsating sounds of the music blasts from inside the car and thumps through my ears.

I open my eyes to focus on the sky above; everything has happened so quickly?

I can hear screaming and the car engine in the background. I'm struggling to breathe and I can taste blood at the back of my mouth. The darkness is all that I can see and an unbearable pain takes over my body. I'm trying to focus but the muffled sounds are fading into the sound of footsteps. I'm confused and in agony. All I can think about is my wife and son.

Five

Jenny

Knocking on the front door awakens me. For the first couple of seconds I contemplate my surroundings because I am confused. I'm unsure if I'm still in a dream – but the knocking continues. This time louder. I glance across to the alarm clock on Michael's bedside cabinet to see it's 10.15 p.m.

'All right, all right,' I shout, pulling the quilt cover away from me and sending a draft across my thighs. 'I'm coming. Give me a minute.'

Michael must have forgotten his keys. I bet he's drunk – or worse, a taxi has sent him home and the driver has had to carry him to the door. I haven't known him to have gotten in that state for years but with our argument from earlier I was kind of expecting him to have a drink or two.

I have a flashback memory to the weeks leading up to our wedding. I can see myself in bed with Michael after a night out with our friends. He was slightly drunk but I was pregnant and I remember what he said.

'You're my everything,' he told me, 'we're going to have an amazing future.'

This was a period where we were out with our friends a lot. We used to go out regularly and have meals out or live off takeaways. Life was very different before Daniel was born. Having a child has instantly turned us into responsible adults. I had no idea how straining motherhood would be at first – and how little help Michael would be after the first year. If I had had the chance again I might have waited a bit longer. I feel guilty for thinking it but because of him I put my career on hold. Without him I could have been more successful.

I want to support my husband because I can see the pressure he is under right now. I accept that he is trying to work sometimes twice as hard to make up for me being part-time. It's his way of paying me back for staying at home most days to be a mother. I wonder too if it is the responsibility of fatherhood that has driven him out of the house more. I know that Michael is trying his best – we both are – but things can't stay this way forever. Maybe I was too hard on him tonight?

I take my dressing gown off the hook on the back of the bedroom door and flick the light switch on. I walk down the stairs and hear the knock on the front door again – but this time louder.

'Yes, Michael, I hear you. I said I was coming,' I say, loud enough for him to hear me. 'I thought you had your keys on you?'

I unlock the door and pull it open, expecting to see my husband's face but two policemen are looking back at me. One of them takes a small gulp and the other removes his hat. My heart sinks as I know something serious has happened. I raise my hand to my chest and can feel the tremble in my body as I struggle to speak.

'Is everything ok, officers?' I ask. Both give me subdued looks that suggest otherwise. 'Do you both want to come inside for a minute or two?'

'Are you Mrs Jenny Clifton?' the taller policeman asks while the shorter one stands beside him not speaking a word. 'Mr Michael Clifton's wife?'

I start to walk back a little as my body language shows signs of worry. I wrap my arms around myself and all I can do is nod. The panic has set in and I don't want them to say the next statement I know is about to follow. I've seen this on television programmes but it can't be happening to me. The chill in the air sweeps through the hallway as I stay silent for a brief moment longer. My stomach cramps with the dread and fear of what could be coming next.

Don't say it. Please, don't say it. Not to me, not now, not here. No – this cannot be real.

'I'm Jenny Clifton,' I mutter. I speak so softly I can barely hear my own voice. 'What has happened? Is everything ok?'

I already know – I just don't want this moment to be real. It has to be a bad dream. We have a son together. He was out negotiating a contract. My husband is at a business meeting. This is a big mistake. It has to be a terrible mistake.

'I'm Police Constable Parker and my colleague is Police Constable Blackwell,' the taller officer says. Lost in this moment of numbness, I stare and listen. 'May we both please come inside?'

Both the police officers step inside our house. Blackwell shuts the front door behind him as he is last to enter. They stand together in their black uniforms. The formality of their presence is unnerving.

'Would you like to sit down?' Blackwell asks. 'We can go to another room if you'd like to?'

'No,' I reply, wanting this done as quickly as possible. My eyes can barely look up from the floor. 'Please, can you just tell me, here?'

I realise I am a trembling, nervous wreck. I'm staring at what they're holding and my mind isn't able to control the tension, or the nerves. I feel sick.

'Mrs Clifton, do you recognise these items?' Parker asks me, holding up a clear bag with a wallet and a mobile phone inside it. 'The wallet as you can see is open with a photo of a young child. Does this wallet and mobile telephone belong to Mr Clifton?'

'Yes,' I respond, 'that is our son, Daniel. It's Michael's wallet and I know that must be his phone. How? Where did you find them?'

I'm shaking head to toe, waiting for the dreaded moment. They have my husband's belongings so I know this must be serious. My eyes start to water as I hold back the tears. I take a gulp to clear the build-up of saliva from my throat and await the officer's response.

'I have some bad news I'm afraid, Mrs Clifton,' Parker says, looking directly at me. 'Your husband has been involved in an accident on the short road leading to the Taverton Estate Hotel. I'm sorry to be the one to tell you that he has died at the scene. I'm really, very sorry.'

The shock is starting to sink in. I can't stop shaking my head. I hold on to the wall to stop me from dropping to the floor – although I was expecting him to tell me this news because from the moment I opened the door it was like something from a television drama. Hearing the words from his mouth make it all the more real. My husband is dead. An accident?

'Mr Clifton has been taken to the hospital morgue,' says Blackwell. 'I'm so sorry that this has happened. We have to inform you face to face.'

I keep looking at their faces. Both officers just stand there looking at me while I have nothing to say. I'm struggling to accept the news that my husband is dead. I only saw him this morning. I made him his dinner and then we argued. He was meant to come home. That argument. I was dreadful to him.

My tears are filled with the guilt and sadness I feel. I hold my stomach and drop to my knees. It's like being lost, scared, unsure, guilty and hurt all at the same time. I remember the last words I said to him. Tears are now dripping down my face. *Just go.* I never meant it. I loved him.

I will never get to see Michael again – speak to him or even apologise. How can he be dead?

What about Daniel? What will I say to our son?

How do you explain to a three-year-old that his father is dead – that he will never see him again for the rest of his life? A whole childhood without his father to watch him grow up. All these questions flood my mind at once, driving me mad.

I get back up off the floor, straighten my dressing gown and then wipe my eyes.

'How did this happen?' I ask both of the officers. 'I don't understand. I hope he didn't suffer. Was it quick?'

'We believe it was a car accident. Your husband was struck by a car going at some considerable speed. He was pronounced dead at the scene after the ambulance arrived,' Parker replies. 'We have a witness who claims to have seen what happened. Some of our officers are currently taking his statement. Unfortunately, we haven't yet been able to find the driver of the vehicle.'

'A car accident?' I ask, confused. 'Did his airbag not open?'

'No, Mr Clifton was struck by a car that may have been stolen. He was walking towards the hotel entrance. He was not in his own vehicle or the suspect's vehicle that struck him.' Parker replies. 'Mr Clifton's car is still parked at the hotel car park. All we know at this time is that the driver of the car has fled the scene. We have a witness who saw him exit the vehicle unharmed and run into the surrounding fields. Our forensics team are gathering all the evidence they can. Unfortunately, the number plate on the vehicle has been tampered with but we're continuing our enquiries.'

'I know this may be difficult for you,' Blackwell says, 'but we do need someone to identify your husband's body. It doesn't have to be right now but we can arrange to take you if you agree. If you wish not to do this yourself is there anyone else we could ask?'

'I want to do it. I need to see him,' I instantly respond without having to think about it. 'I want to see my husband.'

'Would you like to come to the hospital with us now?' Blackwell asks. 'We will be with you every step of the way. You could bring someone with you if you wanted?'

'Not right now,' I reply. 'Not at this moment because I need to speak to Michael's parents. They're looking after our son. I need to tell Daniel.'

'Do his parents know?' I ask the officers. 'Peter and Donna Clifton?'

'No,' Blackwell answers, 'we have only informed you as his next of kin at this stage.'

'I will do it,' I reply. 'They're both in their late fifties. Losing a son like this, it's going to break their hearts.'

I start to have a breakdown again. I walk away from the hallway and into the kitchen. Both officers follow me but Parker pulls out a chair from the table and I sit down with my hands covering my head. The tears still fall from the grief I have been hit with. Even saying it out loud still doesn't make it seem real.

'Michael is dead.'

'I'm so sorry,' I say to them both as they stand in the kitchen and try to offer me support, 'I guess this is just part of your job?'

'This is never easy,' Parker responds. 'It has to be done face to face. We never get desensitised to it, either. The loss of someone very close to you in these unfortunate circumstances is very tragic. We are sorry for your loss.'

I look up, removing my hands from my face. I see Michael's coffee mug on the rack in the corner of the kitchen. I remember how I complained about him leaving paperwork all around the house. Memories of small random moments pop into my head.

Parker pulls what looks like a business card from his jacket pocket.

'Here are the contact details for a family liaison officer,' he says as he places it on the table next to me. 'Please give Sharon Jenkins a call when you can. She will talk about our family support services and you can call the number tomorrow when you want to identify your husband at the hospital. She will arrange everything for you so you don't have to worry.'

I nod my head to accept that I will call Sharon. I don't exactly know when but I will do it in the morning. The most important thing to do right now is call Donna and Peter.

Should I get a taxi to their house?

I have a sense of urgency – wanting to organise everything but not being clear what I need to do. I know I have to call Peter and Donna and I have to see my husband at the hospital. I will have a funeral to organise, work to go to and my son to sort out. Why couldn't Michael have just stayed at home?

I keep staring at the officers. I don't know what else to say or what other questions to ask. I know I'm in a right state but none of it matters. Somehow I'm going to have to sit Daniel down, too.

Both Parker and Blackwell come forward.

'Is there anything else we can do for you?' Parker asks. 'Anything at all?'

I shake my head while wiping my nose. Michael should have been at home tonight.

'I'd like to be on my own now, please,' I say to both of the officers as I get up out of the chair. 'I can show you out. I'll get straight on the phone to his parents.'

The officers leave in silence. Not a single word is spoken between us until I am about to close the door behind them.

'Take care,' says Parker.

I don't acknowledge their parting words. I need to call Donna – who will think I am only checking up on her about Daniel staying over for the night. This isn't going to be easy. I take my mobile phone and sit back down at the kitchen table. I have no idea in my head how to break the news to them other than by being direct. It takes three rings before Donna answers.

'Evening, Jenny,' Donna answers. 'Pete and I were just on our way to bed. Daniel has been a good little boy for us all day – showing us some new dance moves he's picked up from watching the music channels.'

'Mum,' I interrupt her, 'this is really serious. You need to sit down.'

I hear nothing but silence. Then breathing noises down the phone. I take a deep breath myself as my courage wavers.

'It's Michael,' I blub. Now I can't stop the tears as I feel the misery of my own surroundings and the absence of anyone here to support me. 'Mum, he's dead. Michael has had an accident.'

I shudder – the bearer of tragic news.

'What do you mean? What are you saying?' Donna asks, struggling to acknowledge my words. 'What accident – and where?'

'The police haven't long left,' I continue, once I am able to catch my breath. 'It was a hit and run near Taverton. Please don't tell Daniel tonight. I need to do this myself.'

For a moment there is nothing but silence as I wait for Donna to reply. In the background I can hear the television. Peter is coughing. Donna's heavy breathing is a sign of her emotions and her realisation that Michael is dead.

'I promise,' Donna eventually replies, her voice cracking. 'I will leave it for you to tell Daniel.'

We cry together before Donna has to leave to break the news to Peter. Having been reassured that they will bring Daniel to me as soon as he wakes up in the morning, I hang up the phone. I leave his parents to establish the foundations of their own grief. Michael was my world, and now he's gone I don't know how I am going to cope without him.

I sit in the kitchen with the silence. I look around the room and feel detached from my surroundings. It's like I have been placed in the middle of a bad dream. A nightmare that I can't escape from.

'I love you, Michael,' I whisper into the air. I look up as though he is looking down at me from somewhere. If only he would walk back into the house. 'I don't know what I will do without you.'

I cry into my sleeve – still in shock. How am I going to explain this to Daniel?

Six

Jenny

Donna and Peter return Daniel just after the crack of dawn this morning. He looks tired. My emotions are like a cyclone of mental destruction but for Daniel's sake I need to stay focused. None of us had any sleep last night. I spent most of the early hours walking from room to room imagining all the past conversations I had with Michael in this house. I remember the laughter, the cries, the arguments and I keep talking to myself over and over about how I will break the news to Daniel. He must be wondering where his daddy is.

I prepare Daniel a bowl of cereal for breakfast and hand him a spoon. He still gets himself into a mess with his food. I can tell he can sense something has happened. He must have seen his grandparents cry this morning or overheard some of our conversations. The most difficult part of the morning was trying to keep it together in front of him when he arrived home. Donna and Peter smiled at me and we welcomed each other with hugs at the door. Short sentences with minimal eye contact followed as we tried to hold back our emotions. We all knew this was going to be a struggle so Donna and Peter stayed in the lounge while I walked Daniel through to the kitchen.

It is often said on the blogs I read that children can pick up on emotional reactions so I need to explain this to Daniel in the best way a three-year-old might understand. I watch him eat his cereal and then sit down next to him at the kitchen table. I hold his small warm hand while he looks up at me.

'Daniel,' I say, holding back the tears as I desperately struggle to stay strong-minded, 'I have some very sad news about Daddy.'

'Daddy?' Daniel responds. His eyes light up and I know his reaction is to expect his father to be right behind him. 'Where's Daddy?'

I take in a deep breath, preparing myself to tell him the news.

'Daddy has been hurt,' I reply, overcome with emotion and with the lump in the back of my throat becoming stronger. 'Daddy won't be coming back home, little man. Daddy has gone to heaven.'

Death. How can a three-year-old begin to understand?

Daniel looks at me and neither of us speak another word to each other. I bend forwards and cry into his hair as I hold him close to me. I know he has no idea how to understand what I am telling him, which makes my own emotions worse. He is both innocent and naïve but Daniel is hugging me as if he has a need to please me. He is likely wondering why I am crying but he recognises it as a sign I need comforting. It breaks my heart.

'Mummy will always be here for you,' I whisper. 'You will always have Mummy.'

I help Daniel down from the table and watch him run into the hallway.

'You've done it now, I take it?' Donna asks, holding out her arms. 'That poor little boy. Come here and hug me, will you?'

Aware that Daniel is safe in the living room with Peter, Donna walks through to the kitchen and wraps both of her arms around me. The build-up of emotion is overwhelming as I let go of the tears. Together we cry in each other's arms – an understanding growing between us that in life there is death and that neither of us will ever get to see Michael again.

'I can't believe he is gone, Mum,' I cry. 'I can't believe this has happened to us.'

'We will get through this, I know we will,' she replies. 'You are our family and family stand by each other, no matter what. Michael loved you so much – I know he did, we all knew. I miss him so much.'

'I don't know what I will do without him,' I say, letting go of her. 'We had a row last night and I said some terrible things to his face. I keep hearing the last words I said to him over and over in my head.'

I watch Donna frown at me, her solemn expression riddled with the grief of a mother who has lost her son. I know she is trying to hold her emotions together, as am I. We are connected in this grieving torment.

'I'm sure Michael knew that you didn't mean it,' she replies. 'Every married couple have their ups and downs, don't they? Listen, Pete and

I have been married for over thirty-five years and we still argue over petty little things at times. It's normal. Michael adored his family – he wouldn't hold it against you.'

I don't think she understands my guilt. I made some really hurtful comments.

'Why was he at the Taverton Estate Hotel?' Donna asks. 'I don't understand why he was there so late in the evening?'

'It was a work thing,' I reply, keeping it short. 'He was there to meet a new client. I surprised him with a meal but he said he had to go because it was important. If he had stayed at home, then maybe he—'

'Stop it,' Donna interrupts. 'We can't change what's happened. It's a terrible accident. Don't you dare blame yourself for this. I hope they find the bastard who left him for dead.'

Donna sobs until the makeup runs down her face. Together we sit at the kitchen table, clutching our tissues and sharing memories of Michael. I can hear Daniel playing with Peter in the living room. His laughter makes me smile. Our son has no idea what has just happened in his life.

The sound of the letterbox being knocked startles me – a reminder of the police presence last night. I called the family liaison officer Sharon Jenkins as they instructed who has kindly arranged a car to take us to identify Michael but it's too early in the day so it cannot be her.

'I'll get it. Don't worry about it,' Peter says loudly from the other room. 'It's just the paperboy. I saw him walk past the window and put something through the door.'

I listen as Peter starts talking to himself. I try to concentrate but only hear mutters like little whispers.

'Something you might want to see?' Peter asks, walking through to the kitchen and holding out the newspaper. 'It's made the local papers. You might want to read this?'

I take the paper from Peter's hands and lay it out on the table with the inside pages open to reveal the headline in all its gloomy glory.

Taverton Estate Hotel Death

My eyes are fixed on the article as I read the report on the tragedy. I see the local press haven't named my husband but describe him as a male in his thirties and yet to be formally identified. I find it hurtful.

Why couldn't they just wait – or not publish it at all?

Donna cannot look at the paper and moves away from the table while I scan further down the page. She wipes her nose with the tissue and leaves the room to allow me to sit on my own with my thoughts. Michael has barely been dead a day. I'm angry to read this and see it so soon. The reporter was covering a function at the hotel that same evening and was able to speak to the only witness, Gary Taylor, who gave a brief statement of what he saw.

> The car came to a halt after it hit him, but then dragged him even further down the road. I saw another man about six feet tall with a grey baseball cap, run from the vehicle in the direction of the fields behind the hotel. I ran in the direction of the man who was now partly trapped under the car. I held his hand while I called the ambulance and the police. He died in front of me. It was very sad and sudden. I offer my condolences to his family.

I am saddened that in his final moments he died without his family around him.

I sit in silence with my head lowered over the newspaper. Again, a flood of questions race through my mind. I walk into the living room to see Daniel sitting on Peter's lap and holding a toy car. I fixate on it. It's ironic that just such a vehicle killed his father. Donna sits in the chair by the window, staring out at the sky. The atmosphere is awkward as we try to hide our grief from Daniel.

My eyes are heavy and tiredness is starting to set in. I look at the clock on the mantelpiece and I estimate that I have another hour before Sharon arrives. I sit on the sofa while Donna and Peter sit in opposite chairs. No one says a word but instead we all fix our eyes on Daniel who is playing on the living room floor with his cars.

Daniel will never get to know his father.

Seven

Jenny

The drive to the hospital in the back seat of the unmarked police car felt like hours even though in reality it was twenty minutes at most. I looked out of the window the whole journey in a world of my own, watching the scenery and passing cars. We stopped at the red lights leading up to the hospital, where I felt nauseous. Knowing I will come face to face with my husband again after his tragic death has me in floods of tears. I know I have to face him; it's as though I need to do this if only to believe I am not trapped inside this nightmare.

Was he thinking of us when he died: me, his son, his family?

An hour ago, Sharon Jenkins was sipping the last drop of coffee from the mug I made her at our house after she formerly introduced herself as my family liaison officer. For a woman with such a compassionate and sensitive presence, I couldn't help but fixate on how young she was in comparison to myself. I doubt that she could relate to having a deceased husband but I warmed to her northern accent because it reminded me of home. I miss my family. I need my parents.

Peter refused to join us in our journey, instead deciding to stay home with Daniel. Both Donna and I have to face this moment together. I need to say how sorry I am. Michael will never hear my words but I need to say them all the same.

The guilt I carry with me since Michael has died is troubling me. I've convinced myself that I am to blame. I shouldn't have argued with him. The thought of him dying and hating me for what I said that night… I didn't mean it. I can't ever tell him how sorry I am.

Donna sits next to me in the back of the car while Sharon drives up to the entrance of Westbridge General Hospital. We don't speak but exchange looks. I grab hold of Donna's hand while placing the damp tissues I hold into my jacket pocket. This memory, I know, will stay with me for the rest of my life.

'This is it, Mum,' I say to Donna, who looks at me nodding her head. 'We have to stay strong. Michael wouldn't want the fuss. You know what he's like.'

Donna wipes the tears from her eyes.

'You're right,' Donna agrees with me. 'He was such a character. I still can hardly believe it.'

Sharon parks the car, unbuckles her belt and turns to face us both.

'I will walk in with you and speak to the reception desk. Doctor Kaminski is expecting us, and you can both take as long as you need. I'll be here, right beside you every step of the way. If at any time you want to leave, say the word.'

'Thank you,' I reply while Donna continues to nod her head. 'I'll let you lead the way. Thanks, Sharon.'

We all get out of the car. I take in a breath of air to calm myself and follow Sharon. Donna and I remain silent as we are led through to the reception area of the hospital. There are corridors and rooms around us, all interconnected so that I couldn't tell you how we got here if I had to explain it – but Sharon leads us through the maze of hallways and doorways the whole time.

'Doctor Kaminski is waiting for us all down the end of this final corridor,' Sharon explains. 'Once we get inside the room I will introduce you both and then ask if the deceased person is your husband, Michael Clifton – but only at the appropriate time. Remember that if you're not comfortable, we don't have to do this.'

I walk towards the room with a feeling of emptiness. Being here seems surreal. I don't really understand what is happening or what is expected of me. Sharon did explain the formalities but none of it registered. I keep agreeing without thinking. I am desperate to see my husband. My breathing is still erratic from the nervousness and I glance towards Donna who is in a state of despair with her own grief, shock and thoughts. For now, I have to focus on meeting Michael. Facing my husband while he will be displayed to me in a state of death is a thought I never imagined I'd be dealing with.

'Are you ready?' Sharon asks, her hand on the silver door handle. 'This is the room if you both want to proceed?'

Donna places a hand on my shoulder. I feel her rubbing it as a form of comfort. Can I do this. Would Michael want me to see him this way? I have last-minute doubts but I know I have to do this.

'I'm ready,' I respond. No more doubts. I breathe in another deep breath of air to calm my nerves. 'I want to see my husband.'

I'm here, Michael.

The door opens to reveal gleaming white walls with scatters of blue seats and an office desk in the corner. It's like stepping into any ordinary hospital waiting area. I glance at the cabinets against the far side of the wall. The shining steel doors all clearly numbered. In one of those is where Michael must be resting. I keep staring at the numbers, thinking that he is here, in one of them.

I feel emotionally drained.

'This is Doctor Kaminski,' Sharon introduces us, 'and this is Mrs Jenny Clifton and Michael's mother, Mrs Donna Clifton.'

The doctor shakes our hand. Her hair is short, dark with grey patches and tied up behind her ears tightly. I glance at her face for a moment before I acknowledge her. I look at how short she is – under five feet tall. I glance at Donna, who is nodding. I've assumed the constant nodding is a distraction from speaking.

'I'm very sorry for your loss,' Kaminski says, now walking to the cabinets. 'If you would both kindly follow me to the far end of the room.'

Kaminski seems emotionless and formal. I remind myself that she must spend all of her working day around the deceased. She's likely become accustomed to dealing with families and their grief.

'I need to inform you that you will see some bruising and stitching on the body,' says Kaminski. 'We have covered most of him except for his face and left hand.'

Now I am shaking head to toe but I'm not as distressed as I thought I'd be. I am a little overwhelmed. A sensation of dizziness swirls in my head.

'Why his left hand?' I ask. 'How bad is the bruising?'

'This is in case you want to hold his hand,' Sharon says, taking a glance in Doctor Kaminski's direction for assurance. 'Some close family members like to hold the hands of their loved ones. In some cases this is the final goodbye. It's a perfectly normal reaction to want to touch your loved ones.'

Donna and I are stood side by side. I steer my gaze away from Sharon and the doctor to look at the numbers on the doors while the doctor grabs the handle on number five. In one quick swoop the door is opened to reveal the contents and all my eyes take in are the swollen feet and the white sheet covering what is a body beneath.

'I'm going to pull back the cover to reveal his face,' Doctor Kaminski explains. 'Please be aware of the bruising and the stitches.'

The doctor pulls away the cover to reveal the face. In that same moment, a rush of emotion overcomes my senses. Donna throws her hands to her face, while all I can do is stare, wide-eyed, and breathe heavily. The shock is hitting me as a sense of coldness snapping its way down my body. I tremble – but this man is my husband. This is Michael and for a few seconds I am unable to speak a word.

Michael, I'm so sorry.

'Mrs Clifton?' Sharon asks. 'Can you confirm to me that this is the identity of your husband, Mr Michael Clifton?'

We both know the answer but I accept her formalities. I hear Donna sobbing behind me, unable to look at the body of her own son. I wasn't expecting to wake from a terrible dream but on the way here there had been hopes in my heart that maybe it was someone else. A misunderstanding of some sort.

'Yes,' I respond. 'Yes, this is Michael. My husband.'

It is as though I am unable to take in this image all in one glance. I look at my husband's face, realising it is swollen, black and blue with serious bruising. His eyes are shut and with stitching underneath them. I recognise him clearly to be Michael.

How did this happen?

I move closer to touch his left hand. I daren't move any of the sheets to reveal further injuries. The coldness of his temperature surprises me. He remains eerily still – and I realise something isn't right.

It's missing!

'Where is his wedding ring?' I ask. 'He's not wearing it. Did it get taken off for safety?'

'He was not wearing any jewellery on his fingers.' Sharon hesitates, then shrugs her shoulders. 'All of his belongings have been bagged up. His clothing and a designer watch we have logged have all been returned to you.'

'He wouldn't have taken it off,' I say, still confused. 'We are married. It's never left his hand since the day we...'

Donna moves closer to comfort me.

'Maybe it was the accident.' Donna said. 'It might have come away.'

'Maybe... I need to find out,' I reply, trying to grasp at every little detail. 'I know he would never ever have taken that ring off his finger.'

I remember when we both had our rings engraved with the date of our wedding on them. I know he would never remove it. I glance down towards my own wedding ring, rubbing it to remind myself of that moment. He was always full of surprises. On our wedding day he left me a series of notes, like a treasure hunt, but each note contained one of his favourite memories of us together attached with a little heart-shaped chocolate. The final note was taped to a whole boxful. 'Together forever' that last note said.

'If no one has found the ring,' I reply, 'it must have come off somehow in the accident. Maybe someone will find it near the hotel and hand it in?'

'I can ask some questions back at the station,' Sharon states. It's like she wants to shut me up. 'But I am very much aware that the only items on him at the time of the accident were his watch, car keys, mobile phone and wallet.'

I look back at Michael's body. I'm surprised I'm not in floods of tears. His battered face is all bruised and scratched; he would have hated to be seen in such a terrible state. I'm holding it together better than I expected. I don't want to ask any further questions but I can tell from the shape of Michael's body that he must have been crushed to death.

'Would you like some time alone with him?' Doctor Kaminski asks. 'I can leave the room for a few minutes if you both want some privacy?'

I take a look at Donna who is shaking her head and for once I agree with her.

'This is not how I want to remember my husband,' I reply. 'I don't need any more time. I have identified him, and I would really like to leave now. Daniel will be wondering where I am.'

I turn away from everyone and close my eyes as I hear the slam of the chamber that contains Michael's body. The lack of his wedding ring still bothers me but I will try to hunt for it in his car or near the hotel grounds. My gut feeling is that I can't see why Michael would have removed it. He wouldn't have had any need.

Donna and I follow Sharon back out into the corridor.

'I appreciate this must have been very difficult but thank you for identifying your husband.' Sharon says and she too seems relieved this is over. 'It's a brave and emotional thing to have to do, so thank you. When you're ready I can drive you both back home?'

We leave the hospital in silence as we arrived. Sharon seems quite kind with her responses but I know that she has to be impartial. I wasn't expecting her to be full of emotion because this is her job. The police have to deal with this sort of occurrence quite regularly but it all seems so clinical – like Michael is an object.

On returning to the car, Donna sobs continuously while I keep my focus, staring straight ahead. All I want to do now is return home to Daniel. Our little boy will need me more than ever.

We have so much to organise. I don't know how we are going to face the next few weeks.

Eight

Jenny

No matter how many times I tried to put them both off visiting, Samantha and Lizzie would not take no for an answer: first the Facebook messages, then a text message, followed by a series of voicemails. I'm not ready for visitors but I've tried to make an effort to look presentable by having a shower and throwing on some clean clothes. They heard about Michael's death thanks to an announcement about my absence from work. I wasn't in the right frame of mind to visit the office myself so I made one short phone call. I do appreciate their concern. They'll be here any minute. I understand that they are worried about me, as I would them in similar circumstances, but I'm hoping the visit will only be for an hour or so.

They were having none of it when I tried to postpone it. I'm not even sure how I am going to react when I see them. It's not been all that long since I was last at work but my life has changed so much. Practically overnight.

I can't believe the life I had a few days ago is so different to the life I have now. When I last saw the girls, I was in the office staring out of the window waiting for the I.T. team to fix my computer connection issues. I was filing invoices, talking to suppliers, but now my world is upside down and I am thinking about my husband's funeral. Those times when I would talk to Lizzie on break, or we would walk with Samantha to the nearest supermarket moaning about our husband's traits, already feel like another life.

I can't get my head around it. Michael being hit like that was so cruel. I can't shake the image of his body out of my mind. Lying there on the slab, peaceful, with a cold stillness – a shell of his former self.

Why my husband? Why did this have to happen to us?

Lizzie's other half is always away on business but she copes with that; she likes him being away as he doesn't get under her feet. I've met Samantha's husband Tom a few times on nights out but they're both joined at the hip in everything they do. If I'm ever invited to a meal out, it's always the two of them. If I ever arrange a night in with some wine and a rom-com, she can barely keep herself off her phone, checking up on him every five minutes.

Michael and I rushed into our marriage, which surprised my friends. They didn't know at the time that I was pregnant. I kept Daniel a secret until I was starting to show. It was a whirlwind from the moment we first met. Michael was everything I wanted in a partner: good looking, ambitious and attentive. He made me happy. It felt right. He swept me right off my feet – but he was a show-off and extravagant in our dating days. No expense spared. He paid for everything.

Michael proposed to me after six months of us dating each other. We were well established and very serious about being together. He even asked my father for permission, which was so romantic. Michael proposed to me during a picnic, in the days when we would take long walks by the rivers. I will never forget that day in the spring. I stood up to shake the sandwich crumbs from my dress and as I looked away, Michael pulled the diamond ring from his pocket, knelt on one knee and blurted it out the moment I turned back around.

'Will you marry me, Jenny Evans?' he asked, his hands trembling with nerves. I hadn't even noticed the glistening ring for the worried expression on his face. 'Will you?'

'Of course,' I responded, though I thought he was joking at first because it took me off guard. 'I love you so much. Of course I will marry you. Yes.'

He recreated that same picnic when we first moved into this house. He always liked to make romantic gestures – but over the last few months he became distant. I can't even pinpoint when it started. It happened gradually. I think our arguments were down to the pressures we put on ourselves – stressing about what we couldn't afford, what we needed for the house. Michael was working long hours while I was unable to do more than a couple of days work a week. This house seemed a pressurised environment. We should have made more time for each other. We were both at fault for that.

There's a knock on the door. I can hear Lizzie's voice a mile away. Even in the office, everyone talks about how loud she is. We asked her if she was deaf but she seems to be one of those people who shouts when they're on the phone.

'Hey, Jen,' says Lizzie as I open the door. 'You're not going to hide from us that easily. Come here and give me a hug.'

Lizzie wraps her arms around me and I suddenly feel the need to burst into tears. That moment when someone else shows you a sign of sorrow – it triggers me. Samantha smiles and waits for her turn. Of everyone in the office, I'm glad it's these two. We are inseparable in the office.

'I'm so sorry about Michael,' Samantha says while coming in for a hug. 'The office has had a whip-round and a card for you here, babe.'

I grab the envelope and card. I open it to reveal that the whole office has signed it. That's really quite touching. I don't count the names or read the messages in any detail but fold it back up again. I place the online shopping voucher back inside and the three of us stand here staring at each other.

'Thanks for the voucher,' I say to break the ice and the awkwardness. 'How is everyone back at the office?'

'Oh, you know, hun. Mitch is still his old miserable self. Got a temporary team leader role and it's gone straight to his head,' Samantha replies. 'Promotions are coming up and you know how everyone suddenly starts acting super professional when these come about.'

'It feels like I've been away from the office for months, even though it's only been a couple of weeks,' I reply. 'Mitch has always been a bastard. He's fair though. I'm sure he'll make a great team leader.'

I lead them both through to the lounge. I quickly pop upstairs and make sure Daniel is in his bedroom with the baby gate shut. It feels strange talking to my friends about random work chat when I am looking at them wondering how they would cope in my situation. They must feel awkward?

'Jen, if there's anything, you know, anything we can do for you, just ask,' Lizzie says. I know I can count on her too. 'Whether it's babysitting, a chat about stuff, you name it.'

I nod and smile at Lizzie. I know she means well. She's a genuinely nice person who would do anything for anybody but she has a reputation around the office as a gossip. She's usually the first to know about any drama and I'm guilty of being the first to demand what she knows. She calls it her office survival techniques.

'Thank you, Liz,' I reply, wondering if I've been talked about much. 'I bet I'm the talk of the office right now, aren't I?'

'No, of course not,' Samantha interrupts. 'None of us knew Michael that well but we care about you. We can't imagine what you're going through. This is shit you only hear about on the news, isn't it? No, we mean, it. Anything you need, you just ask. We know you're not going to be in work for a while.'

'I had to identify Michael's body yesterday,' I blurt, changing the subject. I'm crying but I need to talk about it with someone other than Donna, who is dealing with her own grief. 'I don't know how to describe him. I knew I was looking at Michael. I recognised him but it was like looking at someone else with his face. He looked so peaceful.'

Lizzie comes over and puts her arm around me. Samantha moves closer.

'I couldn't imagine looking at my Tom,' Samantha says. 'I bet he'd still expect a selfie.'

I smile with them for a second. I know she's trying to lighten the mood. They wouldn't be used to seeing me this upset. In the office I'm usually the bubbly one. I'd walk round Monday mornings asking what everyone got up to at the weekend. Then by Friday I'd try convincing people to do a Mexican wave to celebrate that the week was finally over. I like to get to know people and they're used to my quirky ways. I'm touched that they care and it has been good seeing them, despite my trying to put them off.

'I read about the accident at the Taverton Hotel in the paper,' Samantha continues. 'I didn't associate it with Michael at first. I got to the part about the witness and thought how tragic. I can't remember his name now but he came across very kind.'

'Gary Taylor,' I reply. 'He was the one who called the police – but I struggle to look at that paper now. I've put it away in the bedside cabinet drawer.'

'It just doesn't seem fair,' Lizzie says. 'I hope they find the bastard that did this. I was saying to Sam on the way over that I only saw Michael in town the other week. I recognised him from the photograph on your desk and some of your Facebook pics. I was trying to see if you were about.'

I catch Samantha glancing at Lizzie – giving her that awkward look like she has said something she shouldn't have. Lizzie has noticed it too.

'What, Sam?' says Lizzie. 'It's cool. I think we should mention it.'

'Mention what?' I ask, sitting to attention. 'What's wrong. What is it?'

Samantha shakes her head.

'I'm not getting involved. I told her she doesn't know anything,' says Samantha, glaring at Lizzie. 'I don't think now's a good time.'

Samantha takes out her phone to distance herself from the conversation as Lizzie continues.

'I was walking past the shopping centre the day before Michael died and Michael was at the cash machine. You know, the one by the entrance next to the passport photo booth. I looked around for you but couldn't see you anywhere. It was wads of money, Jen. I know it only lets you take out five hundred pounds but it must have been a right handful of notes. It was eleven in the morning and I was waiting for the bus. You know how late they can be, coming up to lunch.'

I'm anticipating what she has to say, nothing so far seems out of the ordinary, but Samantha puts her head down.

'Liz?' I ask. 'What is it you're trying to say?'

'It wasn't so much him – but the others,' Lizzie replies, slowing down her flow of speech. I nod as if to signal for her to hurry up and tell me. 'Two men came over and I saw Michael hand over the money. It looked like they were having an argument at first. It didn't last long. It seemed a little odd. Just saying.'

I stop for a moment. I convince myself she must have been mistaken, Michael has never mentioned this.

'Are you sure?' I ask, but I don't disbelieve her. 'He's an accountant. He has to deal with all kinds of transactions?'

'I know what I saw, Jen,' Lizzie replies, nodding her head. 'If you'd been at work I would have said something to you then. I just thought you might want to know.'

'I'm so sorry,' Samantha interrupts. 'Her timing is terrible. You know what she's like. I did say it could have been anything. Doesn't mean he's a—'

'A what?' I interrupt. I think I know where this is heading. 'A drug addict?'

'I'm sorry,' Lizzie says, shaking her hands about. 'I shouldn't have mentioned it. It didn't look like anything work related. Michael was in a suit. The others looked a bit rough – but I got on the bus and never saw them again.'

'Thanks for your concerns, though. I'm glad you told me. Don't worry,' I reply. I could have done without this revelation today. 'Knowing Michael it was probably work related. He has to deal with all sorts of small traders. I never get involved in any of his finance work. It's not like I'll ever find out now.'

For twenty more minutes we sit talking about our husbands, reminiscing over some bad girly nights out. With every minute that passes, I want them to leave. I keep wondering if my husband was a drug dealer – but I'd have known. Surely I'd have seen the signs.

All they've managed to do is add to the doubts I have about Michael.

Nine

Jenny

I'm still struggling to sleep which comes as no surprise under the circumstances. The last couple of days have been a living hell. My life has been turned upside down in the blink of an eye. Something doesn't feel right about Michael's death. I can't stop reminding myself about how urgent it was for him to leave the house that night. I know we had an argument but he seemed desperate. Michael was tense and he wasn't normally in that much of a rush to leave.

The image of Michael's body haunts me and I weep and wail through most of the early hours. The vision of his lifeless corpse covered in stitches and bruises is stuck in my mind, while thinking about the coldness of his hand makes me want to cry again. I'm comforted that he wasn't alone and the thought leads me to think about Gary. Knowing that someone was by his side, Michael should have understood that help was at least on the way. I try to imagine that if it was me there with a stranger beside me, I'd have a sense of hope that he would at least try to get some help.

We are too young for this to happen. He was taken way too soon. The thought of Michael on that ice-cold metal slab, before being closed within a confined refrigerated space for his last resting place, makes me feel sick. I hope they find the bastard that did this.

Daniel wakes up, calling for me around one o'clock. He does this sometimes but then falls asleep again after I tuck him back into bed while telling him stories about his father. He listens, although I'm not sure if he's taking it all in. There was a time when I woke up with Michael touching my bump while I was pregnant. It wasn't his hand across my stomach that woke me but the sound of him reading Shakespeare. He had read some blog on the internet that said that reading to your child while it was in the womb helped with development. I laughed about it for weeks. It still makes me smile thinking about that memory now.

'I want our little man to have the best start in life,' he said to me. 'I want him to get good qualifications, go to university.'

Daniel hadn't even been born yet but even then Michael was trying to plan ahead.

'So long as he's fit, healthy and happy he can be whatever he wants to be in life,' I replied. 'We'll love him no matter what.'

All I have now are memories.

It's as though Daniel hasn't a care in the world. At three years old he doesn't know any better. I wonder if he will ever remember his father when he's older. I have plenty more stories I can share. If it weren't for Daniel, I would most likely lie here in bed and forget about the world. The only comfort I could receive right now would be to lock the doors, turn off all the lights and shut the world away while I grieve for my husband.

With the newspaper spread across the bed, I drift between thoughts of my husband walking out of the door, which is the last memory I have of him alive, and the witness who saw the accident. I feel frustrated that this person was the last man to see my husband and to comfort him in his dying moments. I think of this tragic scene and can't break away from having this overwhelming need to speak to the man face to face. I want to ask him if he noticed the wedding ring. What were my husband's last words? I need to know exactly what he saw. I need to hear it for myself.

I keep re-reading parts of the statement over and over until I have built up an image of the deadly scene in my head. The details play out in my mind like a short violent movie. My mind imagines a car racing down the road and crashing itself into Michael's body, which is then dragged underneath the car. I imagine the agonising pain he must have been in. Then, I see the male witness, who I have imagined to be a tall man in his late fifties with grey hair, standing over my husband while calling for an ambulance. I keep visualising Michael's face crying out for me, yet I am nowhere in sight – his wife, the mother of his only child, who has done nothing but argue with him lately. I can't contemplate the pain he must have been in.

It breaks my heart that I couldn't have been there to comfort him at the end. That last breath, his last thoughts play on my mind. I am angry with myself for my part in that whole day. I blame myself for the argument. The last thing I would have wanted was for Michael to die thinking I never loved him or wanted him. My only wish was that we could get back to the way we were before Daniel was born – have random days in bed, long walks on the moors, those times when he used to bring me flowers and I would cuddle up to him on the sofa, forcing him to watch all the soaps. He hated it but watched them for my sake. Memories that remind me that all we needed was to make more time for each other. I'm partly to blame too. I shouldn't have put pressure on him to cover the mortgage while I dropped to part-time hours.

I glance at the clock on the bedside cabinet to see it is fast approaching seven in the morning. The only sleep I have had all evening was a couple of hours after I called my mother again and put Daniel to bed. Already I am thinking about Daniel's breakfast which reminds me that Michael only prepared this for us the other day – the last ever meal he made for his son. I have to accept that everywhere I look and turn there will be constant reminders of his presence, triggering memories of the moments we shared together in this house.

My mobile phone rings. My heart flutters and my stomach sinks. I shake at every noise as I battle with my nerves. I huff at the thought of having to speak to someone, but I don't recognise the number. If it's anyone important, then it will ring again. Having ignored the first attempt, I bolt up out of bed and answer the phone immediately when it rings again.

'Hello,' I mutter, tired and quiet. 'Jenny, speaking.'

'Jenny, it's Sharon, your FLO,' Sharon replies. 'Sorry if I've woken you, I'm literally about to pass by your house on my way into the station. I've got some important news. There's been some developments and I wanted to call you as early as possible but I'd like to see you face to face. I was just checking that you're in, love.'

I remain speechless for a few seconds before I reply.

'I'm not going anywhere. Well I've not planned anything,' I reply, wondering if she could tell me immediately. 'Is this nothing you can share with me now by phone?'

'No, love,' Sharon replies. 'Get a brew on and we'll have a chat. See you soon.'

What possible news could she have to share?

Instantly I am flustered because Sharon is on her way with very short notice. I've not cleaned the house, Daniel is still in bed and I've left the wine bottles all over the kitchen. I don't know why she's doing this. I'm sure she could have told me on the phone. She must be checking up on me and probably wondering how I am coping alone with a child. I can cope. I know I can cope.

In the time it takes me to splash some water on my face and wrap a dressing gown around myself, Sharon has parked the police car on the kerb outside. She is all dressed in uniform, attracting, and has the attention of the neighbours no doubt.

'Come inside,' I say, letting Sharon through the door. 'Good timing, The kettle's just popped. Tea, coffee?'

Sharon glances around. I have left Daniel in his room. I am a good mother. I hope she can see that.

'Tea. White, no sugar, love,' Sharon replies while following me to the kitchen. 'How are you feeling? Stupid question I know but it's always good to ask?'

'Holding it together,' I reply. I can see her glancing at the wine bottles, judging me no doubt. 'Daniel is my rock right now. He keeps me focused and distracted. My son needs me more than ever.'

I set the scene, hoping she's not going to write up some report about me being a terrible mother after my husband has died. Maybe I am being paranoid again but she needs to know I can cope with our son. I have Donna to support me. I have friends who are there if I need them.

'What is your big news?' I ask. We are both standing in the kitchen. I haven't offered her a seat. 'It sounded important?'

'We believe we have found the suspect involved in your husband's death.' Sharon pauses while she watches my reaction. 'The description by the witness and the camera feed from the hotel all tie up. We're just doing some more tests. All the evidence so far points in his direction. The description fits and I am confident it is him.'

'Tests?' I interrupt her flow of conversation. 'What do you mean tests?'

'This hasn't yet reached the press, although a statement will go out today, but the body of a man found within the Taverton Estate Hotel grounds was recovered from a stream last night,' Sharon said, sounding more serious. 'He fits the description perfectly. His next of kin have been informed based on the identification he was carrying. We are carrying out some blood tests to determine what, if any, drugs or alcohol were in his system. I thought you should know.'

Drugs? Immediately I start thinking about what Lizzie told me, wondering if Michael had been there to buy drugs. I'm not going to mention anything in case I open up an unnecessary can of worms. Michael was against drugs, though. He didn't mind the odd drink but never would he touch drugs. He couldn't be an addict?

'Thank you, for telling me,' I reply, shaking nervously. 'Where was he found, how did he die and what happens next?'

I can't really take it all in. I'm not sure how I am feeling. Another man is dead: another body, another poor family having to go through what I am. There are moments during the day when I am pleased. At least he's dead and that is payback – but it's not good enough. I regret having those feelings but also I don't get answers from that low-life being dead. Why did he have to drive down that road at that speed and at that time of night? None of this will bring back my husband.

I fear that Sharon wants to judge me. I can see her still looking at the wine bottles. I'm not a drunk. I'm always sober around Daniel. I wish I was more organised and had cleared away the bottles before she arrived.

'Have you had a chance to contact victim support?' Sharon asks, taking a sip from her tea. 'I can arrange for some counselling sessions if you feel it's appropriate?'

I don't think I could face victim support. It's not just losing my husband that I am dealing with, it's also finding out about what he had been up to the last few months. I need answers, not a counsellor.

'Are you sure that it's him?' I ask, deflecting the subject. 'The dead man, are you absolutely certain this is the same man driving the car?'

'Yes. We believe it to be him,' Sharon said. 'The clothing he was wearing when found matches the description we have of him. Also, we have DNA from the vehicle which we are waiting to match too. I am certain we have found him. It will all be presented with fibre matches from the vehicle and images from the cameras. The witness statements will all prove it is the same man.'

I don't know how I am meant to feel. I look out of the kitchen window and see the sunrise through the cloudy skies. It doesn't feel like closure while I have so many questions running around my mind.

'What about the CCTV footage?' I ask, watching Sharon's reactions. 'Does that show anything more?'

'The team have spent hours going through various stills found on cameras in the area,' Sharon replies. 'In terms of suspect recognition, car recognition, we have evidence he was speeding through some red lights. In multiple areas the car is unsteady and swerving. This at the very least indicates drunk-driving.'

'Why was he in the stream?' I ask, further probing for answers, trying to understand why he might have killed my husband. 'What possesses someone to speed down the lane, drive into my husband and then end up drowned in a stream? I don't understand.'

'Unfortunately, I can only stick to the official line, I'm afraid,' Sharon replies. 'Until the test results come back and we look at the evidence further, I can't comment.'

Sharon is really frustrating me now. I'm certain she knows more than she's letting on. She'll know where this man lives and all kinds of different information that might help.

'Did he know my husband?' I blurt out directly as the idea my husband might have been collecting drugs crossed my mind. I'm sure Michael wasn't a drug user. I'd have known. 'Do you think he intentionally killed Michael?'

'I can't answer that,' Sharon replies, tight-lipped. 'There's no evidence to support that they are known to each other, but I can check phone records.'

'Thank you. I'd like to know,' I reply, but then wonder something else. 'Who found him in the stream?'

'He was found by a member of the public who had taken his dog for a walk within the Taverton Estate Hotel grounds. Our initial conclusion is that he was intoxicated and drowned in the stream shortly after fleeing the scene.'

'So, what happens now?' I ask. 'Do I wait until you contact me again today? Next week?'

'I will follow up in the next few days,' she replies with the same flat expression. 'There will be an inquest too once we have all of the facts. We have to document and follow up all our leads. Again, Jenny, I am very sorry that you have to deal with this. Please, love, reconsider the counselling options?'

I shake my head without answering. I like my own company at the moment. I have my friends online if I need to talk to them on Facebook and there's the forums and Donna and Peter too. Even my own family are there if I need them. I'm not entirely alone.

I have to ask Sharon this question. I know she will not appreciate me mentioning it again but I need some resolution. I can't stop thinking about Gary.

'The witness, Gary Taylor – have you made contact with him?' I ask reluctantly. 'My husband's wedding ring is still missing. Have you found it?'

'No, to both, I'm afraid,' Sharon responds. 'We've been focused around the work associated with the recovery of the body in the stream and also documenting what we have so far. We haven't been able to locate your husband's wedding ring.'

Sharon finishes her tea and places the cup on the side. I look down at it and sigh. The ring is bothering me. It doesn't change anything but the fact that it's missing plays on my mind.

'We might not be able to confirm if Michael was ever wearing it or not at the time of his death,' Sharon says. 'I'm sorry. It may have come off in the accident or he might have even removed it.'

I know that Michael would not have removed it. We had that argument but we loved each other. Neither of us would ever remove our rings. It's not like we haven't had rows in the past. It's normal for us. This just doesn't make any sense. The witness might have seen it, though.

'Can you arrange a meeting for me to meet the witness, Gary Taylor?'

I hear the sound of her breath before absolute silence. I know I am irritating her now with my questions.

'Is this really necessary?' Sharon responds. 'I can be the liaison person between your communications if you have any specific questions you want me to take forward. Let's not forget this man is a witness and any information could be crucial in our investigations. I wouldn't want any complications.'

'I've been thinking about Gary ever since I found out he was with my husband when he died. He's part of this terrible mess. It must have been really awful for him to see my husband like that. I want to thank him for being there.'

I also want to question him about the wedding ring – but I'll leave that until Sharon can hopefully arrange for us to meet. Seeing him, speaking to him might help me get answers. Maybe he saw my husband wearing it?

'I will make some calls and get back to you,' Sharon responds. 'It may take a couple of days. If you are serious about meeting him, and if he agrees, I can be there with you – by your side all the way.'

After our goodbyes, I follow Sharon to the front door and show her out. She places a hand on my shoulder and gives me an apologetic look, the type of look I recognise from when the other officers told me my husband was dead. It's hard to tell if they really mean it when it's their day job.

My gut instinct tells me that Gary might be able to recall seeing a ring on Michael's finger. It would confirm then if it was really lost. I've tried looking his name up on Facebook but there's too many. I can't message them all in case I came across a weirdo. Again, if I show up online, I'd be bombarded with messages from my friends and work. I'm not ready to face talking to them today because I have to focus on collecting Michael's car. That's going to be a real heart-breaking moment for me this afternoon.

I can't face collecting his car alone.

I go upstairs and check on Daniel who remains sleeping peacefully in his bed. I know I must have a good hour before he wakes, expecting his breakfast. He's dealing with Michael's death as well as can be expected too. I have the odd question thrown at me about where's Daddy and he knows something is seriously wrong. He's the spitting image of his father and a constant reminder of my husband. I remember when Michael was at the birth; he took a whole week off work to be by my side so that he never missed a moment. Michael was attentive: patted my head with cool flannels in labour, held my hand throughout and cried with me shortly after the birth.

I will call Michael's parents and ask if they can drive me to the hotel. I can make the journey home with Michael's car – I have no choice – but I'm preparing myself to come nervously face to face with the very spot where Michael died. Another tough day ahead – and many more to come.

Hopefully I might find his wedding ring.

Ten

Jenny

Splashes of rain hit my face while a gentle breeze lifts my hair out of place. Not that I can be bothered to make much of an effort with my appearance. My mental state is constantly reminding me of my loss. I'm fixated on the tyre marks and the indentation in the verge. A muddy bed of earth remains at the very location where Michael had died. I keep my eyes glued on the very spot that changed my life forever.

Why did this have to happen to us, Michael?

The drive to the Taverton Estate Hotel with Donna was emotional. I knew this would be another moment of being faced with the shock of Michael's accident. I hold his car key in my palm while I turn to see the car parked in the bay area exactly where he left it just days ago. The anticipation of having to drive it home has been playing on my mind all day. I'm dreading it. The last thing I want to do is lose concentration and crash the car – which is why Daniel is better off driving home with Donna and Peter.

My breathing is heavy and my chest thumps with the anxiety of being seen in public. I feel that everyone around me is watching my every move as the grieving widow of a man who was crushed to death by a reckless driver under the influence of alcohol or drugs. All I can think about is my husband lying here in the dark with the agony of dying without his family by his side and a stranger comforting him while I sit at home in bed contemplating a break in our marriage.

What sort of wife am I?

The intense pressure of guilt is eating away at me – but it's not like I could have known when he walked out of that door after our argument that I would never see him again.

I couldn't feel any worse if I tried. A scattering of flowers lie close to the spot up against a tree. All these names in the attached cards – unimportant in our lives, but touching that they have taken the time and effort for a man that no one knew better than myself. My perfect husband.

I miss you so much.

Donna kneels beside me, perusing through the cards and reading every message one by one. I hear her read them aloud but her voice is a blur in the distance as I simply stare at the ground, wondering whether, if Michael had taken a different direction on the road, he could have survived; knowing that if he had stayed at home that night, I wouldn't be here now. I go through stages of blaming myself, blaming him and then wishing I would wake up from this terrible nightmare. Never did I expect that I would be dealing with the loss of my husband at my age. I've been robbed of a future in what appears to be nothing more than him being in the wrong place at the wrong time.

'Is this all we have left of him, Mum?' I ask Donna, who faces me with a clueless expression. 'A handful of rotting flowers and cards written by no one we know?'

Donna stands up, walks towards me with open arms and gives me a hug that offers comfort and release. We burst into tears while holding on to each other.

'I miss him terribly,' she replies. 'I still can't believe this has actually happened.'

'Why, Mum?' I respond, shaking with a cold chill. 'Why did this happen to us; what did we do that was so wrong in this world to deserve this?'

'Why was Michael here in the first place?' Donna asked, wiping her eyes dry with a tissue. 'Who was he here to meet?'

I look at her with a distracted glance. I've told her already.

'You already know why he was here,' I snap. 'He was here for work. He was meant to meet some new clients.'

'Yes, I knew that bit, but *who* was he meant to be meeting?' she responds with an attitude. 'I know you have said *why*, but who? Because I still have no idea. I'm going to walk down to the hotel and ask them at reception.'

'Mum. No,' I reply forcefully, then stop for a moment to catch my breath. 'They'll only tell you they can't divulge that information due to privacy laws. We needed the extra money. That's why he was here. It was for work.'

Donna places a hand on her hips and frowns at me. I notice the rain is now dampening her clothing as it starts to pour harder. I remind myself she is grieving too – but I have to do this for myself.

'I'm sorry for snapping,' Donna replies. I can see the disappointment written all over her face. 'You could have asked Michael's father and me for help if you were both in need of extra money. You shouldn't be ashamed to talk about anything with us. You're just as much a part of this family as anyone else.'

I nod my head at her. Little does she know the extent of our issues. I know we had enough with his salary to pay the mortgage and my income helped with the food shopping, but we had no life outside of our own home. All I desperately wanted and needed was a break away to feel connected with my husband again. Michael, for the last year, had put his work before his family. I tried to fix things but he was so obsessed with trying to get more contracts. He said his firm had lost a lot of work.

'Thank you,' I reply to Donna, not wishing to get involved in a conversation with her about our problems. 'It doesn't matter all that much now, but thank you all the same.'

I also have the missing wedding ring on my mind. I fix my eyes on the road, walking down to the spot on the ground where it happened and almost hoping to see a small glistening ring looking back up at me. I check near the kerb. I walk around the scattered flowers and back again. The grass is wispy but not overly long. If there was a gold ring on the ground, you could easily see it from the corner of your eye. I stand still for a second and wipe the damp droplets away from my forehead that have run down through my hair. The rain is starting to pour harder.

Maybe someone has picked it up and returned it at the hotel reception?

'Mum, I'm going to ask at reception if anyone has handed in Michael's wedding ring. It's definitely not on the ground – not that I can see anyway,' I state while still walking around in circles. 'If it had come off in the accident, someone would have handed it in, wouldn't they?'

Donna shrugs and nods. She doesn't understand the importance of the ring to me. I can't accept that he removed it. Our marriage was stronger than that.

'It can do no harm in asking,' Donna replies, looking down at the ground for the ring. 'If you go on inside, I'll head back to the car now and see how Pete and Daniel are getting on. I think Pete has given him his phone to watch those weird little cartoons he likes online.'

'Yeah, we're getting wet out here.' I say. 'Are you still all right to have Daniel in your car while I drive Michaels back home alone?'

'Absolutely, you just lead the way or follow behind us,' Donna says, wrapping her arms around herself to warm up. 'He's our grandson. He can stay with us a few nights if you wanted some time alone too.'

I shake my head.

'No, he keeps me busy. Without him, I'd be too much on my own with my thoughts. He needs me.'

Donna walks to her own car while I slowly move further down the path to the hotel entrance. I lower my head as I see more tyre marks etched into the road with small traces of blood. I shake with emotion as I envisage the brutal scene and imagine Michael dying on the road. Not only am I dealing with the grief and loss of my husband but my mind is playing tricks on me. I keep thinking of him in gory details with his body wrapped around the wheel of a car. I am punishing myself because I wasn't there for him at the end and my grief comes in emotional waves of guilt.

I feel like I was pushing him away.

I must remind myself that Sharon and the police officers said it all happened very quickly. They're convinced that Michael suffered very little pain and died within minutes of Gary reaching him. I keep visualising him on the road in agonising pain and blaming me for everything.

Walking with my head lowered, I see people around me: families, couples, children laughing – those with daily lives and routines that haven't been affected by tragedy in ways that shatter their world.

What I wouldn't give to turn back time. Life can be so cruel.

If I could have just one more day with Michael, I would beg for his forgiveness. I would remind him that money shouldn't have been the most important part of our lives for the last couple of years because I would give anything just to have him here. Even if it meant we had to live in a tent, he'd be here with us as a complete family. All he wanted to do was earn enough to support me staying at home, while taking care of everything to keep me and our son comfortable and give us stability. If I hadn't put pressure on him to pay for all our mod cons in the home, then this could have all been avoided. I feel even more guilty. I could have lived without the large American style fridge-freezer; I could have coped with the old washing machine and its temperamental door. He worked so hard to provide us with everything we needed.

There have been times I knew I took my husband for granted, as he did me. If I had supported him better, reassured him that we could manage, he might never have died. I go through a bitter cycle of blaming him, then me, then back to him again. Despite my thoughts, nothing will bring Michael back – that is a fact that remains unchanged.

Mildly damp through the rain, I head into the hotel and up to the reception. My stomach churns at the thought of standing in a queue of people who I feel are all looking at me as if they've never seen a woman upset before and with mascara marks running down her cheeks.

Eventually, the queue dies down and I am stood alone with the receptionist. Her uniform looks pristine and her long blonde hair hasn't a strand out of place. I admire her youthful beauty before considering my approach.

'How can I help you, madam?' the receptionist asks. I look towards the name badge that reveals her as Kirsty. 'Do you need to check-in?'

'No,' I stutter, 'I, er, I...'

I can feel my heart rate increase as Kirsty awaits my response. For the last five minutes, I had everything I wanted to say planned out in my head word for word. I get to the front of the queue, and my mind has gone blank.

'Is everything all right?' Kirsty asks. 'You look upset. Can I get you anything?'

A sharp, intense stab hits my stomach.

Upset! My husband has died, his wedding ring is missing and my life has been turned upside down. I have a three-year-old son without a father – and I look upset.

'I don't need anything,' I respond calmly. 'My husband was involved in an accident here recently. I need to know if anyone has handed in a wedding ring?'

Kirsty walks out from behind the counter and places her hand on my shoulder. I'm not sure why people do this because I wouldn't encroach on someone else's personal space. I get that she is trying to be sympathetic, but I need her to do her job.

'I am very sorry to hear the news about your husband,' Kirsty says softly. 'Why don't you take a seat for a moment over there and I will go check out the back if anything has been handed in?'

I walk to the seat she has pointed out over to the right of the reception desk, thankful that I won't be surrounded by anyone as the area remains empty. In the short few minutes that she has disappeared behind the reception area into another room, I admire the hotel décor with its wooden panels and bright red furnishings. We could never have afforded to have stay in a hotel like this.

'I'm very sorry,' Kirsty states, walking towards me. 'There hasn't been any jewellery at all handed in recently, not even rings.'

I stand up from my seat and straighten my clothes. There is a disappointed look on my face.

'Can I ask,' I continue, wanting to double-check, 'do you know the name of who my husband was coming here to meet? Are there any bookings for the restaurant under his name, Michael Clifton, or maybe his firm Sphere and Co, that evening?'

'Give me a few moments to check the system,' Kirsty replies, as she walks back to her computer. 'It's not the hotel's policy to give out this information but I can check under your husband's name. I shouldn't be a moment.'

'I thought so, but thank you for checking for me.' I watch patiently as she clicks a few buttons. 'I'm sorry to ask.'

'It's fine. I can't find anything. We're not busy this time of year. I know we had a wedding party that night, but the restaurant was quiet. I can't find anything under his name, or Sphere and Co. I'm sorry.'

I wasn't expecting her cooperation – but when I can find the mental energy I might to call Michael's office. I'll subtly make some enquiries about what they know, if anything.

'If anyone does hand in a wedding ring, can I give you my number?' I ask, before I leave. 'It's important to me, as you might understand.'

'Absolutely,' Kirsty says. 'Just write your mobile number down for me. I'll ask my colleagues to keep an eye out too.'

I leave my number at the desk and power walk out of the hotel to leave as quickly as possible before the tears start to burst. I can't believe Michael's wedding ring is missing. Now I only have the car to look through. I'm dreading driving his car home – touching everything he last laid his hands on while I take the same journey he would have been expecting to make.

Back outside in the fresh air, I compose myself with the help of a tissue from my pocket. I look towards the car park slightly up the hill and head towards Michael's car, which remains parked and untouched since the accident. The rain has died down into a thin drizzle but I cannot stop my fixation with his wedding ring; I hate the thought of it just lying somewhere. It meant something to both of us; it symbolises our marriage. I have to find it.

The sound of the car alarm disarming itself as I press the car key is a familiar sound that reminds me of Michael returning home from working long hours some nights. I remember I would be in bed, browsing through Facebook on my phone, and hear that sound before he walked in the door. The car inside is immaculate, as Michael hated clutter. I pull open the driver's side door further and glance around before fumbling around the inside compartments. Absolutely nothing!

Anxious that I am unable to find his wedding ring, I stretch across the passenger side and pull open the small compartment to reveal a car handbook, a small torch, some mail and nothing else. Initially, I scramble through all the little things: a torch, pens – checking everything, even under the seats. I can't find the missing ring but the notice on the letter in my hands catches my eye. *Important, this is not a circular.* Isn't this what some companies use when they're chasing up unpaid bills?

I tear open the letter and pull out the sheet of paper. I see the value and I'm stunned. It can't be right; there must be a mistake. It details legal action for the unpaid credit card totalling in excess of £5000 before legal fees. I look away from the letter as the penny drops. This is what Michael was hiding from me in his back pocket. The letter he seemed desperate about before going to work. He told me it was a surprise for my birthday. He lied to me?

There's no way I can pay this within thirty days. I'm not even remotely ready to have this stress and I'm concerned about where the money has gone. Quickly lowering it from Donna's view so as not to appear like I have found anything, I read the rest of the page and throw it back into the glove compartment. I'm shaking because not only do I realise my husband has been lying to me but I have no idea what he has been spending any of this money on. We certainly don't have thousands of pounds worth of new furniture or clothes in the house. I know that Lizzie caught him handing money over to some guys the other week. I don't know whether to tell the police but I know Michael sometimes did cash-in-hand work. I wouldn't want to get his boss in any trouble.

Why did he never mention anything? What was he hiding from me?

Michael's wedding ring is not in the car. I sit in the driver seat and the floods of tears now engulf me. I let go of my emotions because I can't control the way that I am feeling. This betrayal, the secrets… I can't pay this much money. My husband is dead. When do I call them? What should I say?

Donna is running towards the car. I watch her as I sit wiping my eyes and blowing my nose into the tissue. I can tell she is concerned but I don't want Daniel to see his mother in such a state as this.

'Come here,' Donna says, moving in closer to comfort me. 'Let it all out.'

'His wedding ring isn't here,' I blub out on to her shoulder. 'It's gone. No one has handed it in. I can't find it in the car, it's gone.'

'I'm so sorry,' she replies. 'One day it just might turn up when you least expect it. It has to have fallen off in the accident. I did try looking on the verge, but there's nothing there either.'

As we embrace another moment in our grieving I feel disappointment that he has let me down. I thought he would have been more honest with me. I was his wife.

'We'd better start heading back,' I say to Donna, who now stands by the door. I can't bring myself to tell her about the statement. 'Let's just go. I just had to come here and find out for myself.'

I shut the car door, place my hands on the steering wheel and feel as though I can still smell Michael sat next to me. A whiff of his aftershave hits my nose. I stare outside the window for a couple of minutes to familiarise myself with the car handling. Prepared to be an emotional wreck throughout the journey, I start the car.

I am accepting that I might never find or see Michael's wedding ring again. The credit card bill proves to me there were things I didn't know about him. I've had Lizzie's words on my mind too.

Who was he paying?

Eleven

Michael

I had my secrets. Of course I did – but then again I was entitled to my privacy.

I wondered if my wife kept secrets from me, but knew that Jenny was far too honest. I loved her sincerity. I admired how she respected me, how she trusted me. She was the perfect wife, the perfect mother to our child. Sometimes I would reflect and feel guilty about what I had done but the guilt soon passed. Lying became easier.

The day I married my wife, I made a promise that I would love, cherish and obey her till death do us part. I meant every word of my vows. It was the happiest day of our lives but underneath the surface she couldn't see the torment in my eyes. That struggle I had endured to pay for the wedding for months on end had now come to fruition. Traditionally it is the father of the bride that pays but Jenny's father couldn't afford it on his basic salary.

I felt as though all my life consisted of was struggling to make ends meet. Jenny had no idea of the extent of our financial problems or the trouble I was in – the pressure that I faced every single day. I never wanted her to find out. I didn't want her to see me as a failure. We were arguing enough already.

Some days it felt like the walls were closing in on me – like there was no escape. I shouldn't have lied in the very beginning. Before I knew it, I was covering up one lie with another, then another. Soon there was no going back. It became easier to deceive her. Jenny believed every word.

I had a wife to support, a child to provide for and a mortgage to maintain. I feared the day when my secrets would catch up with me and expose the extent of my troubles. If I had to admit any of my weaknesses, it would have been that I liked to take risks. Some risks paid off better than others but there were times when those risks failed and I had to walk through my front door and maintain a smile on my face: a smile that hid a secret and masked the problems I had inflicted on my family.

I never wanted Jenny to know the truth.

Twelve

Gary

Dull, heavy clouds overhang the Westbridge skyline. I glance around the street to notice a twitching curtain from the neighbours. I'd better make a move towards Jenny and Michael's house. I'm not sure if this meeting is a good idea. I keep talking myself out of it but I was told how Jenny is hoped that I would meet her.

Jenny's family liaison officer assured me that she was happy for us to meet at her home. I explained how nervous I would be but at the same time I was able to understand from Sharon's reasoning why Jenny wanted to meet me. It sounds from the way Sharon described it that Jenny needs closure – and to thank me in person for being with her husband when he died. Sharon was originally meant to be the one bringing me here but she had to cancel last minute due to other work commitments. I suggested that I could meet Jenny alone but only if Jenny agreed. It sounded as though she wanted to meet me as a matter of urgency.

I can't deny that I am having second thoughts about our encounter. We have been brought together in the most terrible of circumstances. I can't erase the vision from my mind: the blood, the look of fear on his face – his last breath. It's very surreal. I've never had to watch a man die before and certainly not like that.

For the last fifteen minutes I have been stood outside this semi-detached house, watching from a distance and wondering if I can go through with this meeting. Watching Michael die made me think more about my own mortality. Witnessing such a vivid, tragic end made me realise what is important to me. I don't have a wife at home who would grieve – or many friends who would come to my funeral. I'm lonely.

Jenny may have many questions about Michael's death and I may not be able to give much detail or explanation. I'm having second thoughts. I'm wondering if I should wait until I am called upon by the coroner, if, that is, there is an inquest hearing in the next couple of months. I've told the police about everything I witnessed that evening – but it all happened so fast. He died so quickly. I think of the shock that his family must have faced that night. Death is so final.

The sound of the trees in the autumn wind and the crunching of dead leaves under my feet are the only sounds I can hear as I walk towards the front door. I dust down the shoulders of my suit jacket to remove the remnants of any dirt or dandruff; as the last man to see her husband alive, I want to make a good impression on her. I have a brief flashback of him dying in front of my very eyes. I don't know the level of detail that she will expect but it will be safer if she leads with the questions.

I ring the doorbell once. I wait for a few seconds but I hear no footsteps or or other sign that someone is coming to the door to answer it. Impatiently, I ring again.

The front door opens and I stare into her dark brown eyes and smile. She is beautiful – in no way how I imagined her to look. I was expecting someone more formal in their demeanour.

'Mrs Clifton?' I ask, 'Jenny Clifton?'

'You must be Gary,' she responds. 'Yes, it's me. Come on inside, it's freezing out there. We'll head straight through to the kitchen, through the other door straight ahead.'

'Would you like me to remove my shoes?' I ask as I enter the hallway and stand on the doormat. 'I really don't mind, wouldn't want to ruin the carpet?'

Jenny stares at me for a moment. There is an awkward silence.

'No, sorry,' she replies, looking down towards my feet, 'Don't worry about your shoes or the carpet. I have a three-year-old boy. It's hard to keep anything clean.'

I follow Jenny through to the kitchen while taking glances around the hallway and into the lounge. Strange feelings hit me as I contemplate that this *was* Michael's home. That man whose hand I held before he slipped away, lived here in this very house. Pictures of him and his wife hang on the walls. In the hallway I see other family photos with a baby boy. The house seems very small. I hope she can't tell how much of an intruder I feel.

'Can I get you anything to drink?' Jenny asks. 'Would you like tea, coffee, juice?'

I shake my head at her. I'm not at all thirsty.

'No,' I reply, 'I'm fine, thank you. What a lovely home you have.'

As Jenny turns to make herself a cup of coffee, I watch her for a minute while she can't see me. I watch her open the kitchen cupboard and I notice how everything inside is perfectly aligned and organised. It appears that all the jars have their place – but outside of the cupboards it is different. I spot the empty wine bottles on the kitchen side, and the piled dishes. How can she be so organised in some things yet so disorganised in others?

'Sharon, your family liaison officer, said that you were really keen to meet,' I say, breaking our silence. 'Do you mind if I sit down?'

'No, no, go ahead,' Jenny replies, flicking the kettle switch. 'I have thought of a few questions I want to ask – but more importantly, I want to thank you.'

Thank me?

'I don't mind coming round at all, though I was a little nervous,' I say in response and now seated at the table. 'You don't have to thank me for anything. I'm happy to answer any questions you might have.'

Jenny sits down opposite me. I glance towards the tissue in her hand. She comes across sincere and although I wasn't entirely sure what to expect, I like her. Michael was a very lucky man to have a wife like Jenny. She seems caring and kind. I'm good at judging people when I first meet them. I can tell she has a heart of gold.

'I wanted to thank you for being there with my husband when he died,' Jenny says, sounding sincere. 'I needed to say it to you in person. I wanted to thank you face to face. It is comforting knowing that Michael had someone there with him.'

'It's an awful, yet very sad and coincidental, set of circumstances,' I explain, breaking up her flow of conversation. 'I held his hand and let him know I had called for an ambulance. I was never sure if he could hear me but his death was very sudden.'

Jenny takes the tissue and wipes her eyes. The crying is something I expect since she's a grieving wife.

'Did Sharon mention the wedding ring to you?' Jenny asks. 'It might have come off in the accident but I don't know if you noticed it at all?'

'I don't recall seeing it but to be honest I wasn't concentrating on what he was wearing. My immediate thoughts were on calling the emergency services,' I reply, watching her cry. 'It all happened so fast, so suddenly, it was too intense for me to think about anything other than being with him and keeping him comfortable.'

Jenny looks up at me, wipes her eyes and sips from her coffee. Her lips look soft and her mannerisms come across as quite delicate. She must be a gentle person.

'I'm expecting the go-ahead from the coroner's office to start arranging the funeral this week or next. The post-mortem has been completed already,' Jenny continues as I try to stay focused on the conversation. 'Sharon, she has been great throughout all of this turmoil. I could not have done this week without her. She's also signposted me to victim support but I'm not sure about it.'

'I've thought about speaking to them too,' I reply. 'The police officer who took my statement handed me a small card with the contact number. He suggested I might need counselling after the trauma of what I witnessed but I'm not interested. I don't need it.'

For the next few minutes Jenny discusses the importance of the wedding ring. I watch as she removes her own ring from her finger to reveal a small engraved date on the inside. I stare at her with pity, not knowing what else to tell her on the matter.

'I haven't stolen it, Mrs Clifton?' I reply sensitively. 'You are asking me so many questions about his wedding ring that I believe you are wondering if I have taken it.'

'I'm so sorry. Honestly, I really didn't mean it like that,' Jenny replies. 'I didn't mean for it to come across that way. I know Michael would never have taken it off. It might have been lost in the accident but I thought you might have seen it. I didn't mean to offend you.'

We are both sat at the table with our numb expressions. Almost every day, I have reminders of his face staring back up at mine with the blood pouring from his mouth. Like a scene from a horror movie. He was in such a bad physical state that I dare not describe the true gruesome level of detail to her. She is his wife: a gentle delicate-looking soul who needs someone to talk to.

I remember squeezing Michael's hand so tightly, staring straight into his eyes while he struggled to breathe. I focused on his face the whole time because I wanted him to maintain eye contact – but he might have been blinded. His entire body was a complete mess. His last breath came so hard and fast. I don't think he was really consciously aware of the damage that that car caused. Watching the scene was very surreal. It was as if I was playing a small part in a movie. I watched the driver leave the car and run into the distant woodland area near the hotel. He looked drunk.

'Actually, I forgot to ask if you've heard any news on the driver. The local news has been reporting on his death for days and the police suspect he was heavily under the influence of drugs, alcohol, or both, don't they?' I ask, inquisitively. 'Have the toxicology results come back yet?'

'Nothing yet that I am aware of,' Jenny replies, after sipping her coffee. 'Sharon said they can take anything up to six weeks. I think they're expecting them through much quicker judging from the last conversation I had with her. She made it sound more within the next week or two.'

'May I use your bathroom?' I distract her from the conversation. 'Sorry, I'm bursting.'

'Yes, sure. It's just up the stairs and first room on the left,' Jenny replies. 'Are you sure that I can't get you anything to drink?'

I shake my head and stand up from the table to head upstairs. Jenny remains seated, solemn and in grief. Understandable at this time. As I make my way up the stairs, I can see other photographs of them all as a family. There is a small landing with a bathroom on the left and ahead what must be their sons room next to the master bedroom.

The temptation to wander into her bedroom is hindered by my need to pee so badly. I know I shouldn't be looking but I want a little peek. This is where Michael lived. This was his home. It's so odd being in this house where he once walked and got himself ready for work. So surreal.

There is a mix of feminine and sporty shower gels in the bathroom. I also spot Michael's shaving kit on the window next to a bottle of cologne. It looks expensive judging by the extravagant bottle. I take a sniff because I can't help myself. That's a good aftershave.

As I had expected, everything I have checked out in the house so far is typical of a middle-class family – but the child in the photographs is nowhere to be seen.

The sound of the flush conceals my footsteps as I tiptoe around the bathroom. I look inside the cupboard under the sink – just to be nosey – but all I am greeted with is sanitary wear and skin moisturising products. I know this is very wrong but the bathroom door is closed so she doesn't know what I am doing. I compose myself for a moment to not give anything away. I walk slowly down the stairs and see Jenny pop her head around the corner of the kitchen door.

'Are you absolutely sure I can't get you anything to drink?' Jenny annoyingly asks again. 'A nice hot cup of tea or coffee?'

I shake my head. How many times do I need to say no?

'No but thank you for asking.' I reply, straightening my shirt. 'I will be fine. I'm really not very thirsty.'

Together we walk through to the kitchen. On the wall I see the photo of the little boy again with his father. This poor boy has no idea what's happened, I imagine.

'How old is your son?' I ask. 'I couldn't help but notice the family photos. He must be missing his father terribly?'

I witness her expression drop – maybe I shouldn't have said anything about the boy?

'Daniel doesn't really understand what has happened,' Jenny replies. 'Every now and then he calls out for his dad but it's been a difficult time for us all.'

'Poor boy,' I reply, sitting back down at the table. 'It's so tragic, growing up without a father. I'm so sorry.'

Jenny pulls out another tissue from her back pocket and wipes away the fresh tears. I've clearly upset her.

'I don't know how we will ever be able to cope. Daniel and I, all we have now is each other. I will make sure he will always know everything about Michael and how much he loved him.'

'I don't have any children of my own,' I answer, unable to relate. 'I always wanted some, but it never happened.'

For the first time since she opened the front door, I see Jenny smile.

'Oh, kids can be quite a handful,' Jenny says. 'I only have the one and parenting has its challenges at times.'

I see her glance down towards my hands. I think she is checking if I am wearing a wedding ring.

'I'm not married. Well, not anymore.' I reply. 'My wife left me. We got divorced some time ago but I've been focused on my car dealership business. I daren't bore you with all the details.'

'Sorry to hear that,' Jenny says. I can tell from her body language that she feels a little embarrassed. 'Hopefully, it was amicable?'

Amicable? She doesn't know the half of it. I wouldn't even know where to start on that story. I don't want to get angry. If I talk about it in detail, I might not be able to contain myself.

'She was having an affair.' There, I have revealed it. Jenny didn't need to know but I couldn't help myself because there is something about Jenny that makes me want to open up to her. 'I caught her with another man and discovered that she was cheating on me. Our divorce only came through last year but we've been separated for much longer than that. It feels like a lifetime ago now.'

Jenny doesn't say another word. Another moment of awkward silence passes between us for a couple of seconds as we look at each other in sympathy for our circumstances. I can sense from her reaction she wishes she hadn't asked me. I don't want to go into too much detail. I want to remain calm but we are bonded together in this tragedy. She reveals her vulnerability then I reveal mine.

'I'm sorry to have asked,' Jenny says. 'I hope you're ok.'

'Michael called out your name,' I say, feeling the knot in my stomach tighten with nerves. 'He was looking for you, thinking about you too, no doubt.'

Jenny's sobs are so loud they are almost bursts of little screams. I struggle to show my emotions. I thought she might get some comfort from that announcement. Again, this vulnerability: displaying her sadness and letting me see these intimate emotions. I like that she is taking an interest in me. She seems concerned.

'He was looking out for you,' I continue. 'You must have been the last thought in his head as he passed.'

Jenny bows her head and cries into her sleeve. The tormented grief is clearly written across her face.

'Jenny?' I ask, speaking softly to give an indication of compassion. 'Those last few moments of Michael's death... Before I go, is there anything else that you want to know?'

Jenny appears to be an emotional wreck and is now wearing her heart on her sleeve.

'Can you tell me everything that happened that night in every detail?' She asks. 'I had wondered that if Sharon had been here, you might have held back to be polite. I need to know what Michael went through to understand it. If you don't mind?'

She is devastated by the tragedy yet I can still see the beauty in her. Unlike my wife, she seems to be a good person. Michael was a very lucky man. I wonder if she wants to meet me again and if, in time, we could grow to support each other. For the next few minutes, Jenny listens as I reveal to her everything that I watched happen. I purposely leave out some of the detail because I don't want to be distasteful. Her emotions are clearly fragile. These are images I will never forget. Scenes I described that I hope she can draw comfort from.

Thirteen

Jenny

I have woken up in the middle of the night again. This time I am hot and sweaty as the nightmare has played on my emotions. Every second of Michael's death was being played back to me in slow motion. There was no escape as all I could do was look on in horror as he died in front of my eyes. Since Gary told me what he witnessed, I haven't been able to stop thinking about it. That shock is now manifesting itself in my dreams.

I turn to face Michael's side where he has been missing next to me for days – although it feels like months. While placing my hand across the quilt covers to gently stroke his pillow, I feel that I'd give anything to have him back in this bed and snoring again. Those irritating moments are now memories of him that have me in tears. I think of his clothes or the annoying scrunched-up tissues I would complain about him leaving around the house and realise that these are small memories of a big loss.

So many regrets have crossed my mind over the last few days. I regret not telling Michael how much I love him enough. I regret the pressure I put him under to support his family. I feel partly responsible for his death because I could have stopped him leaving that night. I regret the last argument we had because I implied that he needed to change or I would leave him. He died knowing that I might not have wanted him, which adds to my pain.

I'm aware that I am now a widow and a single mother, left to fend for myself. The thought of this takes my breath away with grief when it comes back into my mind. Coming to terms with it is an everyday struggle. I will trawl through the mountain of letters and bills that sit unopened in the next few days. I can't face the world yet. I feel burdened by responsibility but thank god that I have Daniel. My saviour.

I don't know how to cope with this grief.

I listen to the silence that confirms Daniel is still asleep in his bedroom. Donna brought him back around eight-ish this evening after taking him into town. These trips keep Daniel occupied and save him from seeing me upset during the day. I don't want him to live in this misery. No young boy of that age should have to watch their mother go through this pain and grief.

My own mother is trying too hard to be supportive by insisting that we just pack our bags and up sticks to live with her for a few weeks in Leeds. As tempting as that sounds, I need to be here in my own home, surrounded by Michael's belongings. I haven't removed nor touched any of his clothes and it still very much feels as though he lives here. It would be much easier if she came down and supported me – but I appreciate the offer. Nothing can change what has happened but I'm finding it harder and harder to get out of bed each day. Nothing is motivating me except for Daniel and even then I could use some sleep. I like being surrounded by Michael's books. His alarm clock. I like feeling that he is near me. In some weird way I a sense that he is watching me at times.

It's like waiting for him to return home.

I can't stop thinking about how Michael must have felt when he called out my name. It's hard to believe that he is really dead. I know it but accepting it might start to embed more when the funeral has taken place. That burden of responsibility – organising Michael's cremation – will soon lie on my shoulders. Ideally, there would just be me, Daniel and Michael's parents present. No one else has been that close to him or our lives – not even my own parents because they live so far away.

I must have been crying in my sleep as I feel the wetness of my eyes. For now, while I compose myself, I can only stare at the darkness with the shadows from the trees outside faintly visible on the bedroom wall. The clock on the bedside cabinet flashes at four in the morning. I don't know whether to get up and sit downstairs or try to go back to sleep again. I know I am sinking further into my own misery but I have to grieve for my husband. I am lost without him.

Why did we have that stupid argument, Michael?

I wonder if the guilt will stay with me for the rest of my life. Convinced that this is what depression must feel like, I try to remember that it is normal to grieve. I barely have any energy or enthusiasm to get out of bed let alone cook, clean or do the shopping. All these regular routines in my day now have become such an effort and I can't be bothered. It's difficult not to pull the covers over my face and lie there until I am ready to face the world and all its chores. If it was not for Daniel, I think I would actually just sit here and stare at the walls until I passed out. My days are filled with the constant loss of Michael and no wonder. When I sleep, he is all I dream of.

As I lie here still and silent in the dark confines of the bedroom, I hear a murmur of noise.

'Daddy.'

I place my hand on my heart as my body goes rigid. I know I heard it correctly – and then once more.

'Daddy.'

Daniel's muffled call for Michael melts my heart. I curl up into a ball and the tears flow so hard and fast that I scrunch my face without being able to hold back or leave the bed. I hold the pillow to my face to conceal the cries. Devastated by the death of my husband, I now have emotions I never thought I would ever feel.

What can I say or do?

'Mummy's coming,' I shout into the darkness. 'Daddy's…'

I control my breathing so as not to sound devastated in front of Daniel. I place the pillow back on Michael's side of the bed. I am still able to smell his hair wax on the pillow. I know I will struggle to remove the bedding for washing.

'Daddy's not coming home, darling,' I continue. 'Mummy's coming to see you now.'

I pull the covers back and get out of bed to reach Daniel as quickly as my tired, heavy legs can carry me. I switch on the light to his room and find him sitting up in bed, rubbing his eyes.

'Everything is all right now. Mummy's here, little man.'

I sit on the bed and cuddle Daniel, holding him close to me as I hug him. I look down to see his eyes closing.

'Daddy loves you,' I say. 'Daddy will always love you. You were his little man.'

For five minutes neither of us say a word but then I settle him back into bed and pull the covers up to his chest. I watch as Daniel turns on his side and I listen as he gently falls to sleep. Sleep is all I have been craving but I can't stop thinking about Michael. The image of him walking out of that door is the last memory I have of seeing him alive. He gave me a look of disappointment as I turned away. I will never forget that memory as much as I wish I could.

I turn out Daniel's bedroom light on my return to my own lonely bed. I look at my phone. I nervously stare at the screen because I know I will be faced with images of Michael. I open Facebook. While looking at my friends' posts, I notice I have barely responded to any of the messages so I write out a post thanking everyone for their condolences. Images of Michael are on here, stored digitally as keepsakes. At the time I never knew how precious these would become. Pictures of us as a family that I can keep to show Daniel when he is older.

As I scroll further down the list, I stop at one image that jumps out at me. One I had forgotten about. I'd been tagged in it last year by my old colleague Victoria who's now living in Australia. I know it was taken when I was pregnant because I recognise the plumpness of my face but at the time I must have briefly acknowledged the tag with an emoji without looking closer. Maybe it's tiredness and my mind is playing tricks on me. Perhaps it's my insecurities eating away at me?

I can't stop staring at the image, wondering if I am reading too much into it. I'm standing beside Michael, barely twenty weeks pregnant and holding both hands on my little bump. The smile on my face displays all the emotion and happiness of our relationship back then. They were good times. We were so in love with each other and the news of our baby brought excitement and cemented our commitment to each other. Not only were we married but we were a family. Victoria has her arm around my husband. When I zoom in I can see her hand behind his waist. I'm stood slightly in front looking directly at the camera – but that look in Michaels eyes. I know my husband. I can tell when he looks nervous.

Her eyes. They're lit up and the smile in my husband's direction looks like they know each other really well when in fact I am sure this was the first time they had met. It was a barbeque organised by Victoria to celebrate her new job and moving abroad. It looks like she is pinching Michaels bottom but I can't be certain. Maybe it's the angle. She wouldn't tag me in it otherwise, surely?

Perhaps I'm reading it all wrong, although I can't stop this niggling feeling that Michael was hiding something from me. I have to know if he was wearing his wedding ring or not. I stare into the picture, trying to remember it being taken. Michael was probably telling one of his rubbish jokes. He was such an attention seeker and so charming. Michael had mentioned that he went to university with her brother. Westbridge is one of those places where everyone seems to have a connection. I'm likely over thinking it and coming to the wrong conclusion. I remember that I've not spoken to her in months. I'm sure it's innocent.

Oh. She's unfriended me.

I turn off my phone because I'm too tired and upset to scroll through all of the pictures. I spare a moment for Gary Taylor and wonder how he manages to sleep at night with everything that he had to see. I couldn't imagine being in that awful situation. I'm so thankful that he was there. At least Michael wasn't on his own when he died. I only wish I could have been there with him to hold his hand and tell him how much he means to me. When Gary talked about what he witnessed it brought me some comfort. It made me feel like I was a part of his death in some weird way. He seems really nice to talk to.

I'd like to meet him again.

Fourteen

Jenny

The phone call from Sharon sounded important. Again, she has information, but only wants me to know face to face. It infuriates me when she does this to me. My mind has been racing in different directions all morning. I hate the uncertainties – the suspense which only adds to my worries. Sometimes I don't think she realises that she doesn't help me but makes my anxiety go through the roof.

Maybe she has found Michael's wedding ring?

I'm sat on the sofa looking towards Donna who is twiddling her thumbs. She is sat cross-legged on the chair by the window with her eyes peering through the curtain. Leaves are blowing through the air in the autumn wind. I watch the neighbours walking their children across the streets. I see fathers walking their children to school and can't help but think that Daniel has been robbed of a father – denied the love of another parent because of one stupid mistake.

'Where is she?' Donna asks. 'Shouldn't she be here by now?'

I sigh, unable to hide my tiredness. I can see her looking at my heavy eyes. I hold the cup of coffee close to my chest to provide a gentle warmth. In the background, I can hear Peter talking to Daniel as he eats his breakfast. At least, through all this trauma, Daniel still has the same routines.

'It's only nine,' I reply, wishing time would speed up. 'She called me at eight and said she'd be here around ten-ish.'

'Did she hint at what it possibly could be about?' Donna asks. I can hear the tension in her voice. 'She should have told you over the phone rather than put us through this worry. What do you think is going on?'

I shake my head to acknowledge that I am unsure of the situation myself. Donna stands up and walks up and down the living room carpet peering out of the curtains at random intervals to check every car she hears driving past the house.

'Do you think she has found Michael's wedding ring?' I ask, putting out a suggestion for why the call seems so urgent. Sharon knows how desperate I am to locate it. 'Maybe it has turned up after all?'

Donna stands still in her tracks, giving the carpet a break from the shuffling of her trainers. I sense her tension by the look on her face.

'No disrespect, Jenny,' Donna says with her hands now moving to her hips, 'but I think you need to let it go. Stop being so obsessed with his ring. Michael is dead. He's dead and he's not coming back. No wedding ring can fix any of this. We've lost our son and you've lost a husband. Daniel has lost a father. The wedding ring is gone. Accept it and just let it go.'

I place the coffee cup on the floor and a few splashes hit the carpet. I'm a little shocked by her reaction. I wasn't expecting this behaviour. How dare she!

'How dare you speak to me like that?' I respond. 'How dare you tell me what I should or should not do in my own home?'

I raise my voice as the audacity of her comment sets in my mind. I've had very little sleep for days and our wedding day meant something to me. Donna appears equally shocked by my response but who is *she* to tell me what to do in my own house? I've let her talk down to me over the years for far too long.

'You don't have to remind me that Michael is dead. That he walked out that door and the last time I saw him was in the hospital spread out on that cold slab. Don't you dare patronise me, Donna? I know he was your son, but—'

Peter appears from behind the living room door to interrupt the beginning of what could be a very heated argument.

'Hey, hey, hey, calm down,' Peter says, closing the door a little so it's ajar. 'Daniel doesn't need to hear you two going at it like this. Come on, get a grip. Michael wouldn't want this. He wouldn't want us all falling out with each other, would he?'

'I'm sorry. I'm tense and uptight,' Donna apologises. 'Forgive me. I didn't mean it. We've all been a bit tense this last week. I feel bad now. It was insensitive of me. Maybe the ring will just turn up eventually.'

I could mention how little she saw her son in the last few years. I could say how Michael always said how she put her business before her family at times. All that she was interested in since becoming self-employed was money and her constant stream of designer clothes. Michael used to complain that she treated his father like nothing more than a chauffeur. Someone to drive her down to Cornwall, open the shop and watch as she dictated her commands to the shop staff who she wouldn't trust to work on their own.

I will keep the peace and hold back.

'I'm sorry too,' I reply, 'let's put it behind us. Sharon will be here soon and we'll know more about whatever it is then.'

I take a deep breath to calm my nerves. How I have managed to not burst into tears I don't know but the tiredness is taking its toll on me today. All I want to do is go back to bed and sleep. Curl myself up and remember the days when my husband would take care of me. Those times also when he needed me, especially when was ill. We joked about man-flu but he was terrible if an illness came along that hindered his working pattern. I liked to take care of him, make sure he ate well enough to keep his strength up.

I glance at the bright orange mug left on the window sill. It was Michael's favourite. Not that Donna knew this before she made her cup of tea and left it there. I look at the mug and little things come flooding back to me like the time I made him breakfast in bed. That was when our first ever argument happened. He was holding that very mug. I couldn't sit and watch him play the online casino slots, watching all that money go to waste with each spin. I'd rather waste a few pounds every now and then on the lottery but he said it was only a one-off.

Peter leaves the room to return to the kitchen. I hear Daniel talking away to himself, using words he has picked up from the kids' channels on the television. Donna, in the meantime, has returned to the chair and continues to gaze out of the window as if her stares could hurry Sharon along.

'I don't mean to go on about it,' I say to Donna, who doesn't turn to look at me, 'but that wedding ring is now the only reminder of our wedding day that I have left. It's important to me.'

Donna doesn't give an immediate response. She stares out of the window before eventually giving a reply but still doesn't look in my direction.

'I don't have anything,' Donna replies. 'Absolutely nothing except for my memories. Memories of him growing up, leaving university, leaving home. I too have my regrets. I can't change anything though. He's gone and I want to help plan his funeral – to give my boy the send-off he deserves.'

I watch her in silence as she pats her chest while holding back the tears. I have very rarely seen any emotion from her in all the time that I have known her. On our wedding day, she sat and watched, hard-faced, as if she'd seen him marry thousands of times over. Two days before the wedding, Donna took me to one side out of earshot of Michael.

'There's still time to cancel,' she explained. 'You don't have to get married nowadays because you're pregnant. Michael will understand.'

I never told Michael what she said until weeks after the wedding happened. He always made an excuse for her dominating behaviour and explained that she probably meant it in a caring way. Now that I know her better, I believe she was checking to see if I was having second thoughts. That comment upset me but nothing would stop me from walking down that aisle.

I know she hasn't always approved of me because I argue back. When Daniel was a baby, all I would hear was 'in my day' at every given opportunity. Donna would make me feel as though I was a new mother who was doing everything I shouldn't be: the baby milk was always too hot, I shouldn't lay Daniel on his side – as if I didn't know already. It's thanks to Donna and her interfering that I went on to the parenting advice forums. I waited for her other remarks after doing my online research and hit her right back with her own advice. It's a good job that she's not on that website to read all the comments I left about interfering mothers-in-law. I gave her a grandson and for that I know she is respectful of my presence in her son's life. We are a family and we've grown to love each other.

Together we hear the slowing down of a car outside. Donna stands up almost immediately and pulls back the curtain.

'She's here,' says Donna. I stand up and place my empty coffee cup on the mantelpiece, taking a glance at all the unopened mail I need to sit down and sort through. I don't have the energy or enthusiasm for it. I keep putting it off because it reminds me of the huge credit card bill that Michael was hiding from me on the day of his death – but the more I look, the bigger the pile is becoming. I'm concerned I'm going to open the letters to reveal a whole stack of them.

Another day, maybe.

I stand ready by the front door, anticipating the unknown news. Through the glass, I see the outline of her appearance and open the door before she has a chance to knock.

'Sharon, hi,' I say to get the niceties out of the way. 'Come on inside. Michael's parents are here too.'

'Oh, that's good, love,' Sharon replies, holding a black carry case that resembles a laptop bag. 'How have you been holding up?'

'Not good, to be honest with you,' I reply as she walks straight past me into the hallway. 'I have good moments and bad ones. To be expected, I imagine under the circumstances.'

Peter stands by the kitchen door rubbing his hands into a tea towel. My eyes focus on him as I stand there in the hallway, smiling. My smile hides my nerves and anxiety over the uncertainty of what I am about to hear.

'Daniel has just had his breakfast and I've washed up,' Peter announces. 'Shall we all come through to the kitchen?'

I nod my head and follow behind Sharon, who is leading the way. Peter pulls out a chair for her. Daniel is watching us all as he plays with a toy car on the kitchen table.

'Hello, Daniel,' Sharon says as she removes the contents of her bag. A few sheets of printed paper. I see the police logo on the heading. 'Have you been keeping Granddad busy?'

Daniel mutters a few words. His speech has improved a lot since Michael died and continues to get better week by week. He pushes the car forwards and backwards to entertain himself.

'Hello,' Daniel replies and holds his hands to his ear as if he is on the telephone. 'Hello.'

We all laugh with him as he realises what he is doing wrong. Donna is first to sit down, followed by Peter. I remain standing as I am unsettled by Sharon's presence. I want her to tell me what news she has. I want it over with. I look at Daniel to admire his innocence;

unaware of the tragedy, he continues to play with his toys. He's the only thing that keeps me sane.

'Sharon, please tell us all what has happened,' I beg of her. 'My nerves are in tatters as it is. Please, just tell me.'

Sharon holds the paper closer to her eyes. I watch her pull the paper backwards and forwards again while squinting to adjust her vision.

'The toxicology report from the suspect came back much quicker than anticipated, and the results are conclusive,' Sharon continues, as I hold my breath. 'He had a cocktail of amphetamines, methadone and diazepam in his system.'

Donna starts to cry and holds her hands across her face. Peter grabs her hand to comfort her. They both look teary.

'He was driving under the influence, after all?' Peter asks. 'The man that killed my son was off his head on drugs?'

'And alcohol,' Sharon butts in, interrupting Peter's flow of conversation, 'but that's not what killed him.'

The three of us look at each other with this revelation. No one speaks a word until Sharon continues.

'The post-mortem and toxicology results combined have given us the evidence to suggest that after hitting your husband with the vehicle he fled the scene and unfortunately passed out in the stream deep within the grounds of the Taverton Estate Hotel. He drowned.'

Drowned?

'It all seems like a complete waste of life,' I snap, holding back my emotion. 'Some fucking druggy just kills my husband then runs away to pass out and drown.'

I can't deal with this.

'I know the suspect is dead but I don't feel that justice has been done,' I cry, the tears full flow. 'What happens now? What are we meant to do?'

Donna and Peter hold each other. I sit down at the table to comfort myself and acknowledge my own feelings. I look towards Daniel, who has stopped playing with his car to look up at me. He seems confused by what is going on around him, I look at my boy and wish I could explain everything, but he wouldn't understand.

'It's all right, Daniel,' I say, looking into his eyes, 'Mummy's just a bit upset right now.'

'We are compiling a report for the coroner's office. All of the evidence gathered that includes CCTV footage, toxicology reports, witness statements and forensic evidence from the vehicle, all support that Mr Clifton was killed by a man who was driving a vehicle at full speed under the influence of drugs and alcohol. We have no reason to believe it was intentional. Aware that he struck your husband, he fled the scene immediately, but he could not have known if Mr Clifton was deceased at this point.'

'What are you suggesting?' I ask, wiping my eyes. 'That he is innocent, that he had no idea what he was doing?'

'Not in the slightest,' Sharon replies. 'If he were alive it would have been a case of manslaughter — at best — but due to the circumstances we cannot charge him. The events of that evening appear to be a tragic coincidence: your husband being in the wrong place at the wrong time. There's no proof to support anything more than this. Your husband and the suspect were not known to each other.'

I look at her, helpless and disappointed that the best support she could offer was to suggest that my husband was in the wrong place at the wrong time. I have someone to blame, but nothing I can do about it.

I just want everyone to leave. I have that deflated feeling back and I want to be on my own with my own thoughts. I have an urge to tell Gary, see what he says about all of this. He was there, he will understand the injustice.

'His girlfriend is also a known to the police as a drug user and both have been arrested before for carrying class A and B substances,' Sharon carries on. 'The vehicle we suspect was also stolen due to it displaying false number plates and we are confident it did not belong to the suspect. Our records indicate that he had lost his license twelve months ago for drink driving offences too. He was a known criminal.'

'Basically, if he had been locked up for his previous drug use and offences, my husband would still be alive?' I interrupt. 'Why was he allowed to get away with it, surely he should have gone to prison?'

Sharon places the papers back into the folder and puts it directly on the table in front of her.

'A judge had given them both suspended sentences,' says Sharon.

I look at her in disbelief and shake my head. Michael died because of some low-life scumbag who stole a car.

Donna turns to look at me while Peter picks up Daniel and holds him in his arms.

'I'll take him through to the lounge,' says Peter as he carries Daniel through to the hallway. 'He'll pick up on the tension. It wouldn't be good for the little lad.'

Donna and I both look at each other. Our eyes are puffy and swollen from the constant tears and grief that seem never-ending. All Michael wanted to do was better our lives, and it resulted in his death. I wish he never left the house that night. Why couldn't he have just stayed at home? There's absolutely nothing more I can do.

'There's also one more piece of information I need to inform you of,' Sharon tells us both with a look of dread in her eyes. I sense that she's anxious about continuing. 'The post-mortem report and the coroner's certificate approving a cremation have been posted to you. First-class to be signed for. I know you are already aware that Michael died from the injuries he sustained from being hit by the vehicle. The post-mortem revealed he died from being crushed by the car on one side of his body, causing fatal injuries to his vital organs.'

I'm shaking with fear as though this is unexpected news, even though I am fully aware of it. I witnessed his dead body with my own eyes. I know she is doing her job but I really want her to leave me in peace. Both Donna and I nod our heads in agreement.

'I noted your wish for Michael to be cremated from our telephone conversation, so with this release form from the coroner's office, you can now start to arrange his cremation. We can release the body to the funeral parlour of your choice when you have someone in mind. Please keep me updated.'

It couldn't be more real to me than the words spoken.

Cremation. A funeral parlour.

I hold back another emotional outburst. So much to do in what feels so little time. How can I grieve in peace with so much to organise?

'Thank you, officer,' Donna responds. 'We'll start the arrangements as soon as we can. We have so much to talk about between us. Michael's last wishes, his favourite song.'

I turn my head to pull a confused look in Donna's direction. Sharon remains seated with a calm expression as she awaits our indication for her to leave.

'Song?' I ask Donna. 'What has his favourite song got to do with anything?'

'At the service,' Donna snaps back to reply. 'I need to give my son a decent send-off.'

I lower my head and sigh with the stress. This criminal has destroyed all of our lives. I'm glad that he's dead.

Fifteen

Gary

Jenny wouldn't be expecting me to arrive without giving her any notice today but I have taken a chance that she is still at home, grieving. After meeting her for the first time in person a couple of days ago, I can't get the circumstances out of my head. I need to see her again to show my support. I hope she is at home.

I'm standing outside in the rain with a bunch of flowers that have started to wilt. They look a couple of days old. I know I should have picked a better bunch but I was stuck for time. I don't want to come across too forward in these difficult times for her but, from my observations, I wouldn't have guessed she has many friends. In the whole time I was there, not once did I hear her mobile phone ring, nor did I see any condolence cards. I thought she was lonely.

I'm worried about her.

When I think about Michael, I am reminded of how cruel life can be. How another person can take away one's life so quickly without warning. I can't unsee his dying face looking up at me. Unlike Jenny, I am strong enough to deal with death, but it's easy for me to say that when he wasn't my husband.

I knock on the door twice, the second time louder than the first. Soon I hear the footsteps coming closer to the door from the inside. I am pleased that Jenny is home and I hope she likes my gesture. The door opens slightly to reveal her in the small gap she has left ajar.

'Jenny?' I say. 'Sorry to bother you but the police have been in touch with me. Have they contacted you too?'

Jenny opens the door fully to reveal herself in her pyjamas. I notice that her hair is a greasy, tangled weave of long brown locks while her reddened cheeks and puffy eyes signal that she has been crying. If anything is more evident than anything else at this minute in time it is that she hasn't been taking care of herself.

'I'm not really up to visitors today,' Jenny says. 'I haven't had much sleep. I hardly ever sleep now.'

The rain is trickling down my face. It's not a torrential downpour but I am wet enough to have the water from my hair roll down into my eyes. I wipe them dry with one hand while holding out the flowers with the other.

'I brought you these,' I say, hoping she will let me inside. 'Sorry I didn't give you any notice. I don't have your number. I was passing by and took a chance that you were home.'

Jenny opens the door further and takes the flowers. She gives them a sniff – a dozen or so red carnations, now wet and slightly limp in her hands. I thought they might cheer her up. I want to show her that even though we don't know each other all that well, she has my sympathy.

'Come inside,' Jenny now insists. 'I'll put these in water to cheer them up a little. They're drooping slightly, but salvageable. Thank you, you've very kind.'

I follow Jenny through to the hallway. I see the toys all scattered across the living room floor as I walk past. I can't hear him. I look around discreetly and listen out, wondering where he is.

'Shall I get you a towel?' Jenny asks. 'You look quite wet. Had you been outside long?'

'Not long,' I reply, glancing around the room. 'Just a couple of minutes. I parked my transit van the next street over because there's no space outside. It was only a two-minute walk, if that, hardly anything. I don't need a towel, I'll be fine.'

'Take a seat in the kitchen,' Jenny says, leading the way. 'I haven't packed away all Daniel's toys from this morning. He's at preschool today and I still have a few hours of peace left. I was meant to go back to bed but what with everything – I can't sleep.'

I sit down at the table in the exact spot I was a couple of days ago. Nothing has changed except for the pile of dishes by the kitchen sink. Nothing appears to have been cleaned. Jenny pulls out a vase from the cupboard under the kitchen sink and places the flowers within it. I admire them as they are placed in the centre of the window.

'Did Sharon come round here yesterday?' I ask, getting straight to the point, desperate to know what she knows. 'I was informed that the driver of the car was definitely under the influence of some hard-hitting drugs.'

'The whole situation from beginning to end just seems like a whole waste of life,' Jenny replies, now seated at the table. 'In short, from what I know he had argued with his girlfriend, took a concoction of drugs and alcohol. Then I understand he had stolen a car and was speeding around country lanes. Michael was in the wrong place at the wrong time.'

'I didn't get that much detail,' I reply. 'I heard that the suspect's cause of death was drowning. He passed out in the stream at the far end of the hotel grounds. Face hit the water most likely, and gone.'

For a few more minutes we discuss the situation in more detail. Jenny seems more alert than she was the other day and I can see that by talking about the death of Michael she is starting to ask more questions. I like her and she reminds me a little of my ex-wife. She's very trusting, warm and friendly. Wears her heart on her sleeve. Michael had good taste in women.

'You smell nice, is that your aftershave?' Jenny asks. 'I'm sure I recognise it. That's the same designer brand that Michael wore. Is it called Platinum?'

'It is,' I say with a beaming smile. 'Yes, it is Platinum. Everyone compliments it. Michael had good taste.'

Jenny walks towards me, leans over and takes a sniff. We seem to be bonding now and I want her to talk to me more. I can see she has very little support. I want her to know that she can chat to me about anything.

'I am so sorry,' she says. 'I've not smelt that in a while. It's bringing back some memories. Michael's is upstairs in the bathroom cabinet. I can't bring myself to throw it out.'

Jenny starts to laugh. It's the first time I have seen her smile.

'I remember when Michael first bought it and sprayed it on himself in the car. He nearly caused an accident because he thought I was choking to death. I wound down the window and I remember how he was offended because it was an expensive brand. I thought it was a cheap and nasty deodorant at first, but I grew to like it.'

I smile back at her. We are locked within a gaze that I hope is the very start of a new friendship. If Jenny gets to know me better, I might open up to her about my own demons.

'I find it difficult talking about him in past tense too,' Jenny continues. 'Ever since you told me about what you witnessed, I can't stop thinking about it. Some nights I am living it out in my dreams. I've had a couple of nightmares.'

'I didn't mean to give you nightmares,' I reply with concern. 'I was only honest with everything that had happened. I still can't shake the thoughts and images of it from my own head either.'

'Forgive me for asking this,' Jenny says. 'When he called out for me, do you think Michael knew that I wasn't there? I didn't travel with him to the hotel so it was just a thought.'

'I grabbed his hand very tightly as he was calling your name,' I reply. 'I took one look at him and I wanted him to know he wasn't alone. I don't think he knew who was around him or what was even happening. It was quick.'

'He would have known it wasn't me,' Jenny tearfully replies. 'I failed him. I should have stopped him going out that night. I feel partly to blame.'

Jenny buries her head into her hands and the emotions are overflowing. She appears now on the verge of an emotional breakdown. I want to reach out and hold her but it would be inappropriate.

'I tried to tell him that I would find you,' I said, to offer a comforting response. 'I wanted to ask if he had anything to say but it was too late. It was such a distressing cry for you. I am so sorry. So, very sorry. He needed you that night. I only wanted you to know.'

'I can't thank you enough for being there,' Jenny says. 'At least the bastard that did this is dead.'

'If there's anything you need me to do, just ask,' I reply. 'Anything at all. It's been quite a shock to my system too. I never knew your husband but you seem like a lovely family.'

She hasn't taken the hint – or has she?

'I don't think I will ever get over this,' Jenny says, looking up at me. 'I feel like closure would be letting go of Michael and that's the last thing I want. I don't ever want to forget him. A few of my friends from work have said I might never get over it, just get used to it. They mean well. They came over the other day with a card.'

I'm annoyed when I know I shouldn't be.

'That doesn't sound like friendly advice to me,' I reply. 'Does anyone really have those they can call friends at work? People move on so quickly.'

I'm looking at Jenny, who seems confused. They don't sound like friends that care.

'I don't mean to sound rude,' I continue, changing the subject. 'I genuinely care about people but I've been hurt in the past by so-called friends. All I'm saying is, be careful.'

'I appreciate the advice,' she replies, smiling at me, her vulnerability softening my mood. 'Thanks again, I mean it.'

I'm nervous about my next question. It might come across a little strange, but I need closure too. Everything that has happened, all that I saw attaches me to these circumstances and they have brought Jenny and I together. I'm going to put it right out there and ask.

'Would anyone mind if I came to Michael's funeral?' I ask. 'I'll be honest with you. Since being with him when he died, I feel like I should be there, if only as my way of saying goodbye. Even if I am sat all the way at the back – just something.'

Jenny grabs the cuff of my sleeve from across the table. The tears are rolling down her cheeks. All I want to do is reach out and hold her. I can't take her pain away.

'Of course. I don't mind. You were there for him at the end,' Jenny replies. 'It's only likely to be a small cremation service and I know Michael wouldn't have had any objections. His mother might have something to say about it but I'll talk her round.'

'Thank you. That's made my day. I had to ask,' I say solemnly, showing her the emotion in my voice. 'It will mean a lot to me. I don't mean to intrude.'

In those brief few seconds, I feel a connection of friendship. It's been a long time since I could call anyone a friend. I've been on my own for so long. I never expected Michael's death to bring with it these feelings towards her. I'm intrigued, albeit a little scared of how I feel.

'Time I should be heading off,' I say, handing Jenny a business card with my number on it, hoping that she will call me soon. 'That's my mobile in the bottom right corner. Call me if you need anything.'

'Thank you again for the flowers,' Jenny replies. 'It's very kind of you to bring them. Sorry if I was a bit off at the door, I wasn't expecting visitors today.'

I stand up from the table and smile in her direction. I glance one final time at the wilted flowers in the vase as they sit on the windowsill. Carnations are symbolic of admiration, love and affection. I'm showing her that something good can come from something bad.

She doesn't know that I stole them this morning from the scene of Michael's death.

Sixteen

Donna

I'm trying to remain strong-minded but I can see the damaging impact of Jenny's grief on my grandson, Daniel. He may only be a small boy but I can see that it is evident from his behaviours he has picked up on the suffering of his mother. Unable to communicate in ways that we do as adults, Daniel, who is unable to grasp the concept of death and its finality, appears clingier and more agitated to me.

It breaks my heart.

Living with my own torment, the knowledge that I will never see my son again, is something that cuts my heart in two. The only reminder I have left of my son is Daniel: a young boy who has no idea how substantial the event is that has happened in his life.

'Pete, I have to say it. I can't believe I am going to say this out loud, but I have to get it off my chest,' I say to Pete, who is rummaging through the old photographs we have of Michael as a child for the funeral service. 'I don't think that Jenny is in any fit state to really look after Daniel properly. I think he should stay here with us for a few weeks.'

Pete drops the photographs in his hands on the dining room table. He turns to look at me and grabs his coffee as he stands up from his chair. I can tell from the expression on his face that he has been thinking the same thoughts as myself.

'I agree with you,' Pete replies. 'I think she could be on the verge of a mental breakdown. I think it would be for the best if we ask Jenny if she wants to move in with us for a few weeks. We can then take care of both of them – but I don't know how we should approach it.'

'I agree. It can't be healthy just sitting in that house on her own all day and night. She isn't even getting any sleep,' I reply. 'I think if she had some time to herself without having to worry about Daniel's needs, she would have time to grieve. A couple of weeks to really make sense of all this. And I think that Daniel needs to have some separation from seeing her in this emotional state.'

Pete sips his coffee and nods his head.

'Since you put it that way,' he responds. 'it's not good for Daniel. He must be so confused.'

I glance at the box of photographs on the dining room table and a sense of dread looms over me. I'm not ready to face the memories, to remind myself of the pain all over again. I might not have seen my son for a few weeks because he was always out working but he knew I was there whenever he needed me. Michael knew he was loved by both his father and me. I'm so proud to have raised such a hard-working man who took care of his family.

'I'm going to mention it when I next go around. I can't keep quiet about my concerns any longer. Daniel is our grandson, we owe it to him – and to Michael – to think about his welfare,' I say. 'I don't even think that she is bathing him. I collected him from preschool this afternoon and he was filthy.'

'He's a kid though, Donna – all kids are filthy. I wouldn't read too much into it yet but I do think we should keep a close eye on them. Is there anything we can do to support her more?' Pete asks. 'The poor girl has lost her husband so go easy on her, will you? I know how you can go in all guns blazing at times but she won't thank you for it.'

'There's something else bothering me too. I think she's started to drink more,' I say, reminding myself of what Daniel said after I collected him from preschool. 'Daniel mentioned to me that his Mummy has a special juice.'

Pete raises his eyebrows and shakes his head.

'What?' he asks. 'That could mean anything. A medicine perhaps, you know how she struggles to sleep.'

'I'm sure there's been times I can still smell the booze on her breath,' I reply, concerned. 'We've both seen the wine bottles, haven't we. Now that Daniel is noticing it, doesn't that concern you?'

'Like I said,' Pete says, 'go easy on her. It's a difficult time.'

I give Pete the assurance he was looking for but that doesn't hinder my concerns. He hasn't had to hear or see what I have witnessed today. Jenny looked an utter mess. I understand that she has good days and bad days. However, we share similar grief.

As cruel as it sounds, I knew Michael his whole life. I brought him into this world and I was there for his first steps and comforted him through every fall and grazed knee. I supported him through his exams and shaped the man he was. Jenny only knew him for barely just over five years. I don't mean to be so harsh but I am a realist. Michael provided her with a comfortable life through his own hard work.

I'm trying not to shift any of the blame for my son's death on Jenny. She is Daniel's mother and will always be considered a part of this family. But I wonder if things had been different between them, would he still be alive now?

I've never felt a pain like this.

I collected Daniel from preschool and watched as he ran towards me with the biggest smile on his face and excited that his grandmother was there to greet him. It was as though I could see Michael, just as he was at that age, running towards me.

'Michael,' I said aloud and realised my mistake because I was lost in that brief moment within a daydream. 'Come here to Mummy.'

I don't know what possessed me and my cheeks were flushed with the embarrassment. I hoped no one nearby had heard me. No one said anything anyway. Shortly after, I was saddened by the memories that came flooding back to me of Michaels first day at school. I always knew he would be an accountant from the smile on his face when he was given a colourful abacus. As a teen, he was fascinated by the extra buttons on the scientific calculators. Call it a mother's instinct but I always said that my son would grow up to do well for himself. Michael was inspired by his own self-learning attitude in life. He had completed a bookkeeping course by the time he was sixteen. Accountancy for him was destiny.

I miss you, son.

'I'll tell you what else concerns me,' I shout to Pete who has returned to the table to sort out the photographs. 'She seems to be obsessed with that missing wedding ring. I know she's looked for it everywhere imaginable but she will not accept it's likely lost from the accident.'

'Understandable, don't you think?' Pete asks, 'I'd be the same if it were yours. Do you think it's because it has given her something to focus on – a bit of a mystery? It did just vanish, didn't it?'

I ignore him because he doesn't agree with me. I think about how in a short space she has changed and hope that she finds some inner strength to think about Daniel. He will need her more than ever as the only parent able to take on the role of mother and father. Every time I see Jenny, she appears to be looking more and more unkempt. When Michael first introduced us to his then, new girlfriend at the time, I was taken aback by how immaculate she appeared. Jenny was obsessive over how all her clothes had to match. There wasn't even a crease on her. I wasn't keen on her because she was so vain when we first met but now it's like that woman no longer exists.

I don't know her mother and father that well; I've seen them a handful of times in the last few years but not enough to say I really know them. In fact, where are they now? If she were *my* daughter, I would be down here and moved into that house to support her like a shot.

I'm not happy about those flowers I saw in the kitchen either. Something doesn't fit right with what I saw.

'Don't you think this is a bit weird?' I ask Pete, who turns to look at me curiously. 'That Gary guy giving Jenny a small bunch of flowers. I know they're only carnations and some of that cheap green leafy crap they fill the bunch out with but who does that – really?'

'It is a bit strange if you ask me,' Pete says. 'What was he doing round there anyway?'

I give Pete a full description of the events that led to me collecting Daniel from preschool, delivering him to Jenny and stopping over for a coffee and how Jenny mentions in conversation that Gary, the witness, had been round with a bunch of flowers as a friendly gesture while asking to attend Michael's funeral.

'Sounds harmless enough,' Pete replies. 'He was there for our son while none of us could be with him. I should thank Gary really for being there and giving a good description of the bastard that ran away. I don't know how I would feel or react in that situation.'

The stress and strain of the grief and torment we have all been through in the last couple of weeks has really taken its toll on both

Pete and me. I also agree with Pete that Jenny is using Michael's wedding ring as an unnecessary focus point for her grief. When I think about it, she is also distracting herself from the funeral arrangements and the bills. These were all things that Michael took care of but now he's gone she should become more responsible. I've seen the massive pile of unopened mail in the hallway. Letters too, piling up on the mantelpiece and random envelopes in the kitchen. I'm nervous about their contents. Michael had his own way of dealing with things and I'm sure some of the bills might come as a surprise to Jenny. I should be more supportive and mention something when I see her. We could go through them together and that way I can see if my son was up to any of his old tricks.

Pete is dealing with his grief differently to me. I go through stages of wailing at night, random times in the day. At other moments I tell myself to stay strong because Michael would want that. Pete is focusing on the business; I am sure he's doing that to allow me to have some time to myself. It keeps him busy but the hardest part of all of this is that there is nothing we can do other than accept it. I had even wished that I had died instead of Michael so I wouldn't have to feel this loss. I'd swap places any day as any mother would.

To make matters worse, Jenny wants Michael to be cremated. I'm annoyed that she hasn't even consulted his father or me as his parents about what we should do as a family. Jenny was straight in there, demanding a cremation over a burial. I can never recall having a conversation with Michael about his death wishes. I don't think he would be that bothered either way but I want somewhere I can visit. Somewhere I can feel Michael is present. Something physical to remember him by.

The thought of him being burnt and then scattered across a field like waste dust could make me cry harder. I think about myself watching her let him drift off into the wind. I can't stop her either because she is his next of kin. Pete is not bothered about Michael having a cremation or a burial. Either way nothing will bring our son back. I need to tell Jenny how I feel about the arrangements. Maybe she will let me help organise it as she is struggling to cope. Maybe I can change her mind?

Maybe if she hadn't argued with him, my son would still be alive?

Seventeen

Jenny

The post thuds to the doormat. It follows the snap of the letterbox which alerts me it has been delivered. I let the letters lie there and listen with the hope that Daniel has not been woken up. I daren't make a sound to disturb him. Not yet. I'm not ready to start the day with a false smile over a boiled egg with bread soldiers. The minute I look at his little smile and remember that he loved his dad preparing his breakfast soldiers it will tug at my heartstrings.

I'm sat in the kitchen alone with my thoughts, staring at the walls and cupboards – all the places where Michael once stood. The familiar shuffle of his footsteps when he was around has been replaced with utter silence. It's so quiet that I can hear my own breath echoing in the confines of the kitchen. This kitchen has become a safe place: a seat, a kettle, a fridge, my wine and the food all in one place at close proximity. I can escape to this room and become lost in my daydreams. Sometimes a bottle of wine or two helps me through the emotions and my loneliness.

My body aches. The heaviness is all part of the grief. I discovered more about it by looking up a few online blog posts on the stages of loss – but everyone is different, aren't they? This emotional rollercoaster feels like a stab in the heart every time I wake up and face my reality. I go to bed with heavy eyes reddened from the hours of crying and I awake to sadness. If it weren't for Daniel, I think I would pack a bag and head right back up to Leeds but I want to keep things normal for him and to have Donna and Peter nearby who are a stable part of his daily routines. I don't want Daniel to be unsettled.

I expect Michael to be here all the time. Sudden moments pop into my head. I hear the post; *Oh, Michael will get that.* The door will knock; *Michael, will you get the door?* The pile of unopened letters have built up so much over the past weeks that they're overflowing across the mantelpiece. I'm worried and scared about the bills. Finding that unpaid credit card statement in his car knocked me back. I don't want the extra pressure and stress before the funeral. For Donna and Peter and for Daniel's sake I have to stay strong and prepare to say goodbye to my husband: the husband that I knew – and the side of him that I didn't. I'm still coming to terms with him hiding something from me but I'll know in time. I'll get to the bottom of it. I wonder if there were other women?

Victoria's picture on Facebook: I thought about that some more as I sent her another friend request last night. I checked this morning and her profile has disappeared. She's blocked me. Something about that picture of her with Michael sets alarm bells ringing. It's like they knew each other already. I'm annoyed with myself for not picking up on this sooner. I should have looked at it in more detail but I was blinded by trust. I don't even have her phone number and she lives on the other side of the world. I can't even ask her if anything happened between her and Michael. Maybe her actions speak louder than words?

I think back to Donna asking me about Michael's hotel visit. I assumed it was a birthday surprise but now I know that letter he was hiding from me was a credit card bill, I'm trying to join up the dots. Donna implied that he looked like he was going for a job interview but she knows he is an accountant. A job interview for a hotel doesn't make any sense. This was a different hotel than the one he visited on the night of his death: two hotels, two separate times, credit card bills – it makes me wonder if he was seeing another woman. Is that what Donna's question was suggesting?

Was she testing me?

I remember arguments Michael and I had in the past about his controlling ways. He was very organised and proud of that fact but complained at times that I didn't contribute much. He didn't mean it in a financial sense but he said that I never organised anything and that when something needed doing, it was always up to him to sort it. I told him that he never gave me a chance. He took things upon himself without asking for my input. Michael hardly ever liked to admit his own flaws but I loved him and tolerated his outbursts. I took a backseat in our finances because he was an accountant. After time it was easier to let him get on with it to keep the peace. He spent so much time switching companies to get deals, moving money to save interest and renewing the mortgage to save money on fixed rates that I lost track. I never expected him to die, nor to have created this web of deceit.

I know Donna is worried too and has offered her support but I want to do everything in my own time. I have to do this step by step, with the first step to overcome being the funeral. Then, I want to find out who he was meeting that night. I also need to know who he was making cash payments to. I might have to question Lizzie again without Samantha around. See if there's anything else she might remember.

Michael's cremation. I suspect that both Peter and Donna will naturally want a major role but I fear Donna will take over completely. This is where Michael gets his dominant personality streak from. Donna will chip in with her advice. Before I know it, she will take over everything behind my back. I don't have the mental energy to argue with her or anyone else for that matter. I can't shift this emptiness. I never even got to say a proper goodbye.

The flowers that Gary kindly delivered in person have perked up on the kitchen window. He didn't need to bring me flowers but it was a very kind gesture. I don't how he can go to sleep at night either with what he witnessed and I feel embarrassed for crying in front of him: this stranger thrown head first into my grief. He seems really pleasant as a person and I feel like I should do something to repay him for his kindness. Perhaps I could text him later and thank him again.

The chair rubs against the kitchen floor as I stand up and push it back in towards the table. I was hoping to avoid that annoying squeak noise so as not to wake Daniel. I quietly walk to the front door to retrieve the mail from the doormat. I don't want him disturbed. I see the large brown envelope with the coroner's office logo printed in the far-right corner with postage stamp marks. This should be everything we need to now make the funeral arrangements. Michael would have hated how long this is all taking to organise.

When I look at myself in the hallway mirror I hardly recognise the aged emotional wreck that I have become. I can tell I have lost weight too but I've been forgetting to eat. Each day I make Daniel his dinner and think about making mine later. Later never comes.

I head into the living room and slump back on to the chair that faces the window. I've already opened the curtains to let in the daylight and I am ready. With a quick tear, the envelope is open and I stare at the contents. I pull out a copy of the report. Certification of Coroner.

My eyes scan it as quickly as possible as I try to read it all at once.
Cardiac arrest?

Michael died from a heart attack suffered from the trauma of the accident. I read further down the form. I can't take my eyes away from it.

In my opinion, there is not a need for further examination of the body.

It's printed, signed and dated.

I'm upset – but not as emotional as I thought I would be when reading it and seeing it there in black and white. It's a huge step forward in now being able to organise Michael's funeral. That should come as a relief to Donna and Peter. I have no idea how much it will all cost but I know that Michael has some life insurance he took out when we bought the house. I'll hunt out the paperwork from his files in the next few days. It's hard keeping a focus and being bothered but I need to be better prepared for all this organising. I need to get my act together. I'm going to call Donna. I need some help.

The envelope from the coroner's office and its contents with leaflets are left on the arm of the chair. I look at the others and I see another with bold red lettering emblazoned across the front. Not again. Not more credit card bills. I only thought he had the one and Michael never mentioned his spending habits. It was something that was only meant to be used for emergencies. My hands are shaking a little as I tear open the end. I still feel nervous – and in an instant I am confronted by confusion. This can't be real.

'No,' I shout, although no one is here to listen. 'No, this can't be true. What's happening?'

I'm trembling and there is nothing I can do. It's there, staring at me as clear as day. It has to be wrong. I'm looking at the default notice for three months of missed mortgage payments. The shaking still continues but the anger has turned into numbness. I'm sure Michael paid the mortgage every month. Most of the main expenses are set up to come straight out of his bank account by direct debit. He would have told me if he hadn't paid. There must be some misunderstanding?

I read the letter again and total up all the missed payments. I'm reduced to tears. It's as though my world is caving in on me and I haven't got Michael near me to ask him why? Why was he missing the payments? Why was he keeping things from me?

Daniel's crying distracts me and reminds me that I have locked him in his bedroom. He'll be upstairs trying to get out of the door but the baby-gate is locked shut.

'Mummy's coming up to get you now, Daniel,' I say. 'We'll get you your breakfast.'

I fold the letter. I will deal with it another time. I can't bring myself to have to talk to people, to wait on telephone lines when I am not even sure what Michael's passwords are. No one even knows he is dead yet.

Why did Michael put us in a position where we could lose our home? And how am I ever going to fix this mess? What did he do with our money?

Eighteen

Gary

The appointment reminder text is still at the top of my messages on my mobile phone. I stare at it for a minute, wondering if I should have even bothered to turn up. I thought speaking to a therapist would improve my mood but it's made it worse by stirring up memories. Despite the success I have achieved in my life materially. It's only now that I feel like a failure. Some days I can hardly believe my life has turned out the way it has. It is because of the actions of other people who have helped shaped the man that I am today. I've spent most of my adult life giving and forgiving others. But now this is my time.

Fuck anyone else.

Jenny has unsettled me. I wasn't expecting to be greeted with such warmth and care from her. I don't even really know what I was expecting but she's managed to make me think that good people do exist in this world. She reminds me of my ex-wife, too. I thought she was a good person once. I believed her too when she said she cared for me.

What can I do to make Jenny contact me again?

I was a successful man who had everything I could ever need: a loving wife, a beautiful home, a constant stream of income to provide a lifestyle for her no other man could afford – but it still wasn't enough. I wasn't enough. She said I was the only man she would ever need – before leaving me for *him*.

That day hit me like a ton of bricks. I was even contemplating suicide. I felt worthless, useless. I succumbed to the thought of ending my life. But I changed over time; I had to move on with my life. The man I used to be is dead. It can be vile how the actions of one person can impact on another even to the point of no return. She played me for a fool.

I still have the photographs from the private detective. Images I paid for and of them both embracing each other. How could they have done that to me?

I know my symptoms; I know how to deal with them. I sit down in front of the doctor with not a care in the world. He speaks, I listen, he shakes my hand, I smile and walk out of the office door. On top of everything else, I know I have depression, but nothing matters anymore, nothing has more importance than the hatred that has ravaged its way through my mind. It eats away at me daily yet the tablets are meant to control these demons.

Why should the doctor really care about someone like me?

I still keep my thoughts directed to my ex-wife and to the exact moment that ruined everything we had together. I can pinpoint it to the day I caught her with another man. I followed her after my instinctive suspicions and watched as she leant in for a kiss. I forgave my wife but I never knew that the effects of her leaving me would come back to haunt me two years later. I accepted that I wasn't around much for her either. I thought showering her with gifts would make up for my distant relationship. I apologised for all the times I shouted at her and expected her to be a better wife. I wanted her support. I forced her to work with me even though she hated it. In the end I drove her away – to *him*.

We should have both admitted that it was over long before the divorce hearing. She was the only woman I ever loved and probably the only woman I ever will. I still miss her but I mourn more for the life I thought I could have had. Fate, consequence and coincidences ensured I was dragged down to my lowest levels. Destiny dealt me a bad hand on this earth and I'm now running with that hand freely and unapologetically.

If I could rewrite the past it would have me walk away there and then rather than beg her to stay. I believed her when she said it was over. I wanted to trust her again but she couldn't help herself. Whatever it was that he had that I didn't – I might never know now because I have no idea where she lives. We've not spoken since the divorce. I made sure she stayed at home, working, with little contact to the outside world. I thought she would learn her lesson.

'He's like an addiction,' she told me during the last conversation I had with her. 'I don't love him but I sometimes need him.'

'Why did you do this to me?' I asked, pleading for explanations while blaming myself. 'Am I not enough for you?'

Letting my wife go was a struggle because it made me feel like a failure. I no longer blame myself. I blame *him*. He came along and destroyed my life and I shall never forgive him.

After my wife deserted my life the stress took over – along with guilt and emotions and anger I never knew I could feel and which I blame for my illness. And it all started with *them*.

It's all their fault – but I blame him more.

I hit rock bottom in ways I couldn't have imagined. There were days when I couldn't bring myself to get out of bed and all because more than anything else I blamed myself. I learnt from my wife's betrayal that loving someone is a dangerous game. Love is fragile and meaningful but can shatter into disappointment in the hands of someone else. I don't ever want to put myself through that again.

The doctors want to be supportive. I am dealing with my demons, which are now under my control. If I had kept my wife under control at the beginning of our marriage, then perhaps it wouldn't have come to this. She might never have left me. Maybe my demons wouldn't have appeared?

During today's appointment with the therapist, we discussed how I felt watching Michael Clifton die. The therapist didn't want me to focus on the gruesome details of Michaels's body ruined under the wheels of the car, but how I felt about being there in that traumatic moment of his death – that one final moment where life evaporated. He knew it made me think of my own mortality and how delicate our lives are in this existence.

'Everything just stopped,' I explained. I had already gone through this with the police. 'It was like he was frozen in time. Everything from his facial expression to his body had stopped. I no longer heard his choking sounds or the breathing noises and his hand felt limp and lifeless.'

I will never forget being there that night and although I am unsure if Michael could see my face with the damage done to his eyes I know he could hear me. I felt the way his hand twitched when he listened to my voice. I was there at the end of his life and I realise in some strange way that Jenny is comforted by this fact. In the same way that she needs to hear every minute detail of Michaels last seconds. I feel drawn to her.

I'm confident that Jenny will call me soon. I know that she can't stop thinking about Michael's death, which is causing her some considerable pain – naturally – and nightmares too. I was the only one who was at the scene and who can reconstruct for her in my own words the vivid detail of the events. She needs to hear what happened over and over. I know because of this she will eventually call me.

Without realising it, Jenny is going through the self-torture method with her grief. I recognise it from when my wife left me. Although the circumstances are different, Jenny and I share a similar loss. We both have a pain, a void in our lives that we should blame someone else for. Jenny will unlikely ever move on from her tragedy and nor will I. I want to be there for her, a supportive friend. She needs me.

I look at the list of prescribed drugs for my condition. I have to set reminders to take them because this is still all new to me. I feel so alone. I have thought about opening up to Jenny but we've only just met. It's too soon to bombard her with my troubles. She's only just lost her husband and is still yet to arrange his funeral. I have to sit and wait patiently – but confident the right time will come soon.

My mobile phone vibrates in my trouser pocket while I wait for the surgery dispensary to announce that my prescription of drugs is ready for collection. I take a quick glance at the notification. I'm unfamiliar with the number but I know who it is by the message. Finally, she's made a move.

> Thank you for the flowers, they are beautiful. Sorry if I have been offish when you visited. Lots to organise as you can imagine. Thanks again. Jen.

I smile joyfully. I feel perky already. I am smiling and cheerful that Jenny has reached out. I make the decision not to reply straight away because I don't want to come across too keen. It might put her off. I want to choose my next words wisely since the communications channel has now been opened and I don't want her to push me away. I have to think about how I can entice her to invite me round again. I want her to open up to me, to tell me how she feels because I know that we have a connection, even if she doesn't realise it yet. I'm not going anywhere.

'Mr Taylor.' I hear my name as the pharmacist holds up the white paper bag. 'Your prescription is ready.'

I look at him standing there, waiting for me to rush. I stand up, stretch my legs and collect my drugs. I turn to look around the room and wonder how many more are in my position? All of us sat here with varying illnesses hidden from view. You couldn't tell from the outside what's wrong with anyone. I wonder if they've also been let down by people they once love. People they trusted. People they cared for who abandoned them. Jenny and me have so much in common.

Just as well no one can see what's going on inside my head. Nothing but pain and misery. Jenny might have discovered my weakness. Those brief minutes when she opens up with her grief, I feel we are connected. That sense of turmoil and despair we each have is created by different circumstances but unites us with its misery. She doesn't realise yet what similarities there are between us. Friendship is a beautiful thing. I can't wait to meet her again.

Walking out of the pharmacy, I can't say I feel any better but I have to keep at it with my appointments. My therapist admitted that I looked better than he thought I would, under the circumstances. I can see where he is coming from – but Michael's death hasn't kept me awake at night; it hasn't stopped me from eating or running my business as usual but it has turned me in the direction of Jenny. I told my therapist I had a new friend – someone I can talk to about my problems and maybe in time, if I show her what a compassionate, caring person I am, someone who wouldn't need anyone else. She might want to take care of me.

I've decided – after a few minutes of waiting – that now is an appropriate time to reply to her text message.

> I'm glad you liked the flowers. I understand your difficult times, but if you need to talk, I am here. Text me anytime. Gary

I keep looking at the message to assure myself that it's not too forward – but not bland enough for her to ignore. I almost ended with a kiss at the end but she might have been offended. I hope I have planted a seed for future contact and I hope she replies – if not today, then tomorrow or the next day. I look again at my phone, knowing that she would have received the message by now. I wonder what she is thinking, feeling or doing? I hope I haven't frightened her off because there is so much more I can talk to her about.

Nineteen

Jenny

I don't seem to know what is happening in my life anymore or if anything was ever clear to me from the beginning. Each day is morphing into the same routine of constant grief and, emotions that run wild. I have to fake normality in front of Daniel until he goes to bed. Only then, when the sun has set, and the nights draw in, can I really be myself. I even feel guilty at times for sleeping. How can my mind ever switch off from this loss?

Since finding out that Michael had been hiding the post from me to conceal his credit card debt, I can understand the stress he was feeling. It's exactly how I feel now. I had no idea that we are in so much debt. The mortgage, the credit cards, the savings accounts, the overdraft, the whole of our life together I now see as a financial picture of negative balances. This was confirmed when I managed to find some time to open a handful of the letters. I put the statements to one side and stopped reading them. I don't even know where to begin to fix this awful mess.

All the withdrawals, the money transfers between accounts, were unknown to me. If he was stood here in front of me now, I'm not even sure if I would believe what came out of his mouth. He lied to me.

Why?

I keep asking myself why he would hide this from me. I assume he didn't want to worry me or thought he had it all under control. If I challenged him about this, I know exactly what he would say.

'Leave it to me, Jen. Have we ever gone without?'

I wonder if he knew we could end up homeless. I'm not sure how Michael thought he could keep this from me all this time. How was he going to explain to me that he hadn't been paying anything?

I don't even know how to pay for his funeral. I might have to sell our belongings, even though there is nothing of much value here. Most of it came from our shopping catalogue – more debt. *I bought into the convenience and payment plan options, not realising that all the time I had been adding to our financial struggles. I was left in the dark.*

All the different things that I need to consider float around my head along with one worry after the other. I don't know what else to do, who to turn to, what to say or where to even begin. I don't even think his parents have enough to sort out this mess. All I want to do is lock myself away and think about something else. This strain on my living circumstances has me wanting to go to bed and never get out of it again. I'm constantly tired: tired of the lies, the worry and the stress of what might happen next.

What's wrong with me?

I know the bills keep coming in because I'm piling them up unopened. My sick pay from work is not enough to cover everything but I do have another month of compassionate leave left. Even if I were able to return to work sooner, I still wouldn't be able to afford this house on my own. Whether I like it or not, I'm going to have to face up to the possibility of losing it. When the funeral is over, I will find more strength. I have to do this one step at a time. My mental health is already broken enough.

Michael's mother will no doubt judge me and form opinions that will send me into a rage, while my own mother will just pester me to pack my bags and move back up north. That does seem like an easy option and certainly better than homelessness. I don't know the process because I've never had to think about being a single parent with no home of my home. I'm going to check the local authority website later to think about what help I can get, if any.

I am dreading the conversation I am going to have to instigate with both Donna and Peter. I will ask his parents if they could contribute towards Michael's cremation costs. I've managed to find the local crematorium online, which I can show Donna when she's next over.

The telephone is ringing and it distracts me from my depressed thoughts. I'm expecting this call from Donna because she is collecting Daniel from preschool this afternoon. I can't go there and face the other mothers staring at me. The death of my husband makes everyone smile – or glance at me in awkward silences. I'd rather Donna went for the time being.

'Hi Donna, is everything ok?' I ask. 'Is Daniel all right?'

'Daniel is fine,' Donna replies. 'He's always safe at school. The teacher said he was a little grumpy, but that's to be expected. They aren't concerned, and we will be back home in about five to ten minutes. See you soon.'

'Thanks for letting me know,' I reply. I can tell she can hear the concern in my voice. 'I hate this fear I seem to have of everything. I never had this before Michael died.'

'It's only natural. I would be the same,' Donna replies. 'I don't mind picking him up anytime. You know that.'

I hang up on Donna after saying my goodbyes and I feel relieved. I have been thinking about taking Daniel out of preschool to keep him at home with me. I'm scared about losing Daniel too. What if Daniel died in some accident?

Daniel is all I have left. He is our son and I have to protect him. If he went to school and there was some freak accident that killed him too, how could I go on living?

The mental torment from the thoughts of despair, loss, anger and hurt leave me unmotivated to do anything. The struggle to wash and get dressed was something I would never consider difficult until now. Everything in my life is such an effort. My motivation to do anything is dwindling because my mind won't switch off.

I'll get washed later.

I look down at my mobile phone and start flicking through the contacts list: names that are all too familiar and contacts who seem distant strangers after Michael's death. The only recent reply is from Gary. I owe him a thank you for such a lovely gesture. I keep thinking about messaging him again. He might think it strange for me to want to hear about Michael's death all over again. I want to get an understanding of how he was feeling and what was going through his mind. Now that I know the extent of the secrets that he was hiding and the consequences, I want to get inside his head.

Michael wanted me by his side, and I failed him again. Every last detail of his facial expression helps me to come to terms with his death. I get comfort from understanding it – from the fact that Gary is able to be honest with me about what he saw. He understands.

The sound of the car engine shutting off outside alerts me that Donna is here with Daniel. I stand, staring at the wardrobe door with the black bags in one hand and my tissue in the other – wiping the tears from my eyes as I ready myself to start packing away Michael's clothes: suits, jeans, shirts and jumpers, all strewn across the bed as I had left them after emptying the drawers earlier in the day. I'm not ready to see them go but I can't hold it off much longer. What good would keeping them do – these constant reminders all over the house? Daniel must be sick of seeing his mother cry from one room to the next.

Someone knocks on the front door twice. I can hear Daniel's sweet angelic voice from the other side of it. I feel both calm and relieved that he is home and safe. I have this yearning to lock ourselves in the house – away from the world and cocooned in a dream of safety and the reassurance that I will never lose my son. I want to keep him safe.

I open the door to Donna. I watch her eyes wander up and down as she stares at me. At the same time, I take a look into her eyes for one second and I can see she is still grieving too. That solemn look shows she is hurting even if the fancy designer clothes that she wears say otherwise.

'You're still in your bedclothes?' Donna asks. 'Why haven't you got dressed yet?'

Before I can answer, she barges in and walks Daniel through to the living room. I shut the front door and by the time I pull up the handle to secure us indoors, she is stood there with her hands on her hip. She doesn't look impressed.

'I'm worried about you,' Donna says. 'You haven't washed by the look of your appearance. You're not getting dressed; you're barely leaving the house, if at all. Pete and I are concerned.'

I can't believe her at times. My husband is dead. What does she want me to do – act like nothing has happened? I can't just forget him.

'I've had too much on my mind today,' I reply, wishing she wouldn't ask such stupid questions. 'I don't even know where to begin.'

Donna sighs and looks at me as if I'm making excuses.

'Tell me,' she says, 'we're in this together.'

'He hasn't been paying the mortgage. I think I'm going to lose the house. Michael has got us into so much debt and he's been handing money to god knows who,' I blurt out while bursting into tears again, tears that don't seem to want to stop. 'I don't know what to do or who to speak to about this. I don't know why he's been lying to me, Mum.'

The look on Donna's face reminds me of the moment the sheet was pulled back to reveal Michael's body at the morgue. That was the last time I saw her with that dropped mouth expression. I don't care about whether I am washed or dressed and I can barely even cook for myself. Everything in my life is centred around Daniel's needs and surviving day by day.

'How much are the arrears?' Donna asks, hands now removed from her hip with one on her forehead. 'One month, two? What do you mean you are losing the house? Are you serious? Michael's not even been cremated yet.'

'I'm serious, it's really bad,' I respond. 'It's thousands. He's been hiding things from me: credit cards, missed payments. I don't know where to begin. It's not going to be long before the debt collectors start knocking on the door. I could lose everything.'

Donna frowns and shakes her head. I can see she is worried. She must be disappointed about her son – but these are the facts. He was lying to us all.

'I can't believe it,' Donna replies. 'Maybe Pete and I could help. I can see what I can offer to at least keep the roof over your heads. Credit cards, things like that – well people can't get from you what you haven't got. This house has to be your priority. What about the funeral?'

'I have the coroner's certificate now, approving the release of Michael's body. The certificate is on the microwave.' I reply. 'I have to register his death and to get the process rolling with a funeral director. I'm not coping. It's becoming too much. I've tried, but—'

'Stop that,' Donna interrupts me mid-flow. 'That's not the Jenny I know. You have to get through this. You have a son to look after. This is not what Michael would have wanted to see from you.'

We stand together tearful in the hallway. I try not to argue back but I want to be left in peace. Every little thing in my life right now seems like a big hurdle. Some hurdles are too big to jump over. I'm falling flat.

'We need to get Michael's funeral planning underway as soon as possible. Why don't you let us take care of that?' Donna asked. 'We can register Michael's death together now that you have the certificate and see if we can get him buried next week?'

'I don't want him buried. We've been through this before,' I reply, sharply. 'The thought of him being there in the ground, rotting away, is not what I want. I don't think Michael would have wanted that either.'

'Did Michael ever talk about what he wanted?' Donna asks, walking forwards in my direction to get closer. 'If he ever wanted a cremation or burial?'

'We talked about death, Mum,' I reply. 'Of course we did, once or twice when I was pregnant, in case anything went wrong but he wasn't that bothered either way. It's me who can't face the idea of him in the ground. I don't want him to be buried.'

'Don't you think it would be lovely if we had somewhere to visit? If he was in a grave.' Donna sobs. 'I brought him into this world. I think he should be buried. I can't hide my opinion – because he was my son.'

Once more, she is overpowering me. My heart is racing with the temper that is brewing. I'm trying to control it, but she's asking for my opinion.

'I am his wife.' I snap back. 'This isn't your decision. I'm sorry. Really, I am, but he was my husband and I don't want him buried. Can we leave it at that now? I don't want us to fall out with each other.'

Donna stares at me briefly. I don't know what else to say.

'I would rather you helped me than argued with me.' I continue, to console her a little. 'His death has affected us all, hasn't it? We can do something lovely to remember him, even if he isn't buried. Maybe we can plant a tree and have a plaque too as somewhere to visit?'

Donna wipes her eyes and nods in agreement. Then she takes a few steps backwards and turns briefly to check on Daniel who is sat on the chair in the living room playing with his toys.

'I'm sorry,' she says, 'forgive me. I've never been good with my timing. I feel so strongly about it – but respect that it's your decision in the end.'

Donna comes towards me with her arms out. I cuddle her.

'I need your help, Mum,' I explain as we are still locked in an emotional embrace. 'The house, the funeral, I don't know where to begin. I have no idea what Michael has spent our money on. I'm going to wait until the funeral is over so I'll be more mentally up to it. All the phone calls, the letters and people I'll have to deal with.'

We separate and wipe our eyes.

'Another week or so won't make any difference, I agree, but you need to start by looking after yourself better,' Donna says, still wiping her cheeks. 'Let me come around again tomorrow and we will sort out what we can.'

'Thank you,' I reply, sighing with relief, the anxiety of packing up all Michael's clothes still looming over me. 'Did Michael ever mention anything to you about anything?'

'Anything?' Donna replies, 'what do you mean?'

'His debts or gambling. Has he ever mentioned these to you when I wasn't around?' I ask with more detail. 'I know Michael liked the casino before we were seeing each other but he said that was all behind him by the time we got married.'

'He wouldn't talk to me about anything like that – not before talking to you,' Donna replies, 'I know he used to like the odd flutter on the horses now and again.'

'It was mostly cash withdrawals,' I respond, trying to analyse if she knew anything or not. 'Most of the credit card bills statements show he used cards to take money out. I have no idea what he spent that money on, and the interest is higher. Getting higher every month.'

Donna looks surprised and continues to shake her head to give an indication she had no idea.

'Maybe we can go through it all in a few days then,' I say and leave it at that for now. 'My head is constantly thinking, constantly worried, constantly unsure of anything.'

'I'll go back home and have a discussion with Pete,' Donna says, walking towards the door to leave. 'I'll let you know what we can do to help.'

Donna gives Daniel a kiss on the cheek before leaving the house. That moment between us was good to clear the air. Donna didn't seem to challenge anything I told her at all. She brushed off the gambling question and left.

I wonder what she really knew, if anything?

Twenty

Gary

I'm angry. I've been mad for most of this afternoon after calming down from a violent outburst caused by my own frustrations. I've been reflecting on my life, some of the good choices but mostly all of the bad. No one should see me in this mental state of mind. I end up hating myself for my temper. It has always been my downfall and I feel guilty for taking out my frustrations on my ex-wife by hitting her. I blame my violent temper for steering her in the direction of sleeping with another man.

I have been staring at my phone for hours but there is still nothing from Jenny. All morning I've been wondering when she will call me again and if she wants to see me. Maybe I should ask her if she wants to go out for a meal. I think she needs cheering up or a distraction at least. She's ignoring me and it's killing me.

She should have called me by now. I was expecting her to need me and to discuss Michael's death with me because this is what binds us to each other. We can support each other. I have prepared another round of discussions in my mind to help her concentrate on her grief. I get excited when she needs me to tell her what I saw. Jenny has made me feel needed again and I enjoy her company.

Why has she not contacted me? Does she not like me?

I keep thinking about Michael's last moments over and over in my head so that I get the same story without any loss of detail. I told Jenny that Michael was crying out for her. I also made her aware of how much he must have needed her. The guilt she should be feeling was meant to bring us closer together. We are supposed to be friends.

Where are you, Jenny?

I go through different stages with this temper of mine. Stages of rage. Sometimes I accept that some people treat me like shit. It's eating away at me and now my mind too. I'm sat here in the living room with nothing. I've smashed the room in a fit of rage because I feel like I have lost everything. The sofa is torn and with stuffing hanging out either side while the television remains on its stand but with the screen shattered into pieces. I've destroyed everything around me, and it feels good. Finding Jenny has given me a new purpose in life. She should have contacted me by now.

My life was well and truly over the day my wife left me. I couldn't see it then but now it's clear to me. *He* took her from me. Jenny and I are the same but she doesn't realise it. I know what that loss feels like. She doesn't ask me how I am or how I am feeling yet she's my friend.

My heart is racing; I need to control this temper. I have to get my shit together. *He* destroyed my world. I'm trying to calm my emotions by taking in deep breaths and then releasing them slowly just as the doctor advised. All I want to be is normal and accepting that this is now my way of life is hard. The counselling is useless; I turn up just to play the game. It's a tick-box exercise and they're all paid to listen to me. I wonder if they really care.

Does anyone really care?

I need to learn to manage my demons. Some days are better than others but today is a terrible day. I'm in two minds whether to get in my van and drive right over there or not. I am not sure that it wouldn't push her away from me, and that is the last thing I want right now. All my hard efforts destroyed because of my own enthusiasm.

Pull it together, Gary, you can do this.

I cannot even be bothered to eat tonight. My stomach is churning; it feels as though it's in knots. My mind is ticking over like crazy as the hunger starts to gnaw. I am thinking about all those failed relationships that led me to this point in life. My wife is now my ex-wife and I have no idea where she is or even if she is in the country. I fell out with my mother soon after the divorce. Although I am aware that she is in a care home, I've not seen her for years. I don't think she would be any happier to be in my life right now, or lack of one, than I would be in hers. We had a falling out when she needed to go into a care home. The dementia is too bad for me to care for her myself. I keep telling myself that maybe she's even forgotten who I am by now. It's easier to deal with that way.

I was living the high life not so long ago. Now I sit alone in this house and drive round in my van staring at other people. I can't help but watch how others live. Life is so precious yet could be destroyed by circumstance in a cruel twist of fate. No matter how much I had my life under control, nothing could prepare me for this feeling: the shock, the sadness, the anger and the loneliness and the nothingness that fills me with hatred. *That* feeling of wanting to see it all turned around.

I can't let it go. I need it to be over with.

I'm aware that I keep rocking back and forth on the remains of my sofa. I stare at the phone again. I look at the text messages I sent Jenny and then double-check I haven't mislaid her replies. I am tense because I was expecting better from her. I know she is interested, I sensed it. I could see the spark in her eyes when I mentioned Michael's name. When I sat there and described his last breath, I saw her. I saw how she needed to feel a part of that moment. For the first time in years I made a connection with someone – and now Jenny is ignoring me.

Please text me back.

I can't keep sitting here, waiting for Jenny to reply. I should instigate something to make her call me. I need to see her again. Maybe I should drive past and knock on the door uninvited to see what kind of response I get. Jenny doesn't seem a cold-hearted person which is why I thought she would contact me more.

I have a fascination with her. I wonder what Michael saw in Jenny. I have often sat here thinking about the last day he spent with her. Those final hours they had together without knowing what was to come. Those last moments they should have cherished.

What went through his mind? What plans did they make together?

I hope that Jenny understands what I have been going through. I did explain that my wife had been having an affair. Although our situations are not entirely the same, I know how it feels to have your life destroyed that quickly. The cause of my demons.

The buzz from my mobile phone alerts me to the message. I am shaking a little with the anticipation but can see that she has responded. I knew it; I knew she would message me. I was right all along and my trust in my own instincts is restored – then the disappointment shoots me right back down to earth. Jenny was meant to send a text message inviting me over for a chat but instead I receive an update that Michael's funeral service is being planned. I am to expect a date in due course. This was not the message I was expecting but I could use her contact as a means to guide the conversation in the direction I want. I'll send a reply about the missing wedding ring.

> Thank you for letting me know. I am finding it hard to sleep. Can't stop thinking about that day either. The more I focus on it, the more I am sure Michael was wearing his wedding ring. Did anyone find it?

I noticed the obsession she had with Michael's wedding ring and this may be an excellent route to take to force her to meet me again. Come on, Jenny, please reply, will you? I've laid the bait and I need you to take it.

Within minutes my phone buzzes again. I sit up with the excitement of her contact and get myself comfortable on the torn sofa. I read her reply, which asks again if I am feeling any better. Jenny continues to mention that she is struggling to sleep too. She can't stop thinking about Michael, calling out his name.

Holy fuck, she's calling me. The phone is ringing. I don't answer immediately, because I don't want to look keen, but then…

'Hello. Hi Jenny, I just got your message. I was just reading it. How are you feeling?' I ask. She doesn't sound well. Her voice is quiet, soft and solemn. 'Are you calling about the wedding ring?'

'Yes,' Jenny replied, 'I didn't mention it on the text but it has just been assumed as lost in the accident. No one can find it.'

'I am having nightmares about Michael's accident,' I tell her. 'I've been getting counselling too, but it's helping only a little. I think it's reminding me and giving me flashbacks from that evening,' I continue while she remains silent. 'I am sure he was wearing his wedding ring. It wasn't important enough to remember at the time because I was so focused on making sure he was comfortable but now other memories of that evening are slowly coming back.'

'Are you absolutely certain?' Jenny asks. 'It means so much to me, more than I can talk about. Are you a hundred per cent sure?'

'Shall I go back to the police to confirm it?' I respond. 'Add it into my statement as confirmation?'

Jenny hesitates for a moment. There are a few seconds where neither of us talk but I can hear her breathing down the phone. There is a soft and sensual tone to her breath.

'No,' says Jenny, 'don't go to the police. It's not as important to them as it is me because they don't seem to care about the ring. It's irrelevant to them.'

'That's just it,' I reply. 'They know how to provide all the information, how to relay those sad messages and help you with support, but they will not know how you can possibly feel until they've been through this themselves. They can't relate.'

I am beginning to sense she has my trust. I want to see her again, look at her in the eyes and see how she is coping.

'Do you want to come over tomorrow afternoon?' Jenny asks. 'We can have a chat about the wedding ring. If you're happy to talk me through everything again, you can stay for dinner if you like?'

I struggle to hide my enthusiasm but I manage to hold off for a couple of seconds before replying. I don't want to appear overly keen, nor expose my frustrations.

'I don't want to burden you.' I reply. 'I'm sure you don't want me getting in the way.'

'It will not be any bother,' Jenny says. 'Think of it as my way of saying thank you. It's been a strange few weeks but you were there when Michael needed someone. I don't know how to repay you for that. Dinner is the least I can do.'

I ended the conversation with telling her I didn't want to put her out in any way but dinner would be lovely. I'm sure looking after a young boy on her own with all that stress from the accident in her mind is troubling. It's admirable that she still has time to think about how I am coping, yet she is suffering the most tragic loss of her life. This makes me realise the strength of her character and reflect and contemplate on what I want from her.

I want Jenny to feel our connection too.

Twenty-One

Donna

I'm looking at Pete who is sat in his favourite chair with his favourite mug. The television has been playing one quiz show after another this afternoon and while we usually are first to chip in with our guesses while arguing which one of us is right, today we sit in silence, staring at the screen and lost in our own worlds and thoughts. We are united by the loss of our son but separated by our emotions. Today has been the toughest day since the news of Michael's death.

I'm struggling with the choice of cremation for my son. He was my son and today his father and I have contacted a local funeral director who will be collecting his body from the mortuary; a memory that I will never forget for the rest of my life is my son on a slab, cold and lifeless. I don't like the idea that in a week he will be burnt and I can't shift away from the disappointment that we will have nowhere to visit him. I wanted a grave, a place to sit and feel like I could connect and reminisce. A cremation will destroy everything that is left of him and the ashes will eventually disappear. I will have even less of him to remember if the wind sweeps his remains around the crematorium grounds or Jenny scatters him across a field. She hasn't even thought that far ahead.

I should have been given a say in this decision. I'm his mother.

Jenny didn't seem interested in listening to my feelings about the funeral but I am cautious about arguing with her in case she stops me seeing Daniel. Jenny's mental health is getting worse; her physical state is starting to look dreary and unkempt. Daniel is clearly not being looked after properly and from what his school tells me – because let's face it, Jenny has given up taking him anymore – he is having his dinner and going straight to bed every night. I have my fears that he is being left alone in his room for hours at a time. Jenny sits up all night with her bottles of wine, pouring her heart out to Gary. I'm disappointed. She's coming across like she's losing sight of who she is and what Michael would have expected from her. And she's contacting other men. But Daniel is my main concern. I need her to realise that the little boy will be better off with us for a while.

I don't know who to turn to without causing some form of grievance between us. I keep telling myself that I will confront Jenny about my thoughts on everything after Michael's funeral. Pete reminds me that she has a lot on her mind – but we are his parents and as much a part of his life as Jenny was.

Michael's death itself, his money worries, the whole trauma of the last few weeks has changed Jenny drastically. I barely recognise her anymore. She can just about manage to get out of bed. I don't know what to do for the best and it concerns me. I have seen the drastic changes every other day when I support her by taking Daniel to preschool. She was even contemplating taking him out of school for a while until she gets back on her feet. Keeping him away from his little friends and isolating him in the home is not healthy.

'What good is that to Daniel?' I had asked. 'Don't you think that poor boy needs a routine? He's lost his father and doesn't need to lose his friends.'

I didn't get much in the way of a reply: neither an agreement, nor an argument to deter me – but I still turn up and take him. Michael would never have wanted to see her like this. If nothing changes soon I'm going to have to step in. Maybe after the funeral is over she will start to get better. We will see.

I had my suspicions about Michael's debt problem. I didn't want to confirm it with Jenny when she mentioned it on my last visit but Michael asked me for a considerable sum of money last year. He sounded desperate, like he was in trouble.

'Don't ask me any questions, Mum,' he said in a state of despair at the dining room table. 'I know you have it so can you lend it? I am desperate. This is one of those times when I need your support – but please don't say a word to Jenny, not ever.'

How can a son come to his mother with that question and expect not to be challenged?

'I brought you into this world, Michael,' I remember saying. 'If you're in trouble and you don't want anyone to know, you should at least be able to tell your mother.'

Ten thousand pounds is still a lot of money to us. We're not quite ready for retirement yet and the shop has constant stock to re-order and re-sell. I didn't have all of the money to lend him, only half. I promised him that I wouldn't tell anyone and he promised that one day he would pay me back.

'Please don't let Dad know,' Michael begged me. 'He would be so disappointed in me.'

'So long as you can pay me back,' I said. 'At least within the next couple of years because your father doesn't have control of the savings accounts.'

Pete never seems to know what comes in and out of the business accounts. The money just piles up and I am left to transfer it from one account to the other. He is good at monitoring trends with our sales and doing all the talking with our suppliers.

That money I loaned Michael was meant to be for our nest egg. Pete and I were thinking about a world cruise when we retired. But Michael never paid any of the money back. I challenged him and chased him for some of it and he did pay just over a thousand pounds but there will be no way of seeing the rest. Not that I was disappointed, it was only money, and he was my son. I would have given him the full £10,000 but I had to keep something back just in case we needed it. I knew I was going to have to tell Pete the truth.

In my head, I kept thinking about what I was going to say to Pete. He would be disappointed that I had lied to him. He would never have given Michael the money without demanding answers, but I trusted my son. I knew he would have paid me back.

Now Pete sits quietly alone most nights. We make dinner together and support each other with the shop in Cornwall but our son's death has put a gaping hole in our lives. I don't think we will ever return to normality after this.

To have outlived our only child feels unnatural. We've been there right by his side when he qualified as an accountant. I remember how nervous he was opening his results and how I thought he had a whole bright career ahead of him. I've watched Michael grow into a man and was sat right behind him on his wedding day. I might have had my doubts about Jenny at first because I thought she was trying to tie Michael down but I could see how happy they were together. Michael was overjoyed to become a father and that moment where we were all waiting at the hospital for Daniel to be born was unforgettable. It's as though all those magical memories have been tarnished by misery and loss. He had a future and now it's been taken away. Our son is dead.

I remember this same feeling when my father died. It's a loss that only time can heal. I continue to live my life, and carry on as best I can, but the strength to motivate myself came with the support of those around me that I loved. I am keeping this thought for Jenny. She needs our help, even if she can't see it now — she'll thank me for it later.

Throughout the day I have made one list after another. It keeps me focused while helping to remember what it is that I need to do. Although Jenny is Michael's next of kin, I have assumed responsibility for organising everything for as long as she seems to be unable to get out of bed most mornings. I wish that girl would find it within herself to be stronger. She has to keep herself together for Daniel's sake.

The funeral director seems to be able to take care of most things. All I had to do was explain my wishes — well, Jenny's wishes. The word *burial* was on the tip of my tongue but all the time I sat there with the phone to my ear thinking *I have to honour her requests.*

Michael will be cremated in a dark oak coffin. There will be a small service, with his ashes returned in an urn for all of us to scatter at a later date. If only my son had made a will. His wishes could be granted. At least then, in writing, it would have said about a burial. I know my son would not have wanted a cremation. It's something I am going to have to accept and let go of before it destroys the relationship I have built with Jenny. As his wife and next of kin it's unfortunate that she has the final say.

There's no going back now.

Pete is crying on the sofa. I watch his face and the redness of his cheeks that reflect a father grieving for his son. Not only will I have to tell him about the money that Michael borrowed from our savings last year but that I have paid for the funeral expenses directly with the funeral director. From the conversation I had with Jenny about the missing mortgage payments – the unpaid bills and debts that Michael kept from her – it is obvious she is in no financial state to contribute. Michael has nothing left.

I wish I could have helped him more. I wish he could have come to me and been more honest with his problems. He was secretive at times, just like his father used to be.

I feel my admission on the tip of my tongue. It's right there and I want to blurt it out. Pete will be so angry. I am disappointed with myself for keeping this from him but I have to tell him. He needs to know the truth.

'Pete?' I say while staring at the television. I see him place his mug on the floor. 'Will you listen to me for a moment? I have something to tell you.'

Pete turns to face me after lowering the sound. The quiz show is muted, leaving only my voice to fill the room.

'It's about our savings account. I don't really know how else to say this, but Michael asked to borrow ten thousand pounds last year. He needed our help.'

'What was that – did you clear out the account for Michael?' Pete interrupts me. 'Is it all gone?'

'No,' I snap back. 'We still have five thousand in there but he swore me to secrecy. He said he would pay it all back. I never expected any of this to happen.'

I feel the tears start to fill my eyes. The sadness overcomes me and I weep with both grief and disappointment.

'It's all right, love,' Pete says while getting off the sofa to come and give me a hug. 'Surely he must have something in his bank – or maybe some savings to pay us back. Jenny will sort us out, I'm sure she will help. Give it time.'

'That's just it,' I respond, now shaking as the announcement is about to happen. 'Michael has nothing left. Nothing. Jenny has discovered he hasn't been paying the mortgage, the bills, not even the credit cards. He has left her in a mountain of debt.'

There it was. The moment that Michael never wanted and I know he would have been let down badly if he was here. The look on Pete's face as the disappointment with his son sinks in is expressed loud and clear. It hurt me to say it out loud but I had no choice if I was to be honest with my husband. He trusts me to do the right thing.

'He was a bloody accountant,' Pete ranted. 'Wasn't he meant to be good with money? How the fucking hell is Jenny going to keep a roof over that poor little lad's head? She can barely fucking get out of bed and cook the boy his breakfast from what you've been telling me.'

I sit in silence as Pete continues to let out his frustration. We are both left in the difficult situation of needing the money to be repaid for our savings but also needing to support Jenny.

We can't leave her to be homeless with Daniel.

'We will have to speak to Jenny about this after the funeral,' Pete said. 'We should just get that one day out of the way and say goodbye to our son. I know that you paid the directors this morning and I am happy that Jenny doesn't need to pay this back. He was our son and it feels right that we pay for his funeral.'

I nod at Pete while also wiping my eyes dry with the end of my sleeve. At least it is all out in the open now.

'Even if the savings are paid back over a few years, something small here and there will make a difference. We aren't retiring just yet, are we, and we still have a few grand spare. We can sort this mess out between us all.'

'What about their house?' I ask. 'Michael hasn't been paying the mortgage for months. They owe the bank thousands. He didn't have any life insurance against illness or death either.'

'What the hell has he been doing with himself?' Pete asks. 'Where has the money gone?'

'I don't know anything else,' I reply and I can tell he believes me, 'Michael never said. Jenny has lost all mental capabilities to be able to organise anything herself. So, I agree. We just wait until the funeral next week and then take some control ourselves. For Daniel, more than anyone else. That boy needs us.'

I watch now as Pete rubs his forehead with his hand. He is looking confused but I can see him trying to work it all out in his mind. I know he will want to resolve this as much as me. I hope I can get him round to the idea of having Daniel come and live with us for a few weeks, maybe even months. At least I can look my husband in the eye and know I have been honest with him.

If only Michael had been able to be this honest.

Twenty-Two

Jenny

I have been thinking about what to cook Gary for dinner all day, so much so that in my head I had planned a massive three-course meal with the idea of manipulating him to stay longer. But when the reality of leaving the house to shop set in I could only think about cooking something I knew well enough to do without much effort – Michael's favourite meal, a home cooked lasagne. My head is flustered because this is the first time I've cooked properly in weeks. The last time I cooked lasagne was the night Michael and I had the argument. Now I am cooking for another man. I try to remind myself it's only food. This is only a meal and I can't keep thinking about that argument. What I am doing doesn't feel right but I push myself to carry on. I can't avoid cooking. I can't not have lasagne again. There will always be reminders of Michael everywhere I turn so I need to push through this emotion in the hope that it gets easier next time.

I don't know what stops me when I stand by the front door but I get an anxiety attack that destroys my composure. I look at the door with an overwhelming urge to turn back and sit in the kitchen. I place my hand over the handle. My breathing gets faster and the shaking will not stop. Every minute that passes by with me stood there, coat on, looking out of the frosted glass window, makes the dread of stepping over that threshold greater. Everyone will be staring out at me – the widow from the end of the street.

I know the root of my issue is that Michael stepped out of that door and never came home. His last step, the final goodbye, was from this house. He had no idea what was about to happen that night. None of us did.

It was so final.

My mental health is not in a good place. I cannot deny the difference between the woman that I was three weeks ago and the person that I am today. I am afraid of losing myself in this misery. I don't know who I am anymore. I know that when I step outside everyone will look at me as the widow that lost her husband. Inside, I feel safe. I can feel secure that Daniel is safe too – and I don't ever want to let my little boy out of my sight.

Daniel's preschool hasn't seen me at all. I am now used to Donna taking him there and collecting him later in the afternoon. I can see how attached she is to him. She comes back and gives me advice on what I should or should not be doing. I try to listen to her. In my head I am screaming at her *you are not his mother* – but I just agree and nod my head. I don't want the grief or hassle.

The smallest thing can make me feel like I have no fight left in me. I keep reassuring myself that Donna has always been this aggressive with her views. There were times in my marriage when I am sure she forgot that *I* was Michael's wife and that *I* am Daniel's mother.

I mustered up the energy to visit the local shops to buy everything I needed for my lasagne. I know it was Michael's favourite meal and I've cried my eyes out about it for the last hour but I tell myself I must overcome these small reminders. I will never forget Michael; he was my husband. I'm trying to remain stable. His clothes lie upstairs on the bedroom floor, hanging over the doors and falling out of the wardrobe where I had tried to pack everything into bags for a charity shop. I gave up.

Removing his presence from this house takes away other reminders of him. It made me feel as though I was removing memories. I looked at his suits and it reminded me of the pressures he felt at work: the strains of his employer putting timing issues over his client's tax returns. Michael's jumpers brought back memories of when we stayed in his parents lodge that Christmas not long after we had first met. I know I can't keep his belongings here forever but it hurts to hold them and place them into a bin liner. It is as though everything he owned is now worthless.

I'm proud of myself for leaving the house today, albeit not in a perfect state – but I still got washed, dressed and took Daniel with me. The whole process took hours and, initially, I kept talking myself out of it. I can't keep relying on Michael's parents and online shopping orders to help me survive. I know it's not natural. I will get better if I can push through these small steps. Just one step at a time.

All the ingredients are fresh and dinner is in the oven. I have a bottle of wine in the fridge and some ice cream in the freezer should Gary mention dessert. He could have remembered some vital information about Michaels missing wedding ring. I need to know it was on his finger when he died. I have to have a resolution on this issue because otherwise I will keep trying to figure it out for the rest of my life. It will drive me insane. I only offered him an invite to dinner on the basis he might stay for a few hours to go over the incident again.

When Gary describes what happened and what he saw, in some reassuring way that others would find odd, I get a sense of closeness with Michael. It helps me to be part of his last moments. When I hear it back, I can almost visualise being there. I picture Michael in my head. I can practically see him on the road, calling out my name. Some wives wouldn't want these memories but the guilt within me feeds on the knowledge that he died quickly and with someone there for him. I wish it had been me but I will never be able to change what has happened, nor can I thank Gary enough for his support.

Donna happened to be at the wrong place at the wrong moment yesterday while I was having another low moment. I couldn't hide my stress with the mortgage situation. She didn't seem that bothered and accepted that there is nothing I can do about it right now. She assured me that she will support me with organising the paperwork this weekend; that's tomorrow and I have all the piles of envelopes she needs in the living room. It's a mountain of unpaid reminders. A reminder that Michael hid the truth from me.

My head and my heart are both in separate places. The majority of my thoughts are on the upcoming funeral while other parts of my mind cling to the guilt I feel. Then, the anger sets in. The anger of being lied to by my husband is fuelled by my confusion about his intentions. I might never know why he lied unless I assume that he didn't want to worry me. He wouldn't have wanted me to be stressed knowing that I spent most of the time looking after our son.

Would Michael have really left us homeless?

Looking through the mortgage statements, I have noticed that we had been in further periods of missed payments on the house last year. I have been so naïve about our financial circumstances. I was so trusting of my husband that I had no reason to disbelieve him. I have all the letters in separate piles: bank statements, mortgage statements, credit card statements – three interlinking mountains of paperwork that paint a distorted picture of what I once called happiness. I trusted Michael to take care of everything. He insisted that I need not worry.

I cannot make sense of my own thoughts right now. Another niggling worry in the back of my mind is who was Michael going to meet that night? I have been through his phone and called the number that texted him to meet at 7.30 p.m. – but no answer. I tried texting too since there was no answerphone but I've had no replies. I've been contemplating paying his work a visit to see if I can clear his desk and go through his things in the office. I know that I'm looking for reassurance that he wasn't meeting another woman. The debts and the lies that he was hiding make me question if he could have been cheating on me.

Did he take off his wedding ring because he was having an affair?

Michael was in such a rush that day – and came home late most nights. I need to find out. There are too many what-if's that I can't make sense of. I am sure that once Michael's funeral is over, I can start to rebuild the broken fragments of my mind.

Donna's reaction to my admission about Michael has also been in my thoughts. How can she be so casual about it? This confirmed to me that she must have known more than she is letting on – but at the same time she might be the answer to the financial problems caused by her son. I'm going to have to start thinking about what support I might need if I return to work full-time. I don't know if I can afford the house on my own. Do I sell it, rent it out? I'm lost. I don't know where to begin.

Shit. Is that smell from the oven?

The aroma of the lasagne fills the air after I open the oven door. A rush of heat hits my face and from the corner of my eye I can see Daniel running towards me.

'Go and play in the other room,' I tell Daniel who is playing aeroplanes with his arms – another mimicked action from the cartoons he watches on television, 'Mummy will follow you in there in a minute.'

Daniel stops in his tracks, pulls a face and blows a raspberry in my direction. My heart warms as he is enjoying himself. I pull a face in return and force myself to smile. I don't want him to see me this unhappy all of the time. Masking my sadness from him these couple of weeks has resulted in a distance between us. I have had no choice but to rely on Donna.

'Daddy.'

It has been the first time in days, but it still cuts through me like a knife. My eyes are welling up with the anticipation that I have to remind my son that his father is not coming home. All those times that I cried myself to sleep while Daniel was at preschool, out of the way — now I am struggling not to break down in front of him.

'Daddy is not with us tonight,' I reply, unable to look him in the eye. 'He is looking down on us though, sweetheart. Somewhere around us, I believe. Shall we go and watch cartoons again?'

I sound enthusiastic, trying to divert his thoughts from his missing father. I know there will be a time when the calling out will become less frequent and I am accepting that when he is older I will be able to sit him down and tell him everything he could ever want to know about Michael — especially how much his father loved him.

'He will always be in here, my sweet little boy.'

I show Daniel a hand to my heart and the tears roll down my face — hard and heavy as the floodgates open. He comes running to me and clings to my leg to show his affection. Daniel can see that I am choked up and it saddens me to watch him try to make this situation better. Especially since he is so young. He shouldn't have this worry or burden on his shoulders. Nothing can take away the mental pain that I feel day in and day out.

'Mummy will be all right. She'll have some of her special juice. That will make Mummy better.'

I take hold of his hand and walk him into the living room after I turn off the oven. Unbeknown to him, my special juice now consists of the white wine in the back of the fridge. It doesn't ease the pain but it's helping me to sleep better at night. There's something about alcohol that shuts off my thinking mechanism while blocking out the grief, albeit it for short periods. But I'm trying to get a handle on it. I've got enough problems already.

The television is already on his favourite cartoon channel and I manage to get him seated on the chair with his beloved teddy bear. I stand by the door and watch how his mind can divert so quickly between the toy and the television. It's a gift that we leave behind as adults: being able to switch off our concentration on one thing to divert it to another. I wish I could be like that.

I wish I could switch off from the way I am feeling.

I know that I have an hour before Gary arrives. By that time, Daniel should have eaten some of his dinner, gone to his bedroom to settle down and eventually fallen asleep. Michael's wedding ring must be somewhere and I hope that Gary can remember everything in more detail tonight.

I need closure.

Twenty-Three

Gary

My frustration has calmed down in the time that I have walked from the corner of the street to Jenny's house. I can't screw this meeting up. I can't ruin everything this early in our friendship. I parked my van at the end of the street, a few doors down from Jenny's house and concealed behind a few trees. It's far enough away to allow me to compose myself and control my nerves. I want to make a good impression.

I wish I could learn to control my temper. I've reached that stage now with life where I wonder what the point is. No good can come of my actions anymore. I've lost everything that was good in my life and what I had left I seem to have destroyed. If my wife hadn't left me I doubt that I would be feeling this way. I miss her.

Would I have made the same mistakes?

I see everything more clearly now. I can't change what has been done but I can make amends. I can fix this. My brain is working overtime to overcome the battle of Jenny's resistance. I know that she is desperate to know more about Michael's wedding ring. I know exactly what she wants to hear. I've practised the story over in my head a few times before I left the house. It has to be word perfect. I want to draw her in so that she can spend more time with me. Jenny has made me rethink about my life. She's also vulnerable and lonely and maybe we could be there for each other in our current despair.

I knock twice on the front door. I look around to see if anyone is watching me. I spot the neighbour across the road twitching the curtain. I switch instantly into character with a cheerful expression as Jenny opens the door. It's as if time had slowed down as my eyes try to take all of her in. She looks so different. Her hair is tangled. She hasn't even brushed it. Jenny's pale face has patches of dry skin that make me doubt she has washed. Her appearance is so much more unkempt and unattractive than the last time I met her. I was not expecting her to look like she had just gotten out of bed. I thought she would have made more of an effort for me. She knew I was coming over, so why hasn't she got dressed?

'I'm sorry I'm a little bit early. I thought the traffic would be a lot worse than it is.' I explain, disappointed. 'Have I come at a bad time. Should I come back later?'

I hope Jenny doesn't think that I am being rude.

'No, now is fine. I've put Daniel in his bedroom to bed down and dinner is in the oven. Now is as good a time as any so come on through.' Jenny says. 'I've made plenty to eat. I hope you're hungry.'

I remind myself why I am here without getting too caught up in my emotions. I have no idea how a family could live in such a small house. Mine is a four-bedroom detached property with a garage, study and an annexe in the garden that I once used as a home office. It's still in the same trashed state from how I left it. Empty and desolate as am I.

I follow Jenny through to the kitchen. She pulls out a chair and I take my place at the table. If she had been married to me, I could have given her so much more than this. She would have had better.

'Is this where Michael usually sat at the table?' I ask. You could hear a pin drop as the expression on Jenny's face dropped. 'Did you all eat here together as a family quite regularly, or was he too busy?'

I watch and focus on her face as I see that I have unsettled her emotions. I sit here, staring at her body language with an innocuous smile. When I cause a reaction, I like it that she displays a vulnerability that I feel in control of. She reminds me of my ex-wife in that way too. Jenny is emotional, but defensive. I bet she's feisty when she gets going.

'Yes, it was. Michael hardly ever cooked but I didn't mind,' Jenny replies and I watch her hesitate. 'Why do you ask?'

'Just curious because it still feels strange being in his home,' I reply. 'I bet he was a great father to Daniel and a loving husband. Those photographs of you around the house as a family – you all look so happy. Family time together is so important.'

Jenny pauses for a moment but I can see she is thinking. She doesn't realise the pauses give away her moments of concentration. I'm starting to be able to read her like a book.

'He certainly was. We were a family. A solid, happy family.'

Jenny turns around to face the window. I can tell she is lying. She should have been honest with me. From her tense body language I can tell she is uncomfortable. Michael was out of the house, working away. This wasn't a happy marriage.

Why isn't she being honest?

'My wife and I always ate at separate times because I worked away from home a lot. I think that was another reason we drifted apart,' I reply. 'It's odd how hindsight changes everything. If I knew before our split what I know now, I would have spent more time with my wife when we were married. Time is precious.'

The grief has taken its toll on her. I notice how rundown she looks and I'm disappointed because I have made the effort to get smartly dressed in the hope that she was looking forward to seeing me. I don't see any sign of enthusiasm from her.

'Did you like the flowers I brought over last time?' I ask, thinking back to when I stole the best bunch from Michael's memorial spot. 'I hope you didn't think it was inappropriate. I wanted to do something nice. To say thank you?'

Jenny takes two plates from the cupboard, turns and smiles at me.

'No, they were lovely,' she says. 'They didn't last long though. Died in a couple of days.'

'Nothing stays the same forever, does it?' I respond, watching her pull the lasagne from the oven, 'Is there anything I can do to help?'

After insisting that I remain seated because she has everything under control, Jenny plates up and slices the garlic bread onto a separate plate.

'What first attracted you to Michael?' I ask, watching as she serves the hot food. 'I'll be honest with you, on first impressions I wouldn't have placed you two together. No disrespect but you give me the impression that you are home all the time with your son. Did he hold you back?'

I watch her become uneasy with that question. Due to being such a polite woman, I doubt she has the confidence to put me in my place. I hope it makes her realise that her potential was wasted.

'It's complicated,' Jenny explains. 'Michael wanted what was best for me, for all of us. He made some bad choices and I'm slowly finding things out after his death. I mean, he's still surprising me, put it that way.'

I want to ask more, but it's not the time or the place. I'm intrigued by what she knows but I don't want her to push me away. Now we approach the conversation of the wedding ring. Jenny has half eaten her meal and stopped for a break or completely lost her appetite. Surprisingly I managed to eat more than I thought I could but the bread was too tough.

'I had a flashback earlier,' I explain as Jenny concentrates on my every word. 'I remember holding Michael's hand and I definitely think I felt something like a ridge. I remember it now. It must have been the wedding ring. The more I go over and over it in my head the more I can almost visualise the glint of the metal reflecting in the light. I'm convinced he was wearing it.'

'Can you be absolutely certain, though?' Jenny asks. 'I need to know if you are sure. You have no idea what this means to me.'

'I don't remember physically seeing it,' I reply and her expression shows the disappointment clearly. 'I am convinced it was there. I know I felt something, saw something. However, with all the drama, my eyes were focused on his face. I kept telling him to hold on and be strong.'

'Maybe after the funeral, I will go back and look around at the hotel,' Jenny says, still desperate for answers. 'We had an argument but I can't bring myself to believe that Michael would have removed his wedding ring that night.'

Jenny starts to cry but it's only a short outburst. I want to reach out to her, hold her hand and have her cry on my shoulder. The more I watch her, the more I want to make things right but there's nothing I can do to make this any better. Jenny is going to have to face up to the reality one day or another.

'It might turn up eventually,' I reassure her. 'I can always help you look for it at the hotel if you want someone there with you. I don't mind taking you there?'

'Thank you, I appreciate it,' Jenny replies, and that smile gets me every time. 'I could use a friend right now. Thanks for listening.

Sorry if I am going on a bit. No one seems to care about the ring. Everyone assumes that it was lost, but if he took it off, that's a sign to me, a sign that he—'

'Don't say it,' I interrupt her. 'It's ok. I know what you're saying.'

Jenny moves her hand towards mine. I don't hold back and I place it on hers.

'I'm here if you need me, so don't be embarrassed to ask for anything,' I explain. 'I'm only a phone call away, you've got my number. I understand what it's like to feel alone with no support. It's times like these when you find out who you really can rely on, isn't it?'

Dinner has come to a natural end with neither of us touching our plates. Jenny listens as I explain how traumatic it was for me to rebuild my life. I connect with her on some levels because I recognise the loneliness and the confusion. The more she discusses Michael's parents, the more I wonder if they are trying to control her. Donna sounds overbearing and like she is trying to take over with Daniel. Peter comes across as a people pleaser to keep the peace. Neither Peter nor Jenny stand up to Donna by all accounts and she's used to having her own way.

'There is some help I could use if you are free before the funeral?' Jenny asks. 'I have most of Michael's clothes packed in bags upstairs ready to be taken to some charity shops. Could you help with your van? You don't have too?'

'Absolutely, like I said, anything at all,' I reply without any hesitation. I stand up from the table to stretch my legs. 'How about I load up the van now? It's only across the road. Now's as good as any other.'

I see the hesitancy on her expression as I put her on the spot. Insensitive of me, maybe, yet there is no better time like the present. It proves I do mean it when I say I would do anything for her.

'I don't know about now. I was thinking more about when the funeral is over. I've not packed away everything, I just made a start.'

I take the keys to my van from my pocket. I stand beside her. I want her to see the best thing she can do now is remove them from the house. They have no purpose here.

'I understand you. I really do. When I removed all of my wife's clothing that she left behind, it felt like another blow – another reminder that she was not going to be around. It's going to be difficult no matter what the time of day. Do it now, it makes sense.'

Jenny nods but says nothing in reply. She walks past me and heads to the stairs. I follow behind her and can hear her son talking away to himself.

'Let me have a look first,' Jenny says. 'A few bags of the old stuff wouldn't hurt. Things he never wore anyway but struggled to let go of. He was a hoarder.'

I follow Jenny upstairs and stand at the door to her bedroom. I can't help but stare at the black bags filled with clothes. Some are just spread across the floor, others piled on the mattress. I pick up a couple of bags filled with clothes and I turn the other way. It would be better for her if she got rid of his things so she didn't have reminders of him anymore.

'You'll feel better for this in the long run,' I say, heading down the stairs. 'The longer you keep them, the harder it will be to let go.'

Michael's gone. He's never going to be around again, never going to sit at the dinner table or ever hold her back any longer.

I think Jenny and I really are starting to become friends now.

Twenty-Four

Donna

Daniel's behaviour is changing all the time. I know he is reacting to his mother's grief. It hurts to think of her as a bad mother but right now we are the only people in Daniel's life. All this upset is no good for him. I feel responsible as his grandmother, and as Michael's mother, to do the best I can for him.

Michael would be appalled by her behaviour.

We've been parked up outside the house since the crack of dawn. Pete is still sitting at the wheel, twiddling his thumbs while I keep waiting for the bedroom curtains to open. I know Jenny will be out of bed soon because Daniel has his breakfast by half-seven like clockwork. There are a few home truths we need to get off our chest before the funeral next week. I hope that she can see we are trying to help her but if the worst came to the worst – I will take Daniel from her and refuse to give him back. I have to be the strong one, for Daniel's sake.

'I think she's up and about now,' Pete says. 'I can see movement with the curtains. Are you sure we should be doing this?'

I roll my eyes because I want to remind him that we can't hold back any longer. This is about our grandson's welfare. I'm not doing this for him alone. I'm doing this for Michael. He would be devastated to see his son treated this way. Some days I notice Daniel hasn't even been bathed. I'm surprised the teachers at the school haven't mentioned anything before either. I'm starting to feel embarrassed to take him there.

'There is never going to be a good time to tell her that she is neglecting his needs,' I reply. 'We're the only two people Daniel can rely on now to speak up for him. Michael isn't here to do it, is he?'

Pete takes a sigh while winding up the window on the driver's side of the car.

'I just think that we should wait until after the funeral,' Pete says. 'Losing Michael so suddenly has been difficult for all of us but I don't want there to be any bad feeling. She could cut us out of Daniel's life. Think about the potential consequences?'

'Over my dead body,' I snap. 'She can't even face taking him to school.'

I open the passenger side door and step outside the car. The condensation from my breath in this weather confirms how cold it is this morning. Pete follows behind me as we approach the house. I'm ready for tough conversations but Jenny isn't in a great position to argue with me. I blame her materialistic tendencies for driving Michael out of the house to work such long hours. She's about to lose her home if she isn't careful.

I knock on the door with Pete by my side; we're earlier than she is expecting us.

The door opens after a minute. I can see that Jenny has had another night of very little sleep. The redness in her eyes is a giveaway, it always was. Pete and I follow Jenny into the living room. I close the front door and can see Daniel seated at the table, eating his cereal. He looks at us in the hallway, waving his hand to say hello. My heart melts every time I see him. I can see the resemblance to Michael and remember when he was that age as if it were only yesterday.

'I hope you're eating all your breakfast,' I say, walking through to the living room where Pete is already seated, looking nervous. 'I'll come and get you in a minute.'

Jenny is starting to anger me because she has ignored my offer of help. I explained in our last phone call that I could cook some dinners after I return Daniel home some days. I offered to help with the cleaning, shopping, but she took it the wrong way. I wasn't trying to be controlling, I was offering my support. It's about time she saw a doctor. This has to be depression. There's no other explanation I can think of for her appearance and behaviour. She's barely said a word. I recognise that she is becoming withdrawn. I understand her grief from losing my own father but I also know the importance of carrying on. Even if you feel like getting out of bed is an everyday struggle, you have to fight it because the world doesn't grind to a halt. Jenny and I used to get on really well but now, there's a crack in our relationship.

'You might notice, Pete is with me today?' I say. 'I hope you don't mind that we're a bit earlier than you were expecting?'

Jenny yawns.

'No, it's fine,' she replies. 'I've got him dressed and ready for school and I might pop back to bed when you're gone. I've had no sleep, again.'

'I can tell that,' I respond. 'You look dreadful. Have you had any more of your special juice?'

Jenny looks confused. I bet she thought I'd never find out. Daniel might only be three, but he is picking up on her destructive lifestyle already.

'Daniel has been talking about you at preschool,' I carry on, exposing what I know. 'He mentioned to me that you have a special juice. I can only assume it's the wine. I've seen the bottles in the kitchen. I can see the empty two over in the corner there.'

I point in the direction of the cupboards where empty bottles sit opposite a pile of dishes.

'I'm not an alcoholic, Mum,' Jenny snaps at me. 'It's only the odd bottle here and there. It's not every night either. I'm entitled to a drink if I want one. I am an adult.'

'I managed to convince the teacher that Daniel was referring to you wanting your coffee,' I lie, even though I've openly aired my concerns about her potential drinking. 'They send their condolences to us all and hope to see you at the school soon.'

'I'm going to have to face them eventually,' Jenny replies. 'Apart from you and Peter, Gary is the only other friendly person I bother to talk to right now.'

'Have you been drinking with that Gary?' I ask, annoyed that another man is snooping around my son's house. 'How cosy are things between you both now?'

There was no other way to drop the hint than be direct. She knows how direct I can be.

'That's completely out of order.' Jenny genuinely looks shocked. 'Gary was here last night. He only came round and helped me with

Michael's clothes and they're mostly gone now. He's taking them to a charity shop. I had to make some kind of a start. We're not drinking buddies, and he's not cosy.'

I don't answer immediately because I'm annoyed that once again, Jenny has failed to include me as Michael's mother in these decisions. I might have liked to keep some of his clothes. Some of his jumpers I bought him for Christmas. She doesn't seem to understand that I also might want to keep some memories. I am grieving too. I'm now getting angry because she excluded me. I'm trying not to cry.

'How could you do this,' I snap at her. 'Giving away his things. Pete and I should have been able to take some.'

Jenny remains silent, watching me speak with nothing to say for herself.

'I thought this was something we were going to do together,' I say. 'Why was Gary even here last night? You could have asked Pete and me to come over. We'd have helped you.'

'There are still more of his clothes upstairs,' Jenny replies, frowning at me as if I am overreacting. 'You can take some. I still have another chest of drawers to clear out.'

I try to distract now from the conversation about my son's clothes because I want to get more information about Gary. He was a witness at my son's accident but I don't understand all the contact. I don't know why she is befriending this man or giving him the time of day. I'm going to have to try and meet him to form my own opinions.

What is she playing at?

'He remembers that Michael was wearing his wedding ring,' Jenny replies, and her eyes light up. 'Well, he's sure that this means that Michael was wearing his ring and it must have come off in the accident.'

'So, you're still no closer to finding it then?' I reply drily. 'Michael adored you. He loved you. You were his life. Jenny, you don't need his wedding ring to prove any of that.'

In my mind, I keep thinking about Michael's clothes. How could she just give them away like that?

I'm annoyed. Jenny can see that I am annoyed. Pete is sat in the corner and I can tell by the look on his face that he wants me to calm down. How can I calm down when Jenny is not looking after herself? The house could be taken from under her feet. My grandson could lose his home – and all that is in her head is the crap about a wedding ring.

'You've lost your husband, Jenny,' I say. 'Isn't that enough?'

You could have heard a pin drop. Pete stands up from the chair. He is looking angry with me.

'You've gone too far,' Pete says. 'I think that's enough. We're all having to deal with our emotions. We have the funeral next week—'

'That we've paid for,' I say, raising my voice. 'You've given away all his clothes, we've had no say in his funeral plans, but you're quite happy for us to pay for it all.'

Jenny is shaking. I can see the anger she is trying to contain. Her eyes are fixed on my glare. I had to say it. I know that we're all feeling the loss of Michael but that still doesn't excuse her for being so ignorant. At a time like this, and for Daniel, she needs to stand on her own two feet. I want her to find that strength. We can't all close the world off. We have to keep going. We have to stay strong.

'Michael got us into this mess,' Jenny replies. The confrontation has her in tears. 'Michael was the one taking thousands of pounds out of our accounts and not paying the mortgage or the bills. I have no idea what he has been doing with our money. The financial state he's left us in.'

'Did you look through all of the bank statements?' I ask, watching her vague expression. 'How could you have not known? All those letters, all those reminders. How the hell did that escape you?'

Pete remains silent. I think he's given up. I watch as Daniel peers from around the door. Daniel is watching us, standing there smiling, trying to take in all that is going on around him.

'I trusted him,' Jenny says. 'He took control of everything. I had no reason to disbelieve him. Michael never wanted me to get involved, and he always told me that money was tight, due to his work, but nothing to be worried about.'

'Let's stop this, right here, right now. For Daniel's sake.' Pete interrupts our argument. 'We have to take this poor boy to his father's funeral in a matter of days. Whether we have Michael's wedding ring or his clothes doesn't matter. None of this will bring him back, will it? We need to remember we are a family. We have to get through this together.'

For the sake of keeping the peace, I nod in agreement. I bite my tongue and will leave my questions for another day.

'I'm sorry.' I say. 'Pete and I, we're just concerned about you. You aren't well, Jenny. You aren't dealing with this perhaps in ways that I would have expected.'

My voice is softer but I feel better for getting how I feel out in the open. Jenny doesn't say a word but I want to continue my conversation about Daniel.

'Why don't you let me take Daniel from you for a few days until you are back on your feet? Maybe even a few weeks. All the parents at the school recognise me now. They know who I am. I can do his meals, take him to the park, feed the ducks.'

I had considered at first, asking if she and Daniel wanted to move in together, but I don't think that would be a good idea right now. I might start by convincing her to let us take Daniel, then, when our tensions have settled, she could stay too. It might give her some time to concentrate on getting her household finances in order. At least get the house situation under control.

'What?' Jenny asks. 'You want to take my son from me. I can cope with Daniel, he's not the problem.'

'No, I meant it in good faith. I thought it would be a good idea if you had a break and some time to breathe. Maybe until just after the funeral.' I assure her of my intentions. 'We love spending time with him. I don't like the idea of him being alone and seeing all this upset. It's unhealthy for him to live this way. Think about it, Jenny. For Daniel.'

Jenny takes a seat on the sofa. Daniel runs around the living room floor, making his arms into wings. I smile at him, he's so adorable. He reminds me so much of Michael now that I could cry just by looking at him. The shape of his face, his eyes all come from Michael. He's his father's boy.

'We can help with the mortgage too. Pete and I can make a payment to stop any action they might be taking against you. We still have some money in our savings account that might bide some time.' I carry on, 'We don't have much, about £5000. We just want you to think about it.'

'And I will think about you having Daniel, even if for a few days. Let me sleep on it. I don't even know where to begin with the house, or the bills. I will call the mortgage provider and let them know I have a lifeline, I just—'

'There is no rush to decide right now,' Pete assures Jenny. 'We can help where we can. You only need to ask us, and we'll be there.'

'We're his grandparents,' I continue. 'He's safe with us. We wouldn't let any harm come to him. I was thinking of taking him to our lodge down in Cornwall, we can spend a weekend in the outdoors. Maybe a zoo, the arcades, something different for him. A bit of exercise for us too.'

'Let me think about it,' Jenny says, standing up assertively. 'Let's get him ready for school today and I'll let you know by the time you bring him back later on. I'm going to spend some time today informing Michael's colleagues about the funeral arrangements. I need to give my mum and dad a call too. Keep them updated.'

I smile at Jenny; I hope she makes the right decision. Daniel needs stability and a home. He shouldn't be exposed to all this upset. My other concerns are what will happen when the money runs out. That money from our savings won't last very long.

How will she be able to continue to pay the mortgage on her little income? It's inevitable she is going to lose the house. I can't see how she has a way out of this one but these discussions on her living circumstances will have to wait for another time. Something about Michael is bothering me and I'm not sure yet how to get to the bottom of it. What was he doing with all the money he was earning and to leave his family in this difficult situation?

Twenty-Five

Jenny

I haven't left the house in days but I need this escape. The house is slowly becoming a prison but also the place where I am most safe. I don't have the concentration or mental capacity to drive myself all the way to the cafes near the harbour but I've asked Gary to meet for lunch there while Daniel is at preschool.

I am shaking on the bus into town and I can't help but keep looking around me. I am convinced these people on the bus know who I am. They're watching me. It's making me feel uncomfortable.

Why are they staring at me?

During the journey I send some messages to Samantha and Lizzie. I thank them again for their card and gift. I arrange to meet up again after the funeral. I figure if I send a message now it will keep them off my back for a while. As part of dealing with my grief, I'm slowly unravelling the trail of lies that Michael left behind. I have no idea if I will lose the house but I don't want my friends to see that side of my life. It's private.

Gary is the only other person in this cruel situation who I feel comfortable enough to talk to. He listens to me without forcing his opinion down my throat. He doesn't make suggestions about what I should do or how best to cope. He reminds me of Michael too with his mannerisms and his attitude. I like that. I enjoy being in his company. I feel safe around him because he understands me. Gary seems very upset about his wife and he knows what it's like to lose somebody that you love. I cling to him because he's the last link that I have with Michael, so I enjoy our time together.

Donna's words ring true. She is right. I shouldn't lock myself away in the house and I should learn to *find myself again, learn to do things on my own. I know I need to find my independence so small steps like today need to be done.*

After both Donna and Peter left this morning I called the mortgage provider and promised to make a payment at the end of the month. With a few hundred pounds in one of our accounts, as well as the money that Donna and Peter can lend me, it should keep them off my back until after the funeral. I don't like being in debt to anyone but I need to keep a roof over my son's head. I've decided that I'm not moving back to my parents' house. It would feel like I am taking Daniel away from Michael's memories. Starting a new life in Leeds would be like closing the door on my life here. I have my job, my friends, I will make it work.

The bus pulls over opposite Westbridge City Theatre and I can see the crowds of people walking down the streets, some looking flustered, others casually strolling and it reminds me of when I had no stress, no fear, no worry and would leave the house without a second thought. That feels like a lifetime ago now.

I still think that everyone around me is watching me. I hate having that constant feeling of being an imposter. I also get these niggling thoughts in the back of my mind. Nasty thoughts that I can't shift. How safe is Daniel? Could he come to any harm?

School should be a safe place. I remind myself every day that Donna collects and returns him. If I had the energy to take him I would stand by the school gates all day and wait there until home time, so I know he is safe. Michael walked out of the house that night and then ended up dead. I can't shift my thoughts from thinking this could happen to my son, or me. I have to protect him.

I feel vulnerable. I haven't been out on my own in weeks but I know I'm not ready to go back to work yet. If I can't concentrate on walking from the bus stop to the harbour how can I focus my attention on my job?

A small part of me regrets agreeing to meet Gary outside the house but he was persistent. It is strange how we have managed to form a friendship out of Michael's death. I can't see how we would have met under any other circumstances. I think Michael would have liked him too. Sometimes, when I tell him how I am feeling, it's like I am talking to Michael. He's comforting but I don't want to give the impression

I am interested in him romantically. I can tell he's lonely after his wife left without any form of contact after their divorce and I think that listening to my grief is reminding him of his loss.

The cafe is straight ahead, I can see it. It's a quaint little countryesque cottage-style front with a scattering of tables and chairs outside the entrance. I'm here – at last. I hope Gary doesn't want to sit outside because I'd rather be in the corner and hoping that no one recognises me. I'm not overconfident. Today is about baby steps.

I'm standing at the entrance. I can see the staff rushing around tables with cups of coffee and slices of cake. I'm not thirsty. I'm not even hungry and yet I'm trying to appear normal. The woman at the till is watching me as I pretend to look at the menu placed in the window. I feel a hard, heavy hand on my shoulder. I jump and make a squeal of surprise.

'I'm sorry, did I scare you?' Gary asks. I can smell his aftershave. I would recognise that brand anywhere. 'Didn't mean to startle you. Shall we go inside?'

I compose myself, smile and follow Gary into the cafe. The scent of the aftershave has thrown my thoughts into a whirlwind. I bought Michael the very same brand last Christmas. I tried to find it in the bathroom but it's missing. I'm a little tearful but I'm trying to take more control of my emotions. I can't do this in public. I can't embarrass myself like this.

'Where do you want to sit?' Gary asks. 'Inside, or outside. I don't mind?'

I'm glad he asked. The question reassures me that I can make my choice without having to explain myself and the reasons behind it. I scan the room with my eyes and spot the perfect table in the far left corner.

'Over there looks good,' I respond, pointing a finger to the table. 'Seems quite cosy and more private.'

I unzip my coat and hear the waitress tell Gary that she'll be over to our table in a moment. In my head, all I want to do is sit at home and grieve for Michael. I feel claustrophobic, which may be a sign that I'm not ready for this. I look at all the wooden tables, the pots of plants on wooden shelves and a collection of weird and wacky teapots on display across the walls. Michael would like it here. It seems countryesque and reminds me of when we took some drives to the moors and stopped off at a little café on the way. It's quaint and old-fashioned.

Gary sits down opposite me. I am still distracted by the aftershave he is wearing and the jumper. It's exactly what Michael would have worn. He may have even owned one just like it.

'So, come on then, how have you been?' Gary asks. He picks up the menu from the table. 'I've been looking forward to this all morning, haven't you?'

I shake my head, sigh and wonder if he really wants to listen to my troubles. I still can't sleep; I can't find the energy to even bother to get dressed most mornings and the house is looking like a bomb's hit it.

'I had an argument with Michael's parents this morning. His mother is such a cow at times. She had a go at me about a few things and she wants to have Daniel for a few days.'

'Ah, she means well though I imagine,' Gary replies. 'Daniel is the spit of his father, isn't he? I bet in some comforting way having Daniel near her is like being closer to Michael.'

I'm worried she's become too attached. I'm his mother.

'She's helping. I can't really face the mothers at his preschool but I think she's starting to lose sight that I'm his actual mother,' I say. 'She's his grandmother but she's slowly starting to take over my life. Total nightmare.'

'You might want to watch that,' Gary replies. 'Sounds a tad obsessive. If you need any support, I don't mind. I can drive you places, or pick things up for you. Shopping, anything you need.'

'You're such a good friend,' I say. He doesn't feel like a stranger anymore, 'I appreciate the offer, thank you.'

Gary leans forward. 'So, we're friends now. I do genuinely mean it. I can see what you're going through and I know it's difficult. Emotionally. I've been there.'

'You know what I mean,' I say, and together we smile. 'I'm sure Donna is wondering if there's more going on between us. I've told her there isn't. We're just friends.'

Before Gary has a chance to answer the waitress comes over to the table.

'I'll have a black coffee, no milk, no sugar,' Gary says, looking at me, 'and what would you like to order?'

'Just a cup of tea for me please,' I respond. 'Milk, two sugars, thank you.'

The waitress walks back to the counter.

'Donna does need to mind her own business, doesn't she?' Gary says. 'Have you thought about telling her to back off?'

'Plenty of times.' I laugh. 'Believe me, I've thought of a lot worse. She's helping me to pay for the service though so I feel a little obliged to tolerate her at the minute.'

For a few more minutes I sit chatting to him about Donna and Peter. It feels good to get this off my chest.

'The lowlife that killed your husband had his cremation yesterday,' Gary informs me. 'I saw a small section in the local paper about it. Did the police contact you about anything?'

'Nothing,' I say. 'I had a call from Sharon the other day. She mentioned Michael's funeral and when I could expect the coroner's report but she never said anything about him.'

'I didn't think they would let you know. Probably thought you would turn up trying to get revenge but that's why I did a bit of digging around. I wanted to help you and thought you'd appreciate the info.' Gary leans forward again, and whispers to me, 'I called the crematorium and the guy on the phone said he'd been done on the cheap. One of those without any service, nothing.'

To be brutal, I didn't really care. He killed my husband and ruined my life.

'Good,' I snap. 'The bastard. He is still someone else's son though. I'm not sure what kind of family he came from. It didn't sound good by the impression Sharon gave me.'

'I've only ever spoken to Sharon over the phone,' Gary replies. 'Her northern accent sounds a little like yours. She's a bit flat though. She doesn't give anything away, does she?'

'Sharon annoys me but it must be a really depressing job,' I continue. 'She's supposed to be some kind of support person but I can hardly get her to tell me anything. I can't warm to her because she's so black and white with everything. At least talking to you about it feels less formal.'

I didn't want to come all this way to talk about Michael's death. I don't want to cry in public around people who don't know me. People who don't know or care about my circumstances.

'You know, sometimes I think it would have been easier if my wife had died instead of travelling abroad after the divorce,' Gary says, 'but being here with you now, you remind me of her at times. In a good way, she was good-natured at heart. You're great company too.'

For a moment I watch him, and it's like I am sat here with Michael. His demeanour was the same. His body language and mannerisms all remind me of my husband.

'Is everything ok?' Gary asks. He sounds concerned and I snap out of my daydream. 'You've been staring into space.'

'I'm sorry,' I reply, sounding embarrassed. 'This happens at times. I was just thinking about Michael. His funeral is next week.'

'Shall we change the subject?' Gary suggests. 'You've come all this way and I was thinking that every time we see each other we always talk about Michael.'

He isn't wrong. Every waking minute I am thinking about Michael.

'In an alternate reality, say we had just met and this was our first date,' Gary continues, 'what qualities would you be looking for in me?'

That's a bit of a strange question. It has shocked me. The last thing I want is for Gary to think there's more to me meeting him than friendship. I instantly think of Donna and her words ring in my ear about how cosy things are between us. I need to make sure he understands the message. I don't want anyone else. I can't even begin to think about letting another man in my life that way so soon after losing my husband.

'I don't know,' I reply, awkwardly shaking my head. 'I've never thought about another man. I don't want another man in my life. I can't imagine dating ever again at the minute. It's just going to be me and Daniel from now on.'

'That's good, it shows you're a kind, decent person,' Gary replies. 'So don't let Donna get her claws into your son. No one can take him away from you. Make sure you can trust her.'

I think about Gary's words. Donna's interest in Daniel is now coming across unhealthy and disrespectful. I'm not an alcoholic mother who leaves her son in his bedroom all day, despite what she thinks. Daniel only saw that special juice once, twice at most. I've cut back on the wine now.

'I don't trust her, that's my problem. I'm not going to let her keep Daniel.'

In the back of my mind I keep thinking I should have made a move already, I haven't got much time left. Gary continues to ask me personal questions about my childhood and then diverts the conversation to his own troubled upbringing. Michael's office isn't far from here. I should have called them by now but I didn't want to arrange an appointment in case I changed my mind at the last minute. It's been tough doing this on my own.

The main reason I am going in is to tell them in person about the funeral arrangements. I may have to face clearing his desk but I have hopes that his office could hold clues or paperwork that lead me to who he was meeting that night. I haven't forgotten what Lizzie told me either about him handing over a wad of cash to some men near the shopping centre. I could investigate that further but I feel like I would have known if Michael was on drugs. It seems odd that Lizzie was implying he was paying drug pushers and I now know that he was run over by a known drug user who had a suspended sentence. Was Michael there that night to pay the guy that killed him?

Someone out there must know the truth.

Twenty-Six

Jenny

It felt like a mile but it was only a ten-minute walk. After leaving Gary at the cafe and convincing him that I was more than capable of heading to Michael's office alone, here I am, standing at the entrance. All I am thinking is that I have to try to find some answers. I don't want Gary to see me going through my husband's belongings or questioning Michael's colleagues for information. I know he offered his support but these finer details are for me to digest. I'm trying to work out who my husband could have been meeting, who he was handing over money to and why we are in so much debt.

'Every day, Michael,' I say out loud as if he can hear me, 'this is where you spent most of your time, rather than at home with your son and me.'

I cross the road, keeping my eye on the view of the tower block of offices. I've never been here before, although I've driven past a few times and waited outside before to meet Michael after work. I've not been here for months. Never had any need to be either. Michael has never been inside my office but he came along to a couple of the Christmas parties before. I asked him to promise me that he'd never get drunk and show me up in front of my friends and colleagues. He kept his word while I, on the other hand, would forget how much wine I'd had and end up crawling across the floor.

'It's not me you have to worry about, Jen,' he'd say, 'you're the one who can't handle your booze.'

He was right, which is why I've decided not to do a wake after the funeral. I want it over with. I can't celebrate his life when there is so much to it I never knew about. It feels like I am closing the door on a life that I thought I enjoyed and a man that I trusted and loved as my husband, the father of our child. Deceitful memories are now overshadowing the love we shared with each other. I wonder how much longer Michael would have lied to me – how much more debt he would have racked up if he was still alive? Loans and credit cards all out of control. I had an accountant for a husband who couldn't manage our own finances. It doesn't feel right. My gut instinct is that somewhere along this chain of deception is a missing link.

I'd better get inside. I haven't got that much time to spare before catching the bus back home for Daniel. I press the buzzer and wait.

'Hello, Sphere and Co, how may I help you?' A female voice from the system on the wall waits for my response.

'Hi, I'm Michael's wife, Jenny,' I reply, leaning into the wall to be clear. 'Jenny Clifton.'

The buzzer sounds and I hear the click of the lock signalling the door is unlocked. I pull it open and choose to take the stairs rather than the elevator as it's only one floor up. I see the company logo with the door number and I make my way up the stairs. I remain calm and composed because these are Michael's colleagues, a whole room of professionals who might have questions to ask about the funeral. I glance through the window of the office door, see a short woman in her fifties typing away on a reception desk and I go through. That feeling of all eyes on me returns.

'Hi, I'm Jenny,' I say, standing at the desk while the woman looks at me. 'Michael's wife.'

I look around the office and can see rows of tables with laptops, paperwork and filing cabinets everywhere. I wonder which one was Michael's desk.

'We all heard the news about his death,' she replies. 'We are so sorry for your loss. I remember Michael well and he was quite a character. How can I help you?'

I'm not expecting her reaction, which feels a little off. I start to hear the background voices fade as the office draws to silence.

'I'm here to let you know that Michael's funeral is the day after tomorrow,' I reply. 'I'm sorry for not contacting sooner but everyone is welcome to attend. It's at the Westbridge Crematorium, eleven o'clock.'

The receptionist nods her head and writes down the details. I look left and right. There are a few people on the phone but everyone else is looking in my direction. There must have been about ten people in the office.

'Can I see Michael's desk?' I ask, looking at the empty spaces and trying to guess which was his. 'Do you need me to clear out anything?'

The receptionist looks confused. I wasn't expecting to be overwhelmed with compassion but she seems more lost than I am.

'Mrs Clifton,' she responds. 'Would you like to take a seat for a minute while I get Brad, the office manager? Bear with me.'

I don't even have the chance to sit down as I watch her glance and nod in the direction of a large male in his sixties. If this is the office manager, this must be Brad. Michael often complained about the targets and expectations set by him. He's heading over so I remain standing.

'The news about Michael shocked every single one of us,' Brad says after he's introduced himself, holding out his hand for a shake. 'It's terrible, tragic news. What with that on top of everything else.'

I can feel myself pulling away – the expression on my face distorting. What did he mean?

'Excuse me?' I ask. 'Everything else?'

My expression must have spoken for me. I'm panicking. What does he mean? It's a very odd response. What else does he know about Michael?

'The investigation,' Brad replies, looking at me to suggest it was obvious. 'It's no secret. He was suspended six months ago without pay while awaiting the outcome of our findings into his accounting history. There's an investigative accounting team on the...'

I shake my head. I've raised a hand to my mouth to display my shock. The whole office is still looking at me because it's clear now I shouldn't be here. It's not registering with me? What is he saying?

'What?' I interrupt. 'Are you saying that he wasn't working here? You've not seen him in six months?'

It doesn't seem real. I'm shaking again with the nerves and all I can think is that something serious must be happening. Something so big I might need to contact the police after the funeral. Fraud investigation? For six months? Michael lied to me. I'm angry and upset. I feel cheated and deceived.

'No,' Brad replies. 'He was accused of stealing some sums of money. Would you like to come into my office for some privacy. I didn't realise that you weren't aware, I'm so sorry. I assumed you must have known?'

I'm speechless, embarrassed and feel sick to my stomach.

'No, I'm ok, it's ok,' I reply, in barely a whisper. 'I had no idea, I…'

'Take a seat just behind you,' Brad continues, leading me to the chairs, all six of them lined in a row for visitors and thankfully all empty. 'Can I get you anything to drink, water?'

I sit down. I'm overwhelmed by my need to get out of this office and back home to contemplate the sheer scale of Michael's deception. He was even stealing money from his firm. I'm trying to understand; if he wasn't working here for six months, then what was he doing? He used to leave the house every day with a suit on, some days even with a briefcase. All those projects he said he was working on for his clients. I even sent him off with some packed lunches. My mind is overwhelmed with questions.

'I'm sorry, I need some air,' I reply. 'I need to go, I'm sorry.'

I stand back up but I don't look at the rest of the office who stare at me as if I'm an imposter. The wife of a fraudster.

'So, you have no idea who my husband went to meet at the hotel?' I ask – one last burning question before I forget. 'The night he died – he went to meet a new client?'

'Not one of ours,' Brad responds without any hesitation. 'We don't know anything about it.'

The space around me is closing in on me. I can't believe what I am hearing. If Donna knew she would have said, wouldn't she? Something on this scale I don't think she would have kept from me. Michael hid this lie from us all.

I can't expose anything until after his funeral. Just another day to get through. Another long, troubling day of wondering what Michael was hiding from me. All these lies, his debts, the stealing, and his suspension from work. I can't tell anyone what I know, not yet. I've got to try to piece together this puzzle on my own.

Twenty-Seven

Gary

The pile of Michael's clothes is stacked up in the corner of my living room. I look at them from a distance while seated on the remains of my sofa. The house is still a mess because I can't find the energy to clean it. I can't be bothered with this massive house. I should have left it a long time ago rather than rattle around in it all on my own. The silence is calming, it really helps, and I've stopped reading Jenny's texts over and over. I know that we are friends now. I think that she realises that we have a connection. Since our meeting in the cafe, I've got to know her a lot better too. She even said we were friends. That's definitely progress.

I look at the suits Michael has worn: his shirts, jumpers, T-shirts and ties. He had good taste but the clothing I remember the most was what he was wearing when he died. I can't escape that horrific image – a scene that happened so fast. I can still hear that last breath. His body jolted as he became lifeless. I am reminded of my own mortality when I fixate on that gasp. Michael died in what was a personal moment between us. I felt his fingers and grip weaken with mine – and then he was gone. An instant switch between life and death.

On days like today I have a sense of calm and can accept my demons. These moments are rare but I sit myself down and remind myself that I can't change anything. What's happened has happened but I will still get to have my own way. I wish I knew where my ex-wife was. She'll always be the true love of my life. I hope one day she can forgive me, as I have forgiven her.

I've darkened the room by closing the curtains and leaving only a lamp on. The dim light soothes me when I am in this state of mind. I've come to realise that my wealth is no longer important. My business deals – car rental income, a local shop managed by staff selling car maintenance products, a handful of shops I purchased to become a landlord within Westbridge City Centre – made me powerful and wealthy. I grew my business from nothing. I couldn't have done it without my wife, though. We were a team: a force to be reckoned with when we got our minds together. She also destroyed me.

I sit here, stroking the material of the trousers. This suit fits me better than I thought it would. Michael had good expensive taste and this is a rather classy suit. I've been through all of the clothes and most are designerwear which makes me wonder how he could have so much expensive clothing and yet such a small house for his family. It's like someone who was keeping up appearances.

The shirt fits me well but his blazer is too big for me. I'm starting to lose weight. I worry too much. Although Jenny trusted me to take these clothes to a charity shop, I can't bring myself to take them there because by keeping hold of them, I get a feel for how she liked her men to dress. Michael had good style. I've been through all of the bags and tried on everything I could but I'm undecided what suit of his to wear to his own funeral. The one I am wearing now is the most comfortable. Will anyone even notice?

Now that Michael's funeral is fast approaching, I need to come clean to Jenny. I have to tell her how I feel. How she makes me feel. She's too focused on herself and Daniel to even notice me but I want her to know that I thought we could have been more than friends.

'I don't want another man in my life. I can't imagine dating ever again at the minute. It's just going to be me and Daniel from now on.' Jenny's words repeat over in my head. I'm disappointed but she didn't have to make it so blunt. She said we were friends. She's lonely too so I know she understands what it feels like to have no one who you can trust or support. I never expected to meet her and feel this way about her.

I keep wondering whether, if my wife had died rather than left me, my life would have taken a different direction. I blame my demons on the stress and I blame the stress on all those that took advantage of me. They took advantage of my business and my good nature.

I've tried to imagine Michael's funeral. I've assumed Jenny will be seated at the front row alongside his parents. I know that her own parents are coming down the night before. I imagine they will all take up the front row with Michael's work colleagues and friends filling the rows behind. I wonder where Jenny would want me to sit? Not only was I witness to his death but Jenny and I are now friends. Should I be on the front row too?

From the conversations I've had with Jenny, it is coming across that Michael's mother is trying to make all the decisions. Donna is playing on Jenny's vulnerable mental state. I think she wants to have Daniel and will manipulate Jenny until she gets her own way. She's a mother grieving for her son and whose only link to him is her grandson. If Jenny isn't careful, Donna will end up taking control.

I know we are close now. She confides in me and I enjoy our chats. I want to get closer to her. I have had the occasional sexual thought about Jenny too. Especially when I saw her bed after collecting Michael's clothes. There was a split-second moment in my mind where I thought about undressing her and sleeping with her in Michael's bed. It's too soon and we've only just become friends. It's a shame she doesn't take more of an interest in my life. I had wondered if she would go out on a date with me. I've talked it over and over in my own head, telling myself not to be so stupid. Not to be so gullible.

Now that I have picked the best suit to attend the funeral, I have to focus on everything.

Everything that I have lost.

Twenty-Eight

Jenny

My mother and father will be here any minute. I'm nervous about seeing them but it will be emotional for all of us. The last time I saw my parents in person was when Michael and I surprised them with a weekend trip up north. Daniel was barely eighteen months old and he's changed so much in that time. We talked about another visit but life has just got in the way and they couldn't afford to come down. Daniel had chatted away on many video calls but they can now see how much he's truly grown. Donna's got her own way again and will have Daniel for the weekend but I've made sure he will get plenty of time with my parents before they leave next week.

I received a text from my mother about half an hour ago while she was at the service station. My mother sounds excited to see us both; my father has always been quiet – never gives anything away. He works as a postman so his life is usually up early and to bed early. My mother still works in the same biscuit factory she did when I was a child. We were never poor but not well-off either. I had an average upbringing with a happy childhood. I'm glad they've managed to get time off work. I know they'll try to convince me to move back to Leeds.

I can't believe Michael's funeral is tomorrow. It's come around so fast. If it wasn't for Gary and his kind nature, listening to me going on again on the telephone after our meeting in the café, I'm not sure if I could have coped. He's been a real good friend to me lately. A good listener, too. It's nice to speak my mind and not have my views questioned or judged as Donna does. As soon as I get through this funeral I will need to find my strength again. I have to get my fight back. Daniel will need me; we need this roof over our heads.

Donna pressures me into trying to let her help. She talks about wanting to start cooking meals and doing the shopping but I am convinced it's because she wants to keep an eye on me. If she wasn't so domineering I would consider moving in with her and Peter for a while but I know that the minute I let her help she'll be trying to control my every move. She's ok from a distance and I am thankful for how supportive she's been with Daniel but he is my son. I agreed to let her have him for the weekend but after that I might have to rein her in. Maybe she can have him the occasional night here and there if she's not too obsessive.

I know that I have to carry on with my life. I don't even get any peace to grieve. My head is a mess but I want to take things one step at a time: sort the house issues, sort the bills, get back to work, get Daniel into school. I want to try to overcome this constant feeling of flatness and accept I might never know what my husband was doing with our finances. I thought I knew him but I was wrong. The most frustrating part of all is not being able to have him stand here in front of me and explain himself. His mother, his father, my parents, my friends, all of them have this impression of him as a hardworking husband – but I have no idea what he has been up to. I can't bring myself to tell anyone. I feel ashamed for not knowing my own husband. When he said he was off to the office, I believed every word.

My tears still run down my face as I sit here looking at all my wedding photographs of Michael. Happy memories that I cherish, moments I will never get to experience again. I have found all the pictures of Michael with Daniel and others I took on my mobile phone before uploading them to Facebook. I feel betrayed by him. He must have been leading a double life. How could he lie about going to work for all those months? Going to such extreme lengths as to wear his suits, mention clients and be out of the house all day, every day. What else has he lied about?

I miss Michael so much at times it hurts. I've never experienced grief like this but I am managing to sleep better. The nightmares still persist, as do my niggling doubts about that photograph of Victoria holding him, but I'm accepting that outside of these four walls he must have been somebody else I never knew. The only conclusion I have now is that he was possibly cheating behind my back – taking his wedding ring off to meet women at hotels and handing money over to dealers for drugs.

Are drugs the reason for all this debt?

I try not to think about him calling out for me after the accident. Two men lost their lives on a night with so many *what-if's*. I have thought about each and every one of them. I can't change what has happened but I will make sure Daniel grows up knowing that his father died loving him.

Michael only ever wanted the best for his son.

I look at Daniel. He is opposite me with his small backpack. I can tell he is excited about leaving the house and I've packed all his clothes. Donna is going to take him back home to theirs tonight so that I can have some time with my parents. It gives me a break from having to cook, clean and keep my focus on him. I wasn't happy about this at first but they insisted. They're his grandparents and I know they'll take good care of him.

Donna and Peter will get Daniel ready for the funeral tomorrow and after it they will take him for a weekend trip to their lodge. It's only a few days, I remind myself, and it'll go quickly. I think Donna is focusing all her grief on Daniel. It's like she has replaced her son with mine. I wish she would take a step back but I am holding off organising and restructuring our lives until after tomorrow.

I want to get through this funeral in one piece.

'Going to spend some time with Nanny and Granddad tonight, Daniel,' I say, watching my boy smile back at me. 'Mummy will miss you, my little man. You be a good boy.'

I hear a car pull up outside so I lower the television volume. I place the photographs beside the sofa and I stand up, ready to open the door. I peer through the living room curtains. It's not my parents. Donna and Peter have turned up early.

Donna can't help herself, can she?

They were meant to come much later this morning so that my mother and father could spend a bit of quality time with Daniel before Donna and Peter took him. My mother can't wait to cuddle him again. It's all I've heard about in the text messages she's been sending me this morning.

I open the front door. I'm hoping they notice I'm not in my pyjamas today. I want to make a bit of an effort since my mum and dad are on their way down by coach.

'Morning,' Donna says, with Peter trailing along behind her. 'How are you feeling?'

'Not too bad. My Mum and Dad should be here soon,' I reply. 'You're early?'

Donna can barely look me in the eye. She doesn't appear her normal self. She looks tense. I watch for a moment as both Donna and Peter compose themselves. Daniel is still seated on the sofa with his eyes glued to the television. He's been learning so many new words. I keep wondering if Donna knew about Michael being suspended from work. Is she lying to me too?

'I'm sorry we're early,' Donna says. 'I thought we could take Daniel shopping. Buy him a nice little new suit for the funeral tomorrow. We'll pay for it. No bother.'

'My mum and dad were hoping to spend a bit of time with Daniel this morning,' I say, though she already knew this. 'Daniel was going to wear his smart jogging bottoms and a dark blue hoodie. All his clothes are in the small case out at the bottom of the stairs.'

'He reminds me so much of Michael,' Donna replies. 'We don't mind giving him a little treat.'

'I don't mind,' I reply. 'It's entirely up to you. I just want him back here after your trip so he can spend some time with his other grandparents. They're family too.'

I look at Donna. It's like she wants to get her hands on my son. I hate feeling that I owe them because of the money they've paid.

'What time are your mother and father due to get here?' Donna asks, changing the subject. 'They're coming down by coach, aren't they?'

'They should be here any minute,' I reply. 'They got on one of those cheap coaches. They tend to sleep for most of the journey down, then a taxi to here.'

The timing is perfect.

I hear the sound of the taxi parking up against the kerb. Two slams indicate the doors shutting, followed by my mother's voice as she thanks the taxi driver.

'Mum, can I ask you something again?' I say very quickly. 'I know that you said you weren't aware of anything when I asked on the phone the other day but I need you to be honest with me. Did Michael really not mention anything to you about having some time off work, anytime?'

Donna shakes her head. I scrutinise her body language, looking for a sign or any indication that she knew. I believe her.

'No, I am being completely honest with you,' Donna replies. 'He might have mentioned the lodge at some point, but—'

'They're here,' I interrupt, as I look out of the window. My mother sees me and starts to wave, 'Daniel, it's Grandma and Granddad.'

I open the front door again, giving my mum and dad the biggest hug. I have missed them so much. We are tearful but I'm so pleased they're here.

'Where is he?' my dad asks. 'Where's the little guy hiding?'

'He's in the living room. Donna and Peter are here too.' My mother will tell from my voice that something is up. 'They're going to take him out shopping in a bit. Get him a nice suit for the funeral.'

My mother looks at me. She is not happy.

'Don't we get to spend any time with him today?' she asks. 'I thought Daniel was at theirs later.'

I glare at my mother. I'm not ready for an argument. I know she and Donna have had personality clashes before but Donna and Peter are a world apart from my parents: mine don't own their own business, mine don't own their own house and mine have always been working-class. Donna, I know, will see my family as a bit ordinary, but we're not materialistic.

'Can you let it go for now?' I say quietly to my mother to save a row. 'You already knew Donna was having him before the funeral and for the rest of the weekend. You have four whole days with him from Monday. Let's get through tomorrow, for me.'

My mother nods, while my father smiles and winks at me.

'Ok, Jen,' my mother says, 'let me say a quick hello and goodbye then.'

I lead my parents through to the living room where they fuss over Daniel for the next few minutes. Donna has put on his coat while I've put his small case of clothes by the front door.

'Be good for Mummy,' I say to Daniel as he holds Donna's hand while leaving. 'See you tomorrow. It's Daddy's big day.'

I wave them off. Donna turns around. I think she might have forgotten something.

'Is Gary still picking us up tomorrow morning?' Donna asks while Peter places Daniel on the back seat of the car. 'I'm really looking forward to meeting him.'

I know what she's up to, mentioning his name like that in front of my mother. I've already assured her we're only friends. The agreement was for Gary to collect Donna, Peter and Daniel in the morning and bring them back here. Then, all of us would travel in the limousine together. Gary only offered his help because I mentioned how none of us really want to concentrate on driving. Donna and Peter don't live en-route to the crematorium so it makes more sense if we all leave together for one journey.

'He should be with you about ten,' I reply. 'He'll drop you back here and then we will all wait for the limousine to follow behind the hearse.'

I'm absolutely dreading that moment. Another milestone to pass.

With the help of Donna, the flowers have been organised and the order of service printed as handouts for everyone as they arrive. I shut the door on them and brace myself for the night with my parents. We have a lot of catching up to do but I'm going to have to tell them about Michael's lies. My mother adored him. She thought I was so fortunate to have found a man with a great career and that we were able to own our own home. She will be devastated. My mother will instinctively know I am worrying about something. My father will rant and rave. He shook Michael's hand and thanked him for taking good care of me the last time they met.

Tomorrow is going to be an emotional day for us all.

Twenty-Nine

Donna

Daniel is the spitting image of Michael. The way his inquisitive expression lights up his face brings me joy. All he is interested in at this young age is playing with his toys and watching his favourite cartoons on television. Michael was just the same, only he wasn't as switched on with technology. Tablets and mobile phones weren't so freely around in his first few years and they were too expensive when he was a teenager. It amazes me how even at three, Daniel can swipe his way through choices on video streaming apps.

He knows his own mind already.

I look at Daniel now, asleep in the spare room, as I draw the curtains. I can hear his faint snores. He is unaware of what a big day he has ahead of him tomorrow. I hope he grows up to remember his dad. Michael adored him – loved him with all his heart. He worked himself to death to provide for his family. It's wrong of me to think it but I can't help myself. I wonder whether if Jenny had been less demanding, he wouldn't have worked himself to death.

It wasn't until they bought the house that I first started to realise her expectations. When Pete and I moved in here, we started with absolutely nothing. We had a mattress on the floor before we bought a new bed, we lived without a freezer for a year and we decorated one room at a time rather than all at once. I remember the conversations Michael had with me about Jenny: they needed a new sofa, they needed new furniture that all had to match, they needed a new tv but it had to be a large flat screen one. There was no making do or getting by and nothing second-hand either. Michael had never lived that way in his own flat but he bought everything new to make Jenny happy. He spoilt her.

Daniel always feels special to us as our first grandson but now he is all the more precious to me because he will be my only grandson. He's a part of Michael and I owe it to my son to help him have the upbringing he deserves. I would have liked to have seen him have more children because it makes up for my own mistakes. I regret having just the one child. Michael should have had a brother or sister but we were quite poor back then when he was growing up. Michael was an accidental pregnancy and having children is such an expense. Pete and I discussed having one more and we tried at one point but it never happened. We accepted it wasn't going to be after I had a couple of miscarriages. I couldn't put myself through it emotionally. I came to accept that Michael was going to be our only child – and no regrets.

I'm concerned about Jenny's mental health and I know that she needs a break. It's obvious and I am glad she has seen sense and allowed us to take him to Cornwall with us for the weekend. It will do us all some good and maybe, with a bit of space, she will get organised with the finances and get her house in order.

After the funeral, we will take a drive down to the lodge. Pete and I can spend some time away from the hustle and bustle of Westbridge, the neighbours and the shop – just quality time with Daniel. We're all packed and ready to go. I called the holiday park and asked them to clean the place ready for our arrival. I'm going to see if I can get any more information out of Daniel about what Jenny has been up to. I know he's only three but he'll let me know if Mummy has been back on her special juice or if he has spent any time around Gary. That's my major concern. The weather is going to be dry so there's plenty of walks we can take Daniel on. He might even get to see some ducks.

'Nanny is going to help take care of you,' I whisper to Daniel, stroking his hair because I know it settles him down. 'Your daddy loved you very much.'

Daniel remains asleep, blissfully dreaming.

'You'll always have us, little man. Daddy's gone and Mummy isn't herself. She will get better but I will always watch out for you. I'm not going to let anyone I don't approve of near you.'

It's an emotional time for us all and I can't begin to understand her pain losing a husband but I'm not sure she understands ours at losing our son. Of course, if I lost Pete, I'd be devastated but I'm more independent than Jenny. I don't really see her as being as self-sufficient as I would be in the same situation but we all deal with grief in our own way. Pete has to remind me to take a few steps backwards at times. I know I can take charge and be a little overbearing but there's a little boy to consider here. He needs us and I don't think his mother has her eye on the ball with this Gary. When Jenny mentioned he could take us all to her place because none of us wanted to drive, I was hesitant at first. Pete didn't really want to do it but he could have. I suppose it's an opportunity for me to spend some time with Gary. I know I'll be thinking of my son but I have my doubts about Gary and I want to make sure their friendship is purely platonic.

I am not looking forward to my son's funeral tomorrow – but who would be? I'm still in shock but I have to let go of my wishes for him to be buried. I get angry when I think about it. I only wanted somewhere to visit my son. Jenny was so dismissive of our wishes but I'll have to just forget it. Like Pete says, it won't bring him back. I don't like the idea of my son being burnt. I still have bad memories of him in the hospital. His dead body is still in my mind. It's unthinkable to be in this situation. I feel lost but know that I should be in control.

No parents should have to say goodbye to their own son. After the funeral I will see if Jenny will allow Daniel to stay with us for a few weeks longer. She can't seem to see or accept that she needs this time to herself to help get her home in order. Daniel might lose his home. I can't stand by and watch as they move into some rancid council shoebox house. I've lived that way of life.

When Pete and I were much, much younger, and before we started our business, life for us wasn't the way it is now. We lived on the breadline. We struggled and often we would go without so Michael could have his school uniform and everything he needed, like a decent meal in his belly. He made us proud when he got his accounting and finance degree. Neither of us has been to university and for a son of ours to be so academic reassured us that he would always do well. He loved his job but he never knew how to manage his own money as well as he could handle the financial affairs of his clients.

I appreciate that Gary is giving us a lift to Jenny's in the morning. I'm not very happy about how he and Jenny have started to become friends, it's unhealthy. I only accepted the offer of a lift so that I can see for myself how much of a support he really is. I could have asked a number of friends of ours to help but I am determined to meet Gary. I want to see what he is like with Jenny, to see how close they might have become. I'm convinced it's not good for Daniel to see another man in the family home. It angers me.

Pete is thankful he isn't driving as he'll be in a heavy emotional state. He has a long drive down to our lodge for the weekend but Gary will drop us back home here after the funeral. We might take a slow drive down in the evening when the roads are quieter.

If I see that Gary is anything more than a friend, I will be absolutely livid with her. Jenny seems to be isolating herself in her house and I want to check that he's not worming his way into her life – or my son's bed. If that were true, I'd give her a piece of my mind but I need to keep my cool for now. I'm going to have to keep a watchful eye on how their friendship develops. I don't want Daniel near him.

Jenny has informed me that she has allowed Gary to sit in the procession limousine that will follow behind the hearse. What I am annoyed with is that yet again she didn't even ask me – she's telling me instead. She says that Gary needs to be there, that Michael wouldn't have minded his presence – but he's not family. It's too intrusive. I understand that he might need closure from the terrible accident but the funeral procession should have been for family members only. This is my son's funeral and I paid for it. But I don't want to fall out with her again because she might stop me from seeing Daniel. My grandson is going to need me if his mother doesn't start standing on her own two feet. I might have to take matters into my own hands. I won't be able to keep my mouth shut.

If this distress has tainted her mind, I can help her. I hope her parents will make her see sense too, not that I've ever really got on with them – but they should also have Daniel's best interests at heart. I could have a word with them after the funeral about all my concerns. I'm also worried that they will want her to move away to Leeds.

I can't have them take my grandson that far up north. I have to have hope that he will stay in Westbridge. He needs us. I might have to get some legal advice about access rights. I've lost my son. I'm not going to lose my grandson as well.

Leaving Daniel to sleep upstairs, I've returned to the living room. I give Pete a hug as we pass each other in the hallway and we both look at each other and sigh.

'I still can't believe this has happened to us,' Pete says, walking into the dining room, 'no matter how many times I get my head around it. I know he's dead, I know our son is dead, but I can't seem to accept it.'

I start to cry when I see Pete holding back the tears. He was never one to show emotions but this is too big a deal for him and he can't maintain his old-fashioned masculinity. We hug each other again. I place my arms around him and feel how warm he is as we hold on to each other.

'It's going to be one hell of a day tomorrow,' I reply, mustering some words between the sobs. 'I still can't believe he is gone either.'

I let go of Pete, who remains seated in the dining room, looking at all the old photos we have of Michael as a child – those times when we took him to the park, the beach, the moors, and the random snaps on our old polaroid instant camera. He hated having his photograph taken as a child, so many of them are surprise shots but in most of them, I see that he looks happy. I'm glad that even through our more poverty-stricken days he was still happy. It reassures me that he knew he had parents who loved him and provided what they could for him. If we could swap places with him we would do without hesitating.

There are some things I would never question. I'm not sure what it was but there was a time – driving past the Westbridge Central Hotel by the train station in town – when I saw something. This was three days before his death and I saw Michael outside, all suited and booted – nothing unusual for the line of work he was in, all those clients he had to see – and he was there with a woman. She didn't look very old, barely thirty, but he gave her a kiss on the cheek. I mentioned to Jenny about seeing him there at the hotel and I implied he was there for a job interview but she seemed to not know anything about it. Maybe it was just a work colleague?

I have no idea what social circles Michael was involved in but I know that he was away from home an awful lot those past few months. I saw him only a handful of times and I got the impression their marriage was tense. Jenny was only working part-time while staying home to look after Daniel and I now regret not offering more support to them both. Pete and I were so fixated on the gift shop down in Looe that we came to accept that Michael and Jenny led their own lives.

Of course I knew they had had a child together and bought a house together – but Michael had a past. He had a history of being hooked on the fruit machines when he was in his twenties. I know he liked his online gambling, I know he cheated on some of his ex-girlfriends but Pete and I thought Jenny had really made him settle down. She was the one. When I saw him at the hotel I just had that pang of doubt in my mind. I ignored it for a while because it was none of my business but I intended to confront Michael about it. I would remind him that he was a man with responsibilities and that he had a son. He was a father who should start to grow up and he needed to pay me back that £5000 he owed me. I lied to his father to give him that money.

I never had the opportunity to challenge Michael about what I saw that day but in all honesty it could have been a work colleague or a client. I gave him the benefit of the doubt but Jenny may not have done the same and it gave me a little cause for concern.

None of it matters anymore.

There's a knock on the front door. It makes me jump because we're not expecting anyone and the neighbours have given us some peace. A couple of our close friends next door have said their condolences but respect our privacy and leave us alone. I'm tempted to ignore it, but the knock sounds again – only this time louder. I'm annoyed because it might wake Daniel. He needs his rest.

'Don't worry, Pete,' I shout through to the dining room. 'I'll get it. I'll send whoever it is away.'

'Thanks, love,' Pete replies. 'I'll put the kettle on.'

I stand here at the front door. I've not opened it yet but I wipe my eyes to try to hide that I've been crying. I see some flowers through the glass.

'All right, all right,' I snap. 'I'm coming. Keep your hair on.'

All I can think about is Daniel. Now that he is here with us in this house, it's going to be a struggle to let him go. He's made this house come alive and I can see how he's lifted Pete's mood today too. I think Daniel will be happy here with us for a while.

He's the only part of Michael we have left and I can't get that fact out of my head.

Thirty

Jenny

I should be pleased to see my parents but under the circumstances with Michael's funeral today, it's a struggle to keep the conversation flowing. I didn't get much sleep last night but that's a familiar situation that often leaves me grabbing a few hours on the sofa when Daniel is at preschool. I spent hours talking to them both about the last day I spent with Michael, seeing his body at the hospital, his missing wedding ring, and the lies that he told me.

My husband was under investigation for stealing money at work. My mother and father had no words to describe their shock. I agreed with them that Michael did not seem the type of person to commit a crime like that and I also don't know why or how? I believed he was going out to work and earning his salary. I knew he was after new clients but I didn't relate it to him being jobless. My mother still maintains that I should leave everything behind and move back to Leeds. I said I'd have to reconsider my options if I lose the house. Today, I have only the funeral on my mind.

They promised not to cause a scene with Michael's parents. I'm grieving for a man that I thought was a truthful, honest person but I feel betrayed too. Michael was hiding something serious, and after the funeral, when everything has settled down, I intend to find answers. I'm terrified of the truth yet this could have been going on for years.

My mother is concerned about me, naturally, and keeps telling me to focus on the funeral service then worry about everything else in the coming weeks once this hardest day is over with. She had no words about the debts, the lies, it was as much of a shock to her as it was me when I first found out. Michael was prepared to lose us our home and I may never find out what he did with the money. I thought his gambling days were behind him. I never saw the signs. I had no idea what secrets he was hiding.

I don't know what to think anymore. I'm so tired. I feel drained of energy. At least my own parents understand that Gary is a friend. Our conversations are harmless. I'm not out to replace Michael with another man so soon and nor will I let Donna play games with Daniel. He is my son.

My mother suggested that I should let the house go and move back up to Leeds. I'm not keen which upset her but I've not lived there in years. I have made a life for myself here. My work, my son, I don't know if I could detach myself from Westbridge. I'm not ready to move nor am I prepared to have these discussions right now.

'It's a big decision to make too soon.' I explained, 'I want to get through today and say goodbye to my husband.'

I sense the awkwardness of my mother and father because they keep walking around the house, not knowing where to put themselves. They're angry and wish I had told them everything sooner. I see them trying to make sure that I am all right but I don't think I'll ever be the same woman again. I'm focused on the window and I keep thinking that soon my husband will be here. The hearse will park up outside and I am to await that dreaded knock on the door.

I can't make up my mind what to wear. I don't like this black dress nor my black shoes, nor my black coat. Donna was adamant that the service was more traditional and respectful, whereas I wanted to inject colour. My mother tied my hair up for me because I couldn't be bothered. I'm too anxious and nervous to care about my hair. I know that all eyes will be on me today. I was his wife, the woman who should have been by his side, yet I'm expected to stand there and still conceal his lies.

My marriage wasn't always about struggling with money issues. There were so many happy times that we shared. Buying the house together, having Daniel, long romantic walks on the beach or the moors. We shared some good times when Michael wasn't focused on work so much. It was only over the last year that I needed him to know it was becoming too much of a strain. Michael never knew when to admit defeats, he should have talked to me more about the credit cards, the movement of money in our bank accounts and draining the savings account of everything we were trying to save for Daniel's future – all this for our house.

It couldn't have been just the mortgage putting this much pressure on him if he was out of work. He wasn't paying the mortgage and money was going elsewhere.

I'm stood at the window with both of my parents behind me. My mother places her arm around my waist. Pulls me in closer and together we stand looking outwards.

'I'm so proud of you,' my mother says. 'My strong girl, you might not think it now, but you will get through this.'

I don't want to crack and open the flood gates. I hold back the tears and take a breath.

'Thanks, Mum,' I respond, placing my hand on hers. 'I have to stay strong for Daniel. Gary shouldn't be much longer. Then we'll all be here together.'

'I feel for Donna and Peter, I really do,' my mother says. 'If that had been you in the accident, I don't know what I would be like. There's no words. You're our only child so I understand how cruel it must feel to have to say goodbye to your only son.'

Michael and I had never discussed having more children other than passing comments here and there about giving Daniel a brother or sister. I made it very clear I needed a career, especially now that I am in my early thirties, I don't regret Daniel for one minute but another child would have me tied to the house for even longer. I'm not getting any younger.

'I know you don't want to think about moving back home, love,' my father says, 'but we're here if you need us. Anytime. Just pick up the phone, our door is always open.'

'I know Dad,' I reply. 'I might take you up on that one day but I don't want any more upheaval or change in Daniel's life right now. I have a lot to deal with here, this is our home now.'

They should have been here by now.

'Where are they?' I ask. 'They were meant to be here in plenty of time before the hearse and limo turn up. They're late. I bet they struggled to get Daniel ready. I knew he should have stayed home with me last night. I bet Donna's been up all night with him and struggled?'

'I'm sure if there had been any problems, Donna or Peter would have called you, wouldn't they?' my mother says. 'What about Gary, why is he picking them up anyway?'

I'm tense enough as it is without having to re-explain myself.

'He's doing them a favour,' I snap. 'They thought they'd be too upset to drive and it was too inconvenient to stay here last night as you two are here. Also, he has a lot of contacts in the car industry, car rentals, and he has a few cars himself. He just wanted to do something to help me.'

I shake with worry, holding the phone to my ear as I dial Donna's mobile. It goes straight to voicemail.

'Hi Donna, it's just Jenny here, checking that you're on your way. Text or call me when you can.'

I hang up and immediately dial Gary's number. It goes straight to voicemail.

'Hi Gary, it's just Jenny here, checking that you've got Donna, Peter and Daniel with you. Text or call when you can.'

'Maybe they're on their way and got caught up in traffic,' my father says. 'I'm not sure how bad Westbridge roads are at the weekends but I'm sure everything is fine, love.'

I look further out of the window. I'm on edge because the first thought in my mind is that they've all been killed in an accident. I'm reminded of the day that Michael left the house and never returned home. I can't have this happen to Daniel.

I'm shaking now from head to toe and I need to sit down. I'm teary and stressed. I know the hearse will be here soon. I've texted both mobiles of Donna and Peter, as well as texting Gary. I need some reassurance that they're ok.

There's been a terrible accident, hasn't there?

I scramble around the browser on my mobile phone searching for road accident news in Westbridge. I can hear my mother and father talking between themselves in the background, but I've zoned out. I'm nervous and tense but I struggle to find anything recently reported. Maybe everything is fine and I'm overreacting?

Maybe they've run off with Daniel?

'I knew it, I just knew it,' I say out loud, my mother and father looking at me with confusion. 'They've run off with Daniel, haven't they? Donna is always taking over and trying to act like his mother.'

'I'm sure that's not the case,' my mother explains. 'They're his grandparents and it doesn't explain Gary's part in it. Worst case scenario is that they're in the car, on their way and probably driving somewhere where there's no signal. Mobile phones aren't the most reliable of things, are they?'

I don't reply, but instead, I look out the window. I hear the sound of a car driving slowly from around the corner. I stop and stare, my eyes fixed on the road, and my breathing intensifies. Michael is here. My husband's coffin slowly passes my window and a rush of emotion hits me like a ton of bricks. Seeing him outside like this for the first time seems unthinkable, yet it's very much a reality. I try to look away, but I can't.

Where is everyone?

The hearse is black with the coffin on display from every window. I see the flowers around him, even though he hated flowers – it's what Donna wanted. Everything was about what Donna wanted but I could hardly argue as she and Peter paid for everything. If she had all her own way, Michael would have been buried. I never wanted that; I know Michael would not have wanted that either.

My mother and father stand beside me; my mother places an arm around my waist and pulls me in towards her tightly.

'It looks like the limousine has arrived too,' my mother says. 'I can see it just behind Michael. What a beautiful coffin, great flowers. You've done him proud.'

'Daniel should be here by now,' I reply, my eyes flushed with emotion. 'We have to wait.'

'I'll go outside and let them know what's happening,' my father interrupts. 'I'll say we're just waiting on Michael's parents and they're stuck in traffic or something.'

I watch my father leave the room, and as he does so, I speak to my mother alone.

'This doesn't feel right,' I say. 'Mum, I have a gut feeling something is not right.'

My mother hugs me.

'Give them another call and see what's happening,' she replies. 'Have they not even sent you a text or anything yet?'

I try the number for Donna again and it goes straight to voicemail.

'It's me again. Letting you know that Michael is here, the hearse has arrived. We're waiting for you now. Is everything ok?'

I leave a message and hang up. I take a deep breath but I am nervous and confused. They would have replied to me by now. Donna knows that I need to know my son is safe. I'm starting to panic.

The front door opens with my father and Gary, who looks out of breath but nervous.

Something's happened.

'Is Daniel with you?' I ask, looking directly at Gary. 'Is everything ok. I tried calling but it went to voicemail. Are Donna and Peter in the limousine?'

I see the expression on my father's face with his eyes lowering to the floor. Gary doesn't instantly reply. I shake my head.

'No, no,' I say, 'Daniel. Where is he?'

Gary walks closer towards me as I imagine the worst. In my mind, he's dead and they've all been involved in a car accident: another tragedy where in some strange coincidence, I lose the rest of my family. I knew he should have stayed with me. I was stupid to let him go. I trusted them.

'I don't know where they are,' Gary replies. I look at his suit and I can smell the scent of Michael's favourite aftershave, 'I turned up at the house but there was no answer. I knocked and knocked. I even looked through the windows but it's deadly quiet. It's like they've just vanished.'

'Before you think the worst,' my father interrupts, 'I explained after introducing myself to Gary that maybe they have forgotten and made their own way here, or even to the crematorium.'

'They would have messaged me!' I shout. 'Donna would not put me through this worry or stress. She would have said something or even texted me.'

They've kidnapped my son.

'I think they've run off with Daniel,' I tell my mother. 'I know it sounds stupid, but Donna has been taking him to school all the time, helping me out with money issues, telling me what's best for him – she even wanted me to hand him over to her for a few weeks. I'm telling you; she wants my son. She's taken him.'

I could see clearly on my parents' faces that they thought it was absurd. The only one who listens to me is Gary. Nobody is taking this very seriously.

'I would have replied to your voicemail and text but I didn't want to worry you,' Gary says. 'I needed to look around first and then thought best that I explain it face to face.'

'Surely they wouldn't steal their own grandson,' my mother interrupts. 'I bet there's a perfectly reasonable explanation for this, you wait and see.'

'I told you, didn't I, Gary, that they wanted him? I've been saying it for days now,' I blurt out, looking at Gary, who I am sure is wearing one of Michael's suits. 'Is that Michael's?'

'Is what Michael's?' Gary asks. 'The suit?'

I open my mouth and don't have the chance to question it further.

'I didn't realise that I didn't fit into mine anymore,' Gary continues. 'I've lost so much weight, and I still had some of the charity shop bags in the back of the van. I saw this one but I didn't think anyone would notice. I'm sorry, maybe I should have asked.'

'I recognise the stripes and the little marking above the left trouser pocket,' I explain. 'I bought Michael that suit for his birthday two years ago. This is too weird. I guess I was giving it away anyway, I just didn't expect to see it again.'

Then a thought hits me. A light bulb moment.

'Did you see their car, it's a small grey one?' I ask Gary. 'Usually parked right opposite the living room window if it wasn't on the drive?'

Gary frowns and shakes his head, giving me the answer that I needed to inflict more fear in me. My mind now is focused on finding Daniel, yet my husband is outside waiting for us to follow him to the crematorium. What am I going to do?

'I don't remember, I wasn't really looking,' Gary replies. 'I expected them to be ready to all sit in the back of the black Mercedes I managed to loan off an old mate. I have to take it back after the service and pick up the van.'

I look at my father. I don't know what else to do.

'I can't go to the service without Daniel,' I say to my father. 'I need to know he is safe. I need to know where he is.'

'They're pushed for time, love,' he replies. 'I said earlier we would give it half an hour or more but they've got other services booked in after Michael's.'

Shit. I have to think on my feet.

'Mum, Dad,' I say, 'you go inside the limo and follow the hearse to the crematorium. Gary, can you take me back to Donna and Peter's? I need to see for myself if the car has gone and then, if I find them, we rush back to the service. I have to know where my son is. Maybe I should call the police.'

'It's a bit too soon for the police, don't you think?' Gary interrupts and starts to walk forward. 'Try them again on the phone, and if they still don't answer then yes, I can take you back there. Are you sure you don't want to get in the limo, and I go back on my own?'

'No,' I reply, 'I want to go. Daniel could be missing for all I know. He's more important right now. I need to know what's going on.'

I try calling Donna one more time but there's still no answer. We all walk outside to the hearse and my father has a quiet word with the driver to inform him of what's happening and my need to find Daniel.

As I stand beside my husband's coffin, I look at it, knowing that he is inside there. I think the first few minutes realising that he was here upset me more but now I can't concentrate on anything except Daniel. Michael will have to wait. He would have understood that. Our son has to come first.

'Can you open the back door?' I ask the hearse driver. 'I want to say something. I want to feel the coffin.'

The driver nods, walks over to the door and unlocks it with his key. I stand behind him, peering inside. The smell of the wood hits me, then followed by the flowers. I place one hand on the coffin to feel symbolically connected. I know he can't hear me but for my peace of mind I still have to say a few words.

'I love you so much, Michael. You'll always be my husband, always be Daniel's father and I'll always remember you,' I whisper to him. I close my eyes. 'We had so many happy times together.'

'Do you need me to come with you?' my mother asks. 'Maybe your father and I could go instead so you can be with Michael?'

I see Gary turn and stop; he barely knows them. I won't settle until I've found my son myself.

'No, I'll be fine,' I reply. 'I'd rather you got inside the limo. Gary and me will try to find out what's going on.'

I turn around and walk away in the direction of Gary. Thinking about it calmly, I think Gary is right. It's too soon for the police. I watch my mother and father step inside the limousine after giving them a hug.

I have to find Daniel.

Thirty-One

Gary

We are away from her family and in the confines of my car for the first time. I am putting pressure on myself, reminding myself that my demons are at work. Jenny doesn't realise how I feel about her, she's never had any idea all this time, but that doesn't distract me. I am focused and she needs me, even if she can't see it yet.

I gave Jenny the flowers I stole from the scene of Michael's death. Handing them to her while she had no clue where they had been was satisfying. I manipulated our friendship and gained her trust by wearing Michael's aftershave which I stole from her bathroom. I wanted to cling to her good nature, have her want to know more about me. I hooked her with some lies and I thought we were going to be friends but I don't think she cares enough about me. All those times I kept staring at my phone, looking for replies, amounted to nothing but disappointment. I realised she wasn't interested in me at all.

I can feel that Jenny is tense. From the corner of my eyes, as I continue to drive down the road, I can see her fixated on her mobile phone. The atmosphere in the car is undeniably upsetting for her: potentially missing her husband's funeral service while their young boy is nowhere to be seen. Naturally, she has to find Daniel first, any mother would do that, but the not knowing what has happened to him must be driving her insane. I know how that feels too. I remember the days when I had no idea where my wife was, no idea that she was fucking another man behind my back. I also was robbed of a life and deprived of a future. We're not all that dissimilar.

'I told you she wanted my son, didn't I?' Jenny asks, holding onto the phone. 'No answer. I've tried calling and texting her, she's not responding. Something's happened, hasn't it? Something's not right. They wouldn't miss their own son's funeral. I should call the police, or Sharon?'

'No,' I snap. Shit, it was too forceful. 'They're not going to take it seriously. Daniel is with his grandparents, he's not officially missing. All the police will do is ask a load of questions and take up a lot of time when we could be looking ourselves. Trust me.'

I can see she's come round to my way of thinking. Jenny does at least trust me now.

'Your parents will call you if they turn up at the crematorium, won't they?' I respond, still keeping my concentration on the road. 'Grief does some funny things to people. If they did take him, do you have any idea where they would go?'

I try to keep her talking, distract her.

'The lodge,' Jenny says, holding her hand to her head with the stress. 'It's down in Looe, on a park in the middle of nowhere. They might have taken him down there and got stuck in traffic. It still doesn't explain why they aren't answering their phone or why they didn't tell me. Donna is a stubborn bitch at times. Just like Michael was.'

'It's only about forty-five minutes away across the bridge,' I reply. 'I know you get traffic build-up at the weekend. Yeah, they could be stuck in traffic, sounds logical.'

'I should call Sharon and see if there's anything she can do,' Jenny says, still clutching on to the phone for dear life, staring relentlessly at the screen. 'Report that my son might be missing with Donna and Peter.'

'No,' I say loudly and firmly. 'Trust me on this. Didn't you say that you didn't trust Sharon anyway? Why would you waste your time with her, she can't help you right now, but I can.'

Jenny places the phone inside her pocket and turns to look at me. I glance briefly at her face. She looks tearful. Her mind must be in overdrive but we're almost at Michael's parents' house.

'They won't even be interested until they've been missing twenty-four hours or more, think about it,' I explain. 'You gave Daniel to his own grandparents who love him dearly. It's been less than a day and although they're not answering their phone it doesn't mean the worst has happened. At least wait and see if they turn up at the service. Their heads could be all over the place, or likely they're stuck in traffic. Give it a bit more time.'

Jenny nods. She listens to me when I make a firm decision. It must have been how Michael manipulated her.

'Here we are,' I say, pulling up on the driveway, 'this is the right address that you texted me the other day, isn't it?'

'There's no car,' Jenny says, her mouth is open in surprise. 'They aren't here. They've got Daniel and they've taken him from me. I know they have. I knew all this time she was acting too much in control. It's my fault for letting her take him to school. I've let her take over.'

I watch her pain, the suffering in her mind, and it excites me. This is how we connected when I thought we could first be friends. This pain and mental torture is what we share as something in common. We are both victims.

'It's not my place to tell you to calm down, but I think if you did, you might start thinking more clearly,' I reply, trying to calm her nerves. 'You said they might have gone to the lodge. We need more proof. Do you have a key or any neighbours to contact? Maybe we should see what the neighbours saw or heard – if anything.'

'I'll knock on the door again anyway,' Jenny replies. 'Donna isn't the type to mix with neighbours. She's usually too busy with her shop.'

We both get out of the Mercedes. My hands feel cold. Jenny walks to the front door and I keep thinking of ways to distract her from contacting the police.

'There's no answer,' Jenny says, now looking through the letterbox. 'Donna, Peter, Daniel, are you in there?'

I stand beside her and wait.

'I'll give Donna another call,' Jenny says, looking up her contacts list on her mobile while still lifting up the letterbox. 'Answer your bloody phone, will you!'

We both hear the ringing sound from the other direction. Jenny runs towards the living room window and starts banging on it loudly.

'Did you hear that too?' Jenny asks, her panic mode in full throttle. 'It's Donna's phone, she's in there. Maybe she's had an accident.'

'Maybe she forgot to take her phone with her?' I reply. 'They couldn't have both had an accident. What about Peter?'

'That makes sense. My nerves are making me overreact. I just want to know that my son is safe. I'll call Peter.'

I don't know what else to say. I need to lead the conversation or keep her talking more. I watch her as she looks lost and out of control. I see the panic across her face and can tell she is on edge. I have to think of something and fast.

'Shall I take you back to the service, or you'll miss it?' I ask. 'Maybe they've turned up there?'

'There's no answer from Peter either, but I'll call my mother,' Jenny responds. 'She would have called me if they had.'

For barely a minute, Jenny talks to her mother who confirms no sight of Donna, Peter or Daniel.

'I'm going to try the back door,' Jenny says, walking away from the window to the garden gate. 'They might have left it unlocked.'

Jenny leans over and pulls up the catch to the gate, then we squeeze in beside the recycling bins that lead to a perfectly mown lawn. Plant pots and flowers are tucked in every corner, with a set of chairs and a table on the patio. You can tell by the garden that whoever lived here was a perfectionist.

'It's locked,' Jenny says, pulling at the handle. 'I have to call someone. I need to call the police. Enough is enough, no time for games now.'

I wish Jenny would trust me when I say they wouldn't be interested. Her son is with two people that she handed him over to. The police will not be interested in this yet. She'll have to discuss it over the phone or down at the station for hours.

'Maybe they're at the lodge, just like you suspected. Donna probably left her phone behind,' I reply, watching helplessly. 'I've got Sharon's number, so I will call her as a heads up if you like. If we don't find them in the next hour or so, then we can report it officially.'

I see Jenny roll her eyes upwards; she's thinking about something.

'I'm going to break in,' Jenny says. 'I have to know they're safe. There are a few rocks over there, I'll smash the back-door window and that should allow us both to get inside.'

I walk towards the corner of the garden where the rocks are scattered among the small bushes. I pick one up and hand it to Jenny. It's her decision, not mine. I hold my phone to my ear after I watch her walk towards the door.

'Hi Sharon, it's Gary. Gary Taylor. I'm with Jenny Clifton at Michael's parents' house. They haven't arrived for the funeral service and Daniel is with them. Jenny thinks they are missing, or might have taken him somewhere.'

Jenny is looking through the window, shouting out their names.

'Ah ok. Yeah, I already explained that,' I continue. 'We will, thank you.'

'Exactly what I said,' I inform Jenny. 'Sharon will log it, but if we don't find anything in the next hour the police will put out a search for a vehicle check.'

'But they could be anywhere by then,' Jenny replies. 'Is she on her way?'

'No,' I answer. 'Like I said all along, there's not enough time passed yet. We are better off looking ourselves. They're only going to be here, the lodge or on their way to the service, aren't they? Peter can't use his mobile phone while driving and Donna left her phone in the house. We might be overreacting.'

Jenny doesn't hesitate and smashes the back-door window, unlocks the back-door catch, and the door is open within seconds. She rushes inside and I follow behind her. Jenny shouts for Daniel, then Donna, then Peter. Nothing but silence follows – the house is empty.

'What shall we do now?' I ask, looking at Jenny as we stand inside the hallway. 'There's no answer, no one around?'

'Daniel had his suitcase,' she responds. 'I packed him to be all ready for his weekend away with them. Wait here while I look around a sec.'

I stand in the hallway, staring at the front door. I can't take my eyes off it, nor the plush carpet. Then I turn to face the kitchen. Jenny has reappeared, looking flushed and breathing heavily.

'They've gone, their clothes are out all over the bed, but their cases aren't here. They usually keep them on top of the wardrobe. They've gone. There's nothing of Daniel's here either. With the car not being on the drive, and the clothes and cases, it looks like they might have gone to Looe.'

'Ah, that's not far from here,' I reply. 'And the lack of communication is down to the phone being left behind. Maybe she didn't want you to call her?'

I've dropped a bombshell. I'm interested to see her reaction towards Donna's potential game plan.

'So, thinking about it, I bet she pressured you into letting them have Daniel for the night and then ran off with him to Cornwall while you were meant to be at the funeral service.' I continue, 'Maybe they did want him from you after all. They don't own any other properties do they? Nothing abroad?'

'No,' Jenny says, breathing heavily in panic. 'Just the one in Looe, that lodge down in Cornwall. It's their pride and joy and where they spend most of their free time.'

'I can take you there,' I reply, 'but I will need to take the Mercedes back to the car hire shop, it's en route, and get my van. We can drive down in that. It doesn't matter about getting any scratches then down those country lanes and we wouldn't be pushed for time.'

'I'll call my mother again and let her know what's happened. I don't care about going in the van, I just want to find my son. I need to know he is safe. Donna has obviously taken him somewhere.'

Jenny walks into the living room and picks up Donna's phone which had been left on the table next to a laptop. She proceeds to call her mother from her own phone and I still stay, leaning against a wall in the hallway. There are no keys on the hook.

'Give me five minutes to check their computer if that's all right?' Jenny asks after she hangs up on her mother. 'There might be some clues on here if I look at their browsing history or emails.'

'I'm not in any rush,' I reply, 'What's happening at the service? Is it delayed?'

'Apparently everyone is talking about us because we aren't there, but I don't care about that. Daniel is all that matters,' Jenny responds. She appears calmer, more focused. 'I will do something special when I get Michael's ashes back. He will understand that I need to find Daniel over anything else. This is so frustrating. Donna knows full well that I could have done without this today. Putting me through this worry and stress.'

Jenny sits down on the sofa with the laptop; after browsing around for a few minutes, she discovers something useful.

'They've sent an email to the park,' Jenny says enthusiastically. 'They've asked for it to be cleaned for their arrival. That's something at least. I wish they would have phoned me or contacted me.'

'Let's go then,' I reply. 'It all makes sense, the sooner we leave now the better.'

Jenny needs me.

Thirty-Two

Jenny

I hang up the phone again from my mother who has told me Michael's service has come to an end. Now, on my drive down to Looe in Gary's van, an intermittent signal constantly drops my connection, only adding to my frustrations. I was told the curtains closed around his coffin and I sob my eyes out, not only because of how anxious I feel, but for not being there. The grief, and intense worry for my son Daniel, is all I have on my mind. I should have been at Michael's service but Donna has deliberately sabotaged this day because of not getting her own way. I never wanted a burial for Michael because I hate the thought of him being trapped in the ground. She must have made sure that her, Peter and Daniel were no part of it because this wasn't what she wanted.

My parents are in a frenzy. I told them all the suitcases are missing from the house. Gary is trying to make me see sense that the only place they can be is in the lodge. I hope that he's right. It has always been their go-to place.

I keep thinking about the last few moments when Donna and Peter left the house last night. Was there a conversation I missed, was there anything that I might have forgotten, but no – I just remember waving at Daniel. Nothing in their behaviour seemed out of the ordinary.

What have they done, and where have they taken Daniel?

We're only about five minutes away from the holiday park site. I notice that my battery is low and I'm anxious about finding Daniel. The phone signal isn't great in these rural areas and I'm stressing out because if they aren't there, I'm going to have to find a phone and call Sharon to update her and report them all missing.

'Donna knows I wouldn't go to the service without Daniel,' I say, while Gary is driving. 'She's done this deliberately because of the cremation, I bet. She doesn't want any part of it. There's no other reason I can think of for not going to your own son's funeral.'

'I think you're right,' Gary replies. 'She didn't get her own way and is now making you suffer for it. I wouldn't want her as my mother-in-law.'

'My mother said that it was only them, some of Michael's cousins, and a small handful of Michael's work colleagues who turned up at the funeral,' I say. 'Not that she recognises anyone. She got chatting to a few people on the way out. They were all asking about me.'

I'm disappointed that not many people bothered to turn up. That such a small handful was all there was to show for all his years of life. Was Donna behind that too, is that why only some of his cousins made it?

I'm angry with myself for giving them Daniel. I wonder if she has been overcome with grief and can't part with him. I have gone through so many different scenarios in my head but how do I explain Peter? He does as he is told. If Donna says he should drive to Cornwall, then he's unlikely to argue with her.

Why isn't Peter answering his phone?

'You take the next left and then the next left again after that,' I say to Gary. 'We're almost there now.'

We arrive at the entrance of the park and I try to remember where Donna and Peter's lodge is located. It's been a while since I have stayed here but I've barely had a chance to catch up with my own emotions.

'It's towards the back of the site,' I tell Gary while pointing to another turning, 'I know it's number forty, I remember that much.'

I'm flustered and anxious to see my son. They have to be here. I need to know that he is safe.

Gary parks the van beside lodge forty and I immediately unbutton my seat belt with such a force that it flies backwards instantly. I opened the van door and step down onto the soggy grass. It had been raining in Cornwall but the site is eerily quiet. I am glad to take in the fresh air as the strong, pungent smells from Gary's van were giving me a headache. Every now and then I'd get a whiff of rotten eggs but it was soon replaced by a chemical scent like mild bleach. I asked Gary but he said he had been clearing his house out and it was boxed contents from an old fridge in his garage. His van was unclean and nothing as luxurious as the Mercedes we were in earlier.

'I still don't see their car,' I say, masking the panic in my voice. 'If they were here at the lodge, it would literally be just here.'

Gary closes his side of the van door, walks up towards the lodge but from what I can tell externally, there is no one here.

'I'll knock on the door anyway,' I say, while Gary watches me, 'and I'll look through the window to see if anyone has been here.'

'Didn't you say Donna and Peter emailed the site earlier?' Gary asks. 'You could check at reception if they've been in and got the keys?'

I respond with a shrug of the shoulders and go on ahead to knock on the door. There is no answer. I see through the windows that it appears no one is inside. I try the door handle a few times, just in case, but the lodge is locked. I have an idea.

'They would have their own key on them,' I explain to Gary. 'I could go and ask though. I can tell them to call me if they see anything.'

'Do you want me to drive you back down?' Gary asks. 'I don't mind?'

I shake my head to acknowledge that I don't need him. I look out in the distance over the small hill. There's a short footbridge and it should only take me a couple of minutes at most.

'I can manage it,' I reply. 'I shouldn't be too long. It's only over the hill, over the road.'

I watch as Gary returns to his van. I think if it wasn't for the convenience of their gift shop close by in the area, Donna and Peter wouldn't have bought anything on this site. Maybe they're in the gift shop?

As soon as I mention my name in reception they recognise it because it's the same as Donna and Peter's. It doesn't take much persuasion for a key either and I am informed it has been thoroughly cleaned for our arrival. Another short walk back to the lodge. Gary is now sitting on the step by the entrance door.

'They let me have a key,' I say out loud from a short distance. I keep walking closer and closer, almost to the lodge. 'I had a thought that maybe they're at the shop too, but if they were, I know they'd drop all their stuff in here first.'

I go to the door, place the key in the lock, and for a split-second a nervous rush of anticipation comes over me. I'm not expecting to see anyone inside because I looked through the windows earlier, but I have a feeling of uncertainty. It makes me nervous. Gary follows me inside.

'Donna, Peter, Daniel?'

No answer, but I shout anyway.

'If there's no sign that they've been here, I might have to call the police, or at least give Sharon a call.' I say, filled with anger. 'My child is missing. I have to do something.'

Gary closes the door behind me. I leave the key on the lounge table and head out into the kitchen. I open the fridge and notice that it's empty. Not a sign of any milk, or that they've even been here. It's eerily quiet.

'I'll look in the bedrooms to see if they've dropped off any of their cases but it doesn't look like anyone has been in here either,' I say. 'I'm getting a really bad feeling about this. It's not like them. Something is wrong.'

Gary doesn't reply. I turn around and head into the bedrooms. I hear him open the door again. I can see grass marks on the carpet, even the odd piece of mud. It seems like someone has been in here. Maybe the cleaners had dirty boots on?

I walk into the master bedroom. I see the double bed has been made up with a fluffy grey throw over the bottom half of the bed for extra warmth. I open the wardrobes and nothing inside. I don't see any suitcases but I turn around and notice that one of the pillows is lying flat compared to the others. I see a ring in the centre. I place a hand over my chest and I can hear my heart thudding. The closer I walk towards it, the more it seems real. It can't be. Again my mind is in overdrive. I need to sit down.

I pick up the small gold wedding band and look for the engraving. It looks worn and scratched but it is definitely Michael's. I'm confused, panicky and full of scared emotions. I can feel the tears starting to flood my eyes and I sit on the bed in shock. None of this is making any sense. Surely Donna didn't have it here all this time?

She's been keeping it from me and hiding it in this lodge the whole time.

How, what, why?

I stand up, straighten my coat, compose myself for a few seconds and cling on to the ring so tightly. I hold it to my chest because I know Michael would never have taken it off. This still doesn't explain why Donna, Peter and Daniel are all missing but it does confirm that Donna must have been playing games with me. Did she find it at the hotel when I wasn't looking? That day when I had to collect Michael's car?

'Gary, look what I have just found on the bed,' I say as I walk out into the hallway. 'Michael's wedding ring. It doesn't make any sense.'

I hold out the ring – then drop it on the floor. If I wasn't shocked enough by finding the wedding ring on the pillow I now want to scream – but the sheer disbelief of the image I am seeing has me silenced. I can't even speak. I'm frozen on the spot. I can feel my body shaking head to toe. The fear in my mind has overtaken all my thoughts.

What is happening to us?

Daniel is on the sofa with his hands and feet bound by cable ties. He wasn't there when I walked in so Gary must have placed Daniel there when I was in the bedroom. His mouth is taped and his eyes barely look open. He is alive – but my eyes are fixed on him. My first instinct is to run to protect my son but I stop in my tracks because a knife is pointing in my direction. A million different questions flood my thoughts. I have no idea why this has happened, no idea what he is doing with my son.

Where are Donna and Peter?

My son is a mere few metres in front of me and we are both in immediate danger. Gary is trembling but he seems malicious – with an intent to harm. All I can focus my eyes on is the knife that he is pointing in my direction. It already has blood on it but Daniel doesn't appear to be injured in that way. Daniel appears unharmed. I have to make Gary focus on me. I need to think to survive. I have to keep my son safe.

'Please don't hurt my son,' I say. I still don't move any closer. I remember my mobile phone is in my pocket but in this rural area the signal is hit and miss. 'Please don't harm him. He's all I have left. Daniel hasn't done anything wrong.'

I have a sudden urge to run towards Daniel, but there's no escape. Gary is blocking the door and I can't think of a way to grab my son without getting hurt. I would have to run, pick him up and then somehow make it to the site reception for help. It's not possible. By the time I get to Daniel, Gary would be able to stab me, or worse, Daniel. Reception is too far away, he has a van. It's not going to work.

'What's going on, why are you doing this to me?' I ask. I know he can hear the nervousness in my voice. 'How did Daniel get here, where did you find my son?'

'Give me your mobile phone,' Gary demands, pointing the knife in the direction of Daniel. 'Hand me your phone now, and Donna's too. I know that you have it on you. Otherwise, I will hurt him. I promise you. I will hurt him. Just as I have hurt Donna and Peter.'

I take out my mobile phone and Donna's, then throw them onto the floor in Gary's direction. I feel helpless, but my mind is in overdrive. I struggle to take everything in all at once. He's done something terrible to Donna and Peter, the knife is stained with blood. I fear that moving forward will cause him to harm Daniel, so instead, I have no choice but to talk to him. Try and make him see sense. I don't know how I will survive this.

'Please let him come to me,' I say. 'Daniel is a small boy who's already lost his father. Let him come to his mother.'

Gary holds the knife higher and points it in my direction.

'His father was a liar and a cheat,' Gary replies, watching me cry, while drool spills from his mouth. 'Don't even get me started on his fucking father. Do you want to know more about his father?'

Gary storms closer to the kitchen. I slowly lean backwards as he waves the knife in my direction. I am threatened, angry too, but helpless. There's nothing in these few split-seconds that I can do. The look on Gary's face is of rage and anger. I place my hands up closer to my face to protect myself should he lunge at me. I know there's a knife in the drawer – but by the time I reach for it, it would be too late.

'His father was having an affair with my wife. Michael was sleeping with MY god damn fucking wife. There, so now you know the truth about your dirty husband.'

I gasp with a breath so hard I fall to my knees. I shake my head in disbelief. I don't understand why this is happening to me – or even if he is telling the truth or not. My husband, his wife, the knife. I struggle to take this all in. My tears burst and I still struggle to scream. I fear for our lives.

'Let's talk about this together,' I sob. 'Just you and me, let Daniel go free. He's a toddler. He's my baby. He doesn't need to be involved in all this. Where are Donna and Peter?'

Gary wipes his mouth, coughs and splutters a bit, before turning to look at me again.

'They're both dead.' Gary replies. 'They're outside in the van. DEAD.'

Gary states this truth in an emotionless manner. I don't recognise him anymore. I can tell from the look in his eyes, with that pent-up rage, that he's not right in the head. He could now be capable of anything. My whole concern is getting Daniel free, even if it means harming myself in the process. I keep looking at the door and wondering where he has put the keys. The door behind me at the back of the kitchen will unlock with the turn of a catch. I just need to get Daniel. I'm not leaving this lodge without my son.

I tremble and stumble a little. I can feel my feet move beneath me. I almost faint, so I put my hand out to hold onto the nearest thing beside me which is the kitchen worktop. I am filled with turmoil and confusion, combined with fear and anxiety. Every minute counts.

He's going to kill us both if I don't act fast.

Thirty-Three

Gary

I glance in the direction of Daniel who is motionless on the sofa. I've tied his arms and legs with cable ties, covered his mouth in tape, but left enough space for him to breathe through his nose. He still appears drowsy from the sleeping tablets I gave him in his juice. His clothes are dirty. Blood stains from Donna are splashed on his denim jeans, yet I don't think he realises the reality of his danger.

This innocent three-year-old boy is a victim of his father's behaviour and need not have suffered this trauma if Michael had kept his dick in his pants. We wouldn't all be here now if it wasn't for Michael. He should have left my wife alone. He should have known better. He owed me.

I blame Michael for everything: the stress of my demons, my mood swings, and that my life is crashing down in this domino effect. I have nobody left because of the destruction that man caused in my life.

I've got no family, no kids, no wife, and a car business I'm in the process of selling. I have a house on the market and a will and testament still detailing that all my assets are to go to my ex-wife, should anyone find her. She deserved better than me. I still love her. If Michael hadn't got his claws into her, we might have worked things out. Michael was a good manipulator but in the end, never saw me coming.

I'm convinced the stress that he caused me is the reason for my illness.

Jenny is on her hands and knees, sobbing on the kitchen floor. I've locked the door and she's handed me the mobile phones as I asked. She has no escape. She needs to know the truth.

The only setback I encountered was the boy. I thought I could kill him – but I couldn't do it. He watched me from the top of the stairs at

Donna and Peter's house. I stood outside holding a bunch of flowers, so as not to look suspicious. I didn't notice Daniel until I watched Donna slide down the wall holding on to her chest: one quick stab to the heart after she let me inside and she was gone. I shut the door behind me and had a brief struggle with Peter who was so shocked to see his wife dead on the floor it gave me a few seconds' leeway to grab hold of his throat. I squeezed with all the strength I had left. The job was done in less than two minutes. He went to a dead weight and both of Michael's dead parents were sprawled across the hallway. I was more concerned about the blood than Daniel watching me. I knew that little boy couldn't call the police.

'Please let me get to my son,' Jenny pleads with me. 'He is scared. Let him go.'

'I've drugged him,' I reply, holding the knife at a reasonable distance to her neck. 'He's been out for the count all night in the back of the van. Sat there among the bodies of his grandparents. He isn't scared. He's too sleepy to be scared. Plus it keeps him quiet and still.'

'Why?' Jenny screeches. 'Why are you doing this to us?'

'Because I want to destroy everything that is associated with Michael!' I shout at her. 'Did you not fucking listen? Your husband fucked my wife. She was my bookkeeper; he was my accountant. He manipulated her into bed. He took advantage, and after she left me, after the divorce, I got sick. I couldn't see things clearly then because I was too traumatised, but I see everything clearly now. He caused all of this. I blame him for my demons.'

'What are your demons?' Jenny asks. 'You're lying to me, please let us go. You're not well. I trusted you!'

'After the divorce I developed pains, some constant sickness and migraines that weren't going away,' I say, holding the knife out towards her. 'I have a tumour eating away at me. Attacking my brain. It's terminal and I'm dying.'

I watch every muscle of her face, hoping to see a glimmer of concern, but nothing.

'I've only got a few months left to live, if that,' I state. 'There's nothing anyone can do for me now. I've lost everything and I'm going to die. I've got nothing left to lose.'

Jenny moves slowly forward. It's not enough to move me off track but I wonder in that split-second if she's going to try anything stupid.

'Don't move,' I say, firm and forceful. 'Stay exactly where you are, or I will kill him.'

Jenny nods her head and stands up, letting go of the kitchen side.

'This has nothing to do with Daniel,' she replies, wiping her eyes. 'Please, I am begging you to let my son go free. He might need a doctor. Look at him, he's not well. I can see it. He needs medical help.'

'Every time I look at him, I still see Michael,' I reply to inject more fear into her. 'You should be thanking me that he's still alive. He wasn't meant to be here. He watched everything.'

After I cleaned up the blood and went through the house with a fine-tooth comb to ensure it looked like everyone had gone out, I found the sleeping tablets in the bathroom. I crushed some into Daniel's juice and waited patiently until he fell asleep. When he was out for the count, I drove their car to a nearby street and walked back to the house. I parked my van on the driveway and bundled their bodies into the back in the dead of night. I had three large boxes ready for each of them. I struggled to drag them one by one while taking breaks, and was lucky that no one saw me. I threw in all their luggage, closed the lid on Donna's box, shut Peter's box, and placed Daniel inside his own box with the lid open. I drove away and it was that easy.

I've not slept all night. The adrenaline is keeping me awake. I checked on Daniel a few times in the night to allow more air into the back of the van. He was sleeping on his side but the smell of urine was overpowering. He's dehydrated.

'I'm so sorry that you have cancer,' Jenny says, keeping her voice calm. 'I don't see how Michael could have caused all this?'

I know what she is trying to do, but it won't work. I can tell she is trying to manipulate me. How dare she? I'm not an idiot. She's not getting me side-tracked into any other conversations. To think that I'd be that stupid to fall for a trick like that. Sorry that I have cancer – like she's stood on the back of my heel or something.

I'm raging. I thought we could have been friends if she had made an effort to get to know me better. I didn't want my last few months to be a lonely existence with no one to turn to. Every person I cared about has left me; my own cheating wife abandoned me.

'I never wanted to kill you at first,' I say. 'I thought we had a connection when I first met you. You opened up to me, it felt special. I thought we could have been friends. I thought you were different.'

She's looking at me in disgust. It hurts, this rejection all over again. Just like my wife. I can't go back – not now that I've started this, now that I am a killer. I can't stop here.

'You never once ask me how I am, how I am feeling,' I snap, while she looks at me in shock. 'I thought smelling like Michael, dressing like Michael, you might have paid me more attention. I wanted to get your attention. All you want to talk about is Michael, the wedding ring and the same old crap over and over again.'

'We barely know each other, I'm grieving for my husband,' Jenny sobs. 'You were there when he died. I wanted you to talk to me about his last moments. It made up for me not being there with him when it mattered. You helped me understand what he might have been going through. I thought we could have been friends, in time, but…'

'The stress,' I reply, short sharp, and ready to unleash my annoyance. 'My diagnosis came after the divorce. I have a brain tumour and I've had to accept that my life is over. I blame it all on the stress. My demons. I'm grieving too.'

Jenny's body language is tense. She remains silent but shakes her head at me as a sign of disappointment. I don't know how she could still love that man after everything he has done to her. Everything he has done to me.

'What started as a constant cough, something I thought might have been asthma, has now evolved into my death sentence,' I continue, riling myself up. 'All of it, I blame on the stress. My demons. Demons put there by your filthy, cheating fucking husband.'

Jenny moves a little bit closer.

'Don't you dare come near me,' I shout, waving the knife. 'Do you want me to kill you before you've even heard the rest of it? More secrets about your loving husband?'

Jenny stops dead in her tracks, and her body stiffens. Her eyes are bright red from the teary state she is in – but she still doesn't even know the half of it.

'Michael had a gambling habit,' I announce, 'Did you know that?'

'I know about the debts,' Jenny replies, 'on his credit cards and—'

'He borrowed a lot of money from me. Thousands, in fact. He was meant to be paying me back but failed to deliver,' I interrupt her, knowing that she hasn't got a clue. 'I promised to keep his dirty little fucking secret while my marriage was breaking down, my wife fleeing the area, but I put the debt up after I found out about the affair. He had no choice but to continually struggle to pay me if he never wanted anyone to find out. He paid me to keep my mouth shut – if he ever wanted to keep his family. I thought it was fair to make him pay.'

I watch the torment, the confusion, and the look on her face as this news starts to sink in.

'How long had it been going on?' she asks me, sobbing. 'How much money did he owe you?'

'Twenty thousand pounds or thereabouts at last count,' I reply. 'It doesn't matter now though. He came begging to me months ago. Practically on his hands and knees when he was suspended from his job on suspicion of fraud.'

This next bombshell should be another stab to her feeble emotional state.

'Who do you think organised calling his office, providing them with the doubt? Showing them hints of evidence that Michael was taking some of their business for himself?' I continue. 'I lost him his job knowing full well that he'd come running to me for more money. By then I had already planned his death sentence. He worked for me now. All I had to do was witness it, to make sure the job was done.'

'Why?' Jenny screeches in an attempt to scream at me. 'Why are you doing this?'

It's time for the truth.

'When I accepted my prognosis, all I wanted was payback on Michael. He knew I ran a dodgy car lot. He knew I ran a bent car hire firm. He helped me save thousands in tax bills for a few back-handers here and there. He also knew about the drug runs. All he had to do was deliver the right package to the right address. Sometimes pick up the odd envelope full of cash.'

'Drugs?' Jenny asks, glancing towards Daniel. 'You made him deliver drugs for you?'

'He should have kept his filthy hands off my wife, then all of this wouldn't have been necessary.' I reply. 'All this stress on me, he is to blame. Not me.'

For a few seconds, Jenny doesn't do anything other than look at me. I see her eyes glancing in the direction of the knife, and then back to my face. I take a quick look out of the kitchen window and can see we are still alone.

'I still don't understand what this has to do with Daniel and me,' Jenny says, the panic in her voice clear as day. 'Why are you doing this to us?'

'Because you're both a part of *him*,' I snap at her. 'Because piece by piece and bit by bit I've wanted to watch Michael's life be destroyed and everything that was part of him. Just as mine is coming to an end. Call it my dying wish. It's all been for payback.'

Jenny starts to cry again. I've trapped her in a corner with no way out. She has to listen to me and I want her to understand my pain. Michael destroyed my happiness. I would have expected more of a fight. I have her son bound and sprawled on a sofa but if she runs towards me, I will jab the knife into her. Daniel can sit there and watch his mother die – if he can keep his eyes open. I doubt I've given him a lethal dose, but he doesn't look well.

'Daniel watched both of his grandparents die, and soon he will watch his mother die,' I say calmly. 'I get more satisfaction now at the thought of him growing up with no parents, traumatised by the memories he may have of this day and knowing that he has no parents in his life because his dad caused all of this mess.'

'I thought you were my friend,' Jenny replies. 'You watched my husband die. You even held his hand. You came to our home and talked to me. I told you how I was feeling. I believed you. I thought you were traumatised by his death.'

'I really thought we could have been friends, but we're not, are we?' I say. 'I took off his wedding ring that night purposely to show that his marriage was worthless. The flowers I gave you too, those carnations, were from the scene of his death, left by some work colleague who probably didn't give a toss about him. The aftershave I am wearing is Michael's and look – it's his fucking suit I am wearing too. I also managed to make damn sure that even his own family didn't turn up to his funeral.'

Just saying it all out loud gave me some satisfaction. The truth was told. Jenny should understand now that I am also a victim of Michael's lies. I wasn't bothered when he died. I watched and wished for it to happen. I set the whole fucking thing up. I wanted that man dead the minute my own death sentence was confirmed by my doctors. I am not dying with the man who caused all of my problems still out there living his own life. I've achieved what I set out to do. Destroy his and his family's lives.

'I'll tell you what else you didn't know about your precious Michael,' I shout. 'His own mother fucking knew about his debts. Donna lent him some money to help pay me off. He told me that he asked her, that he had to go begging to his mother and that she knew. It was their little secret.'

'No, no, you're lying,' Jenny snaps, tension in her voice. I see the anger brewing. 'You're lying. Michael was a good man. Whatever it was he was doing was to provide for his family. He loved us.'

From my pocket, I whip out the photograph of my wife and Michael kissing each other. I want to rub it in her face but I hold it out clearly for her to see. I'm not sure if Michael's mother knew about the affair, or even about me. She didn't recognise me at the door but I know she knew more than Jenny realised. She lied for him and would have done anything for him.

'Look at them,' I tell her. 'Look at this picture of Michael kissing my wife. Do you not recognise the hotel in the background? Take a real good hard look at it?'

Jenny puts her hands to her face and cries more. I know there's no coming back from this. She has to know the truth.

'That's the Taverton Estate Hotel. Look at it, go on,' I say. 'That's the hotel where the private investigator I hired watched them kiss. The first picture I saw of them both together and the last place that I stood over him and watched him die. He slept with my wife at that very hotel – paid for, no doubt, with *my* money, the money that she took from me.'

Jenny should start to see the penny drop. I want her to realise. I want her to tell me what is going on in her head. I want her to be angry. I want her to react. I organised the death of her husband. He is dead because of me, and soon the penny will drop.

'It wasn't an accident, was it? All this time, and it was you?' Jenny asks. 'Did you kill Michael?'

I nod in agreement, smiling. I took great pleasure in killing that bastard.

'I arranged his urgent meeting. Dropped little hints that I knew would get to him. I implied it was big money, a big job with a certain accountant needed. A dodgy bent one,' I explain. 'I knew that he was so desperate for money it would get the better of him. It was no accident, and that junkie who mowed him down owed me money too. All he had to do was to wait until I gave the signal. He was off his fucking head, desperate to clear his own drug debts. They both were.'

'But he's dead too,' Jenny says, breathing heavily and with an irate tone. 'He died in the stream. Sharon explained to me that he drowned after he ran away from the scene.'

'I pushed his dirty fucking head under the water until he silently started to float a little,' I respond, and she moves a hand to her mouth in horror. 'Collateral damage. It all looked like the perfect accident in a quiet little village on the outskirts of Westbridge. No one even suspected a thing. He ran exactly to the spot where I arranged our meet, out of sight of the cameras. So many drugs in his system that the police could only have assumed that was the cause.'

I take a look at her while she is digesting all the information, before throwing one more revelation at her. I visited the hotel a few times before organising everything. I found the quietest day, the best time and the position of the cameras. I wanted nothing more than to be there, stood over him as he died. The last face he saw was mine.

'I even supplied the vehicle that killed him.' I watch her squirming with fear. 'Everything was planned right down to his last fucking breath. If the car hadn't hit him hard enough, I'd have strangled him with my own bare hands that night. You should have heard the last words I spoke to him.'

Throughout the short investigation into Michael's death, I was surprised that the police didn't ask more questions. They were too blindsided by me being a witness to a terrible accident, believing I was there for a dinner date. The links between us were not known to the police and my well-established lifestyle of luxury and businesses,

I assumed, made them believe that someone like me couldn't do something like that. That junkie thought he was repaying his debts. Michael thought his life was going to get a whole lot easier with a new contract.

'This is your fault, Michael,' I said, while his eyes blinked and his bloodied body shook as I gripped his hand. 'You fucking asked for all of it.'

I see the wedding ring on the floor where Jenny dropped it. I had slipped it on the pillow when she went to the site reception. I found the lodge keys on the hook by the door of Michael's parents and knew it was a great distraction to get Jenny away from the funeral service. My instincts were right. She did focus on Daniel and his wellbeing. As any mother would in the same position. She was trusting and misguided and I was confident I could manipulate her out of calling the police.

'Help me!' Jenny screams at the top of her voice. 'He's got my son, he has a knife, help, help.'

I look out of the kitchen window and see the workman standing there. He's staring at me with the knife in my hands. He looks confused, but now he knows what he has seen. Me, holding up the knife. I don't have time to capture him. That loudmouth bitch has ruined everything. Why couldn't she have just kept her mouth shut?

I turn towards Jenny and run at her as if for a rugby tackle. I've got limited time before he possibly comes back with backup, or the police. She falls to the ground and I'm trying to stick the knife in. I'm stabbing her, I can feel that I have pushed it with ease into her side as she pushes her arms to try and force me off her. I see blood on the kitchen floor but I've no idea how bad she is. I hope she feels the pain as I hear her scream for help.

I'm a dying man with nothing to lose.

Thirty-Four

Jenny

The stab from the knife didn't hurt at the exact moment it penetrated my side. I didn't feel it at first — but now there is a pulsating stabbing pain with an ache as the blood comes out of me. I can see it smeared on the kitchen floor. I see the wedding ring beside me as I lie here in my struggles. It glistens in the sunlight that is coming in from the kitchen window. I can't die, not here, not today. Not in front of my son. I have to protect him even if it means dying to save him.

The smell of Gary's breath hits my nose as he is forcing himself on me. I have one hand on his chest and another behind his back as I am trying to push him off me. I'm using what little strength I have to try and roll on to my side. I know the man at the window saw me and I can hear him banging on the door. I need him to call the police or get help. He must have seen the knife.

Why isn't he doing anything? I know he heard me scream.

I feel the knife as its sharp edge hits me again. I don't think he's managing to go in deep because of my coat is a layer of protection, but my abdomen is in agony. My heart is beating faster and faster and I'm not sure how much damage my body is taking or how much blood I am losing. I don't feel faint, but the adrenaline is pumping around my body. One more push in the right direction should get him away from my chest.

Gary is strong, he's forcing his body weight on mine, but my arms restrict his movement. I can hear my mobile phone ringing; it could be my mother, checking up on me. Checking if I have found Daniel. All I can think about is surviving this hell.

'No, get off me,' I yell as I manage to tense my stomach muscles and force through the pain. 'Call the police. Help me, my son is in danger.'

I manage to push Gary off me and the banging at the door stops. I'm confident the man who looked like a workman understood everything clearly. As Gary gets to his knees, he struggles for a moment to find his balance and stand on his feet. My mobile phone, which landed down the other end of the room, is continuing to ring. It has to be my mother; she is the only person I know who would continue to call me rather than leave a voicemail.

'You stupid fucking bitch,' Gary raises his voice. 'Why did you have to shout like that? You should have let him walk past.'

I glance on the floor and hold my side. Bloodstains cover my hands. I can feel the warm dampness seeping from the wound. It hurts really badly and I'm running out of time before he tries to kill me. I need to distract him from heading in Daniel's direction.

'He's going to call the police,' I reply, holding my side and standing back up on my feet. 'It's over, Gary. Put the knife down. The police will be here soon, he must have called them.'

'It doesn't matter,' Gary replies. 'I've barely got six months left to live. None of this matters to me. Michael had to pay for ruining my life. It's not over, not yet. I'm not done.'

The phone has stopped ringing but I know my mother will instinctively know it to be strange that I haven't returned her call. She will know something isn't right. I'm hoping that she doesn't blame it on the bad signal down here. She wouldn't know that. Donna and Peter are missing; their grandson is missing and now I could be missing. I hope she calls the police; I hope somebody will help me.

I look at my son as he lies on the sofa, restricted in his movement. He still looks sleepy and I'm not sure he has taken anything he has witnessed in. I hope, if we survive this ordeal, he will never remember this moment. The heart-breaking image of my boy in danger fires my need to protect him. He has lost his father, watched his grandparents get murdered – but he's not losing his mother. I am all he has to protect him. I would die for him, and I would kill for him.

I stand up, though not fully, because of the pain. I look at Gary, who is struggling to compose himself. The glare in his eyes exposes his madness. He looks angry but he holds all the power because the knife is in his hand. One arm is raised, while the other with the knife is by his thigh. The sharp edge covered in blood that drips to the floor is all that is stopping me from running to my son. So long as he is looking at me, it's an extra minute of survival for Daniel. I hope that the police are on their way.

There is another knock at the door; the workman is back. Gary turns his head and I use this moment to lunge forward to try to grab the knife. I push him. He falls to the ground and now my hand is holding onto his arm, my nails digging in hard. I want him to drop the knife.

'Let it go,' I scream. 'Drop the fucking knife.'

'The police are on their way, they're coming,' I hear the male voice from behind the door shout. 'Let her go, they won't be long.'

I see for a brief moment the figure of the workman in the glass and the door handle jolt as he tries to force open the door. The key is on the side in the living room, I see it by the television. I get closer to Gary's body and manage to place my right hand on his shoulder. I push downwards with such force that he stumbles and lowers himself. I'm clinging to his arm because, although I can't reach the knife, I need to make sure he can't use his arm to stab me again.

Gary coughs before catching his breath. The look on his face tells me that he too is in agony. I think about my actions because I only have seconds to react.

'It's not over,' he wheezes. 'I'm not done.'

I raise my leg and kick him hard in the stomach. The agonising stab of pain in my abdomen forces me to let out a short scream. Gary falls backwards and the knife drops to the floor. This is my moment. I have only one chance and I am about to seize it. Gary gets back up to his feet and turns around to face Daniel. I'm shaking with fear.

'No,' I shout. 'Leave my son alone.'

My heart is thudding in my chest; my breaths are short and sharp with the pain I am feeling. I see my blood oozing through my clothes – but I manage to grab the knife.

'Daniel, don't look,' I yell. Gary turns his head but is now leaning over Daniel. 'No, no, no.'

I can't see his hands very clearly but fear they could be around Daniel's throat. I take the knife and thrust it into his back. I feel the rage inside me, an anger that's been unleashed for the sake of saving my son.

'Stop,' I shout. 'Get off him.'

I keep stabbing the knife into his back. I can't bring myself to stop. I'm enraged and in agony all at the same time. I hear behind me the smash of a window, a few raised voices, all shouting at the same time. In fast and ferocious lunges, I stab Gary at least three times in the upper back. The knife slides through his suit with ease and he falls on top of Daniel. In that moment of agony, in that urgency to protect my son, I can't feel any remorse. I want him dead.

'Daniel,' I say out loud while pushing Gary away from him. I'm not even sure if this monster is breathing – nor do I care. 'I'm here. It's all going to be ok. Mummy's here now. Mummy's got you.'

I rip off the tape from his mouth, drop the knife to the floor, and am relieved to see that he is still breathing. He is still looking tired and his eyes appear heavy. I don't know what concoction of drugs Gary has given him but I am relieved to see him breathing. I hold him tightly in my arms – but I need to get those cable ties off.

I feel a hand on my shoulder that forces me to move backwards. I hear muffled words that aren't making sense to me as a crowd gather. I look behind and see that the window to the door has been smashed in completely and the workman is looking at me. It is a look of fear and confusion. He walks past me and I stand in silence. My son is all that matters to me – and he's alive.

'The guy's not breathing,' the workman says. 'I think he's dead. There's also some blood drooling from his mouth. I've checked his pulse and I can't feel anything.'

A young woman rushes past me with a pair of scissors in her hands. She doesn't say anything to me but looks at me sympathetically and aware that I've been injured. She cuts the cable ties and Daniel's hands and feet are free. I can't lift him because of the pain. I'm starting to feel faint. I don't think the knife went in too deep but one side of me is in agony.

'I'm a site first-aider,' she says. 'You need to sit down and apply some pressure on the stab wound. Are you hurt anywhere else? Is there anyone else in the lodge?'

I shake my head twice. I still can't speak. I don't know what it is that is restricting me but I don't want to express how I feel with words. The emotion and fear are combined with confusion and I am in shock. I place a hand on my side where I was stabbed and apply pressure just as she asked. I nod at her to signal that this is where the pain is.

'I don't know exactly what has happened here,' the workman says, 'but I called the police. I explained that he was waving a knife and they said they'd bring an ambulance in case. They should be here any minute – that's the problem when we're so rural down this way. It can take a bit longer to get to us.'

I start to cry with a release that I can't control. My breathing is calming itself down and I look around the room. I see the workman holding his mobile phone; I see the woman holding Daniel and cuddling him to reassure him that everything is all right. I know she is talking to him but it's as though I've now zoned out into a world of my own. That same feeling that I felt when the police arrived to tell me my husband had died. It must be the shock.

I can hear the sirens in the distance. A breeze blows through the open door with its smashed window and there's a crowd of people outside. None of them enters the lodge and I know that it's a crime scene now. Gary's body is slouched on the floor. I look around and realise how much blood is sprayed on the carpet and the kitchen floor. Thankfully my boy is in the hands of the first-aider.

'Is this yours?' the workman asks, handing me the wedding ring. 'It was on the kitchen floor?'

I nod to agree, close my eyes and open them again with my focus entirely on the wedding ring. I hold out the hand that isn't applying pressure to my painful, bleeding abdomen. I grab the ring and hold on to it tightly.

'That was my husband's,' I reply. 'Yes, it's mine.'

'Was he your husband?' the first-aider asks, pointing to Gary. 'The one who attacked you with the knife?'

'No,' I respond, shaking my head. 'That man is a monster. He killed my husband, he killed...'

I stop speaking. I haven't even thought about them.

'Donna and Peter,' I say. The first-aider looks at me, confused. 'He said he killed Donna and Peter. They're in the van.'

'That van out there?' the workman asks. 'That one?'

The workman points to the van that is parked outside. It's the one I meant, and the only one in plain sight.

'Yes, the one outside,' I reply. 'They're inside. He said they were dead.'

The sirens have got closer. I can hear them so loud it's piercing. I look down at my hand holding Michael's wedding ring. Today was meant to be a day focused on his funeral service. I look at my own hand wearing a similar ring with the same engraved date and I feel broken. Gary told me about the affair, the debt problems and the secrets Michael kept with his mother. I loved Michael so much and his loss is still affecting me. I might never get answers or the real truth – but I have to protect Daniel. Nothing else matters but Daniel.

'I need to call my mother,' I say, looking at the workman and the first-aider. 'Where's my phone?'

Before they have a chance to answer, three policemen and a crew of paramedics storm inside. One paramedic comes to look at my side while another rushes to Gary who I stabbed to death. The police are advising that nothing should be moved or touched, while another officer is outside talking to the small gathering of people. They're moving them backwards.

I watch as the first-aider hands a paramedic my son. I go to stand up but the pain is too severe and I struggle.

'That's my son,' I say, 'that's Daniel, my son. He's been given sleeping tablets.'

'We need to take you both to the hospital,' the paramedic says. 'You have two stab wounds to the abdomen; blood loss is not severe and there is swelling but no major arteries appear to be impacted. We need to get that checked out. We'll do an ultrasound scan in the ambulance. This is just to check no piece of the knife has broken inside you and then we'll get you cleaned up and stitched.'

One of the policemen holds out a writing pad. He is looking around the room and then also at me. I watch his eyes as he tries to inspect the scene with multiple glances. He looks worried.

'I understand this is a traumatic time but do you approve of giving evidence on the way to the hospital if I join you? While it's all fresh?' he asks. 'We have witness statements in hand to confirm that you were attacked. If you don't mind?'

I shake my head.

'I don't mind,' I reply while the paramedic helps me to my feet. 'It was self defence. He tried to kill my son and me. I had to do it. I had to somehow get the knife off him.'

I walk out of the lodge door. The air hits me – and the silence. A gathering of people watch as I take small steps across the grass, aided by the paramedic. The policeman is behind us as we walk to the ambulance, which is parked up beside Gary's van. The door of the van is open. I don't even know how they managed to get inside but I feel my mouth drop as I glance at the view of its contents. Three boxes appear side by side. Two, that must contain Donna and Peter, are smeared with blood. I lower my head and look away.

I didn't have a choice. We survived a monster.

Sitting in the ambulance with my son, who is being checked out by another paramedic, and the policeman, I realise how lucky we were to survive this ordeal. I hear them tell me my boy will be fine. That's all I want to hear, all I need for the reassurance that I acted like any other mother would have done.

I thought Gary was a friend. I trusted him. I shared personal details. I let him into my home while all the time he was plotting to destroy our lives. I can't believe what has happened today. I don't know where to begin when I tell this story to the police.

If I am guilty of anything, it is being too trusting.

Epilogue

Michael

I never wanted my wife to find out about my affair. Jenny trusted me, yet with the stress and the strains of fatherhood and with the expectations of contributing to our home, I needed an escape. I thought I'd never get caught but I regretted every minute of it by the time it was over. I lied to protect my family – but in the end I lost everything.

I was first introduced to Gary's wife when we were working together through piles of receipts and invoices. Gary had offered me some money on the side to help him reduce his tax bill. I knew of ways to do this: loopholes and practices I picked up on through my accounting work. His main car dealership business accounts were under the responsibility of my firm, Sphere and Co, but as my client, his side-line businesses shouldn't have been under my control. I was losing Sphere and Co money by not reporting the work and taking the charge and cash payments for myself.

His wife was a bookkeeper for his smaller business. She was self-taught through online courses and asked for my guidance. We'd spend hours alone rummaging around his files to hide traces of his financial dealings. A few bottles of wine later and a few more weeks of spending time with each other and I let my guard down. What started off as harmless flirting turned into an attraction. I couldn't get her out of my head; I fancied her; I wanted her and the hints she dropped made it obvious what she wanted me too. This escalated into an affair. It felt exciting, something new and different. I liked the attention. She used me.

The very last time that I cheated on my wife was at the Taverton Estate Hotel. Gary's wife was there for a work conference, touting new contracts with the hotel, and I made excuses to Jenny that I was going away with a work convention. I lied. I had packed nothing more than a fresh pair of boxers, a clean suit and some fake presentation files – and away I went. Gary's wife and I had dinner at the hotel restaurant in the evening, before retiring to the bedroom. It was so luxurious, and all expenses paid by Gary under his business name. This was the first time we had spent the whole night away together. It was also the last time we saw each other. He made sure she never contacted me again. I tried texting her but the replies soon stopped.

I had no idea that Gary had his suspicions about us. He sent one of his henchmen to follow his wife to the hotel. At that time, I didn't know everything about the strains in his marriage. She hinted about his violent nature but I didn't experience it myself until he confronted me. He took me into his office and revealed the pictures of me and his wife kissing. I didn't know what to say. No lie could detract from the obvious. The confrontation was aggressive and I felt threatened when he locked me in his office and hinted that he could, if he wanted, have me killed. I didn't believe he was capable of that but all I could do was listen and try to explain everything without being beaten up. The last thing I wanted was for Jenny to ever find out. I begged him not to tell my firm or Jenny. No matter what the cost. I promised to pay him back everything that I owed and then I'd be out of his life for good.

Not only had I been sleeping with Gary's wife but I also owed him thousands of pounds; my gambling habits that I had struggled with on and off for years had landed me in trouble. There would be months when I could go without betting or chancing my luck at the roulette table – but then I would relapse. With every spin of the wheel, I would pray that it would be the big one, that I'd win thousands. It was a form of escapism that had slowly ruined my life.

Gary and I had both spent time together in the casinos when we first struck up a friendship after he joined my firm. He was a show-off and spent hundreds on roulette, poker and blackjack. I couldn't keep up but he offered to loan me some money to play the tables. I shouldn't have taken it, yet I had this urge. I was convinced I'd win. The whole time he was getting me more and more into debt.

Gary seemed to be my only hope in the desperate times when I was suspended from work. I thought I could easily find another job before Jenny found out. I had no concept of the seriousness of my suspension. No one was going to employ an accountant in the middle of an internal fraud investigation. Gary offered me even more money and I wasn't in any position to turn it down. It was a vicious circle that seemed never ending. Gary had me exactly where he wanted me.

So when I got notified by phone and email about a new client looking for accounting work and who had heard I was now freelance, I had to jump at it. I'd been told by the contact lead who called me that this was big business and they'd headhunted me. When I was given the address as Taverton Estate Hotel, I admit it sent a shiver down my spine. It brought back memories of Gary's wife. I wondered if it she had set up this secret encounter – an offer of work to fix my money issues. I knew she must have had a big payout in the divorce. All kinds of crazy ideas were spinning around in my mind. I was desperate.

Desperate for an end to my problems. All I wanted was to make a new life, a better life, for my wife and son. My family. My world.

A Letter From J A Andrews

Hello Reader,

Thank you for taking the time to read my novel, this is my second thriller, and another thank you if you've now read both.

I couldn't begin to imagine when I started planning this novel early September 2019, that by the time it was completed in June 2020, I'd have spent three months in lockdown due to a pandemic. In that time also, my debut, *Mummy's Boy*, was published, I have moved house, reached the age of 40, holiday's cancelled, a wedding postponed, and had to adapt so quickly to a new way of working from home. I've definitely gained weight! I hope that you and your families are well and keeping safe too.

You would have read that this book is set in a town called Westbridge, with included location names such as Taverton and Looe. Looe is a real location in Cornwall, and I used to clean caravans every Saturday on some holiday parks there over 20 years ago, it's a beautiful little place with a small beach, but cleaning was tough. Westbridge is a fictional town I named in this story because Looe is actually west of the Tamar Bridge that links my hometown of Plymouth to Cornwall. Taverton doesn't exist either and is inspired from the river Tavy, not far from where I lived when I was writing the first draft.

If you enjoyed my novel, it would be great if you could leave some feedback and a rating for me as a review. It doesn't have to be extensive, unless you want to, but a few lines if you could spare the time, and a shout-out on social media if you're feeling generous. I appreciate your support, and it feels like we're in this together with my writing journey – so thank you.

Have a great day,

J A Andrews

Acknowledgments

Having a book published is a real team effort. I've learnt about so much in the publishing process, and because of that I owe a great deal of thanks to everyone who has been involved with the publication of this, my second thriller. Keshini Naidoo and Lindsey Mooney at Hera, who are absolutely fantastic publishers that work hard to support their authors, and for answering my random questions. Keshini deserves an extra special thanks too as my (very hands on) editor for the structural edits, I've really appreciated the feedback. Thank you also to Dushi Horti, as copy-editor for helping me iron out the kinks. Thank you to Andrew Bridgmont for ensuring that before publication it is as error free as humanly possible, and to Lisa Brewster for the striking image. One broken glass, while the other is standing, cracked and half full (or half empty if you prefer), for this story it is perfect. As soon as I saw it, I loved it and it could relate it instantly to Jenny's journey.

I also have to thank those who have heard me rambling on about the plot during the whole time I was writing. Thank you to Peter Kewley, who has provided words of wisdom, offering advice to stay positive – and keeping me entertained with his bad jokes. Thank you also to my boyfriend Gary Mullen who initially inspired some of my ideas for the witness. If you ever met him in person he would tell you I steal all of his ideas, but I don't. I just stole his first name instead for the character. He doesn't mind.

A huge thank you to my mother, Susan Barry, my sister, Sarah Parker, and my little nephew, Ryan Reyes for their continued support in everything that I do…

…and also to Google, for pointing me in the right direction with search results that make me appear like a serial killer!

Thank you to everyone xx